Deceiver

BOOK 6 IN THE SERIES

Time of Jacob's Trouble

By M. Sue Alexander

Deceiver

This book is a work of fiction. Names and characters in the story are a product of the author's imagination. Any resemblance to actual persons, living or dead, events or locales, is coincidental. Should you purchase a copy of this book without a cover, be aware this book may be stolen property and neither the publisher nor the author has received payment for a "stripped book."

Deceiver

BOOK 6: TIME OF JACOB'S TROUBLE
FIRST EDITION 2020, USA
Copyright © 2020 by M. Sue Alexander
Suzander Publishing

Book Cover by Christine Roszak

View M. Sue's Website and Facebook Page

www.msuealexanderbooks.com

M. Sue Alexander

Series Titles by Author

Time of Jacob's Trouble
Book 1: *The Four Horsemen*
Book 2: *Beast*
Book 3: *Witness*
Book 4: *the Word*
Book 5: *Judgment*

Resurrection Dawn 2014 Series
Book 1: *Resurrection Dawn 2014*
Book 2: *The Christian Fugitive*
Book 3: *Rebels in Paradise*
Book 4: *Veil of Lies*
Book 5: *The Anointing*
Book 6: *Countdown to Justice*
Book 7: *All Rise*
Book 8: *Unlikely Suspect*
Book 9: *Lethal Snapshot*
Book 10: *Purgatory*
Book 11: *April Fool's Day*
Book 12: *Reign of Errors*

Independent Titles
Adam's Bones
Encounters of the God-Kind
The Forum
The Minister's Haunting
Tomorrow's Promise
Out of Time: The Vanderbilt Incident

2027

1

Friday July 9

Nashville, Tennessee

THE NASHVILLE INTERNATIONAL AIRPORT had only six functional runways following the earthquake that devastated West Tennessee. Cracks in the tarmac had been filled in and resurfaced according to federal regulations. The terminal was virtually vacant.

Detective Andrew Taylors's American flight landed the third day after the Tennessee shakeup. Unable to reach Tom Rave by phone due to downed cell towers, Drew employed an UBER driver outside the terminal to take him to the Greyhound Bus Station.

After purchasing a one-way ticket to Fernwood, Drew waited forty-five minutes before the antiquated bus rolled into the terminal. He boarded with four other passengers and found a seat mid-way. Counting him, there were fifteen passengers aboard.

He glanced at his bus mates. They all had trauma embedded in their expressions. Puffing diesel, the lumbering bus pulled out of the station, through town, and crawled along bumpy Highway 100.

Not an ideal time for travel, Drew presumed sensible folks were at home getting quotes from insurance adjusters so they could order repairs. Hopefully, his condo was still livable. Groaning, he gained the attention of the guy wearing a jogging suit seated in front of him. Big-and-tall turned around. "You all right, feller?"

Drew waved him off. *I'm okay.*

Not really. He leaned back in his seat, wondering if Mary was still in California. This was one time he was grateful she was out of the state. But now, they needed to talk and get some things straight.

Two hours later, Drew got off the Greyhound Bus with his duffle bag and dragged himself for two blocks to the Fernwood Police Station. One look told him nobody was there.

Needing caffeine, Drew ambled on over to Wendy's Pastry Station and ventured inside. Despite cracks in the ceiling and scuffed floors from falling tiles, the popular coffee bistro was fully staffed and crowded with adults, boisterous teens, and visitors.

People appeared joyful, talking and laughing, willing to sacrifice a couple weeks of summer school or normal working schedules. Life goes on, so they were adventurous and hungry.

Drew glanced around for a table, or a friend he might join for a cup of Joe. He spied an elderly couple vacating a table for two near the front window and claimed his seat, parking his crutch against the window sill. No need to see a menu, he knew what he wanted. Two chocolate covered donuts with the biggest cup of black coffee offered. A young waitress Drew had not seen before hustled over to take his order. Her nametag read TESS.

"I guess you were one of the lucky ones," Tess said, her pencil and pad poised for a carbon-copy order entry.

"What do you mean?" Drew looked up at Tess.

"I don't see any battle scars." She laughed.

"No, I was out of the country." He winked at the brown-eyed beauty. "Just got back in town, are you a newcomer?"

"Yeah, from Somerville," Tess replied. "We got it a lot worse there than you all did here. What can I get 'cha?"

Drew told Tess. While waiting, he checked his phone for a working cell tower. *Nada.* Tess sauntered back to his table within ten minutes with his order. "Thanks." He dove into the coffee.

The door chimes went off as customers entered the bistro and left, many of them newcomers to town. From recent news reports, Drew knew the quake had instantly redesigned West Tennessee's topography, enlarging populations in towns east of its epicenter.

He could only imagine how Memphis was coping with its landmass loss and some half-a-million deceased or lost residents.

While perusing a copy of the *Weekend Press* left behind on the table next to his, Drew felt a presence lording over him.

No, he smelled the presence.

Glancing up, he laid the paper aside and spied Officer Priscilla Dunn taking a seat at his table across from him.

Drew was dumbfounded at the woman's boldness.

"Detective Taylor!" she spouted. "Imagine running into you here." She snagged a paper menu. "What'd you order?"

Startled by Dunn's interruption, Drew tipped over his mug.

"Coffee with chocolate donuts," he replied, swiping the spilled liquid off the cuff of his blue shirt with a paper napkin.

"Heard you missed all the fun—what's that sparkling pink stuff on top?" Priscilla studied Drew's half-eaten donut.

"Uh, sprinkles." His mind whirred, trying to grasp how the female cop managed to outsmart him in East York, Canada.

Is she here now, to throw it all up in my face?

"Too many calories, I'll pass." She made a face.

"How bad is the damage at the station?" he asked.

"Pretty bad, don't think we'll be using the building for work."

Tess stood patiently beside Dunn, waiting to take her order.

"Shall I come back?" Tess asked.

"No, no," Priscilla said. "Bring me a yogurt health-shake."

"What kind?"

"Fresh strawberry," Priscilla replied.

Drew felt awkward, did not know what to say. Dunn knew he knew what she'd done. This was some kind of weird standoff.

"So . . . your new nanny said you took a trip." Dunn's icicle-blue eyes danced with speculation. "Where did you go?"

Drew scrambled for a lie. "I went to Nashville to visit a friend." He stared at the deceitful cop. "What've you been up to?"

Cat-and-mouse games . . .

"Besides going through a disaster?" She sarcastically piped. "Crime's rampant, but nobody's bothering to report it."

"Has Sheriff Boswell determined where the PD will set up its operations?" Drew inquired. "I've been out of the loop."

"I heard, personal leave—word gets around."

Drew frowned. "Yes, it does."

"Sheriff Boswell signed a lease on an old building out on Highway 64 East," Dunn replied. "Former owner/artist used the space to design and sell concrete figurines and statues."

"That old barnlike structure?"

"Big enough, that's for sure," Dunn said. "Soon as I get my shake, I'm on my way out there. Need a lift?"

"No thanks, but I may stop by later. First, I'd better see if my condo sustained damage." Drew reached for his crutch.

Tess delivered the yogurt shake to Dunn.

"Looks like I'm leaving, too," she said.

They walked to the cash register together and paid their tabs by debiting their Mark accounts. "Good you're back," Officer Dunn remarked as they exited the bistro. "Stay safe."

Is that a threat? Drew cursed under his breath.

It was a cooler day for July. Hobbling down the street with the help of his crutch, Drew assessed the damages to local businesses. Peeking through cracked windows, he spied ceiling tiles scattered across dirty floors, shattered light fixtures, and overturned furniture. Businesses had posted closed signs on their doors.

Maintaining law and order was difficult for cops in normal circumstances, but if electricity and cell towers stayed down, the criminal element would flourish. This was not something residents wanted. But these were unprecedented times.

Not yet ready to go home, Drew crossed the street to the Hardeman County Courthouse and boarded the elevator to the so-called dungeon. The lights in the basement hall strobed on and off. A decade ago, a dual battery back-up system had been installed with state funds. Drew walked past fallen ceiling tiles swept into dark corners and located the District Attorney's office.

Greg Diamond was seated at his desk sorting folders.

Drew cleared his throat. "Is this a bad time?"

Greg glanced up, smiled. "No, Detective." Greg waved him in. "Find a seat if you can." He shoved a stack of folders to one side of his desk and rested his arms on the smooth surface.

Drew took a few steps into the office. "Are you sure. Looks to me like you have a pile of information to plow through."

"I'm sure, I need a break. Let's talk a bit," Greg said.

"Looks like Fernwood got pretty shook up during the quake."

"Appears that's the case all over town," the D.A. said. "Two of my cabinets overturned, so now I have to sort through every folder to assure they contain the right papers." He quirked his lips.

"Don't you have a secretary to help with that?"

Greg shook his head. "She didn't make it."

Drew blinked. "Is there a body count yet?"

"Two-hundred thirty souls countywide," Greg replied.

"Have you seen my wife?" Drew asked.

"Mary? No." Greg threaded stout fingers through his thick mane of graying hair. "I heard you were out of town when the quake struck." He abandoned his desk, stood up and stretched.

"Yeah, I took a little trip—tried calling Mary recently but the cell towers were down," Drew said. "She was to California."

"Well, if that's the case, she's safe." Greg scrutinized Drew.

"I hope so."

"Where were you when it happened?" Greg asked.

"At an airport, quake was all over the news," Drew remarked.

"Yeah, that freakish volcanic eruption at Reel Foot Lake, followed by a 9.7 quake, created a crater the size of the Grand Canyon running down the entire length of Mighty Mississippi River. All bridges between Tennessee and Arkansas are down."

Greg grabbed a breath then erected a folding chair. "Sorry, Detective, forgot my manners. Please sit down. Would you care for some coffee? I can call Wendy's and have some delivered."

"No, I was just there, thanks." Drew dropped his weight in the hard metal chair, leaving his crutch parked against the front of Greg's desk. "I heard the station moved to a new location."

"Yeah, it's put Sheriff Boswell in a tizzy." Greg chuckled. "I know it's not funny, but her antics are first-class humorous."

Drew smiled. "So, how did the jailhouse fare?"

"Not so well," Greg replied.

In the next few minutes, Drew learned that Caroline Sullivan had walked out of the county jail when the earthquake shook the building and opened the doors of all the cells. The news only added to Drew's subliminal anger over failing his mission in Canada.

"Sullivan has not been spotted since," Greg added.

At the news, Drew thought his heart might stop beating.

"Sorry, Detective. Wasn't anybody's fault."

"Is Sullivan a witch or not? How in the world can one woman be so lucky?" Evil people got the breaks while the good suffered.

Greg shrugged. "A quirk of Fate, I suppose."

Fate . . . ? Drew's bitterness toward God escalated. "Yeah that, too," he muttered. Fate had not been favorable to him. Straight out of Sullivan's pistol, a shot to Drew's head produced a stroke that had turned him into a partial invalid. Yet, the serial killer had walked free because Fate was kind to her. It sickened him.

"I know, I know," Greg empathized. "We all wanted to see Sullivan fry for her murderous rampage." He jerked a breath.

"She killed your wife, Greg! Tracy would still be alive if that woman wasn't walking on the earth! You would be the father of twins! My God, how can you just sit there and rationalize?"

Drew's voice escalated with even greater passion. "I swear, Greg, I will track down Caroline Sullivan and kill her with my bare hands!" He was shouting by the time he finished.

Greg blinked. "Better rethink that one, buddy."

"You think I care if I fry? I don't."

"What about your family?" Greg posed. "What about Mary and the boys? You have to think of them, Drew."

Without answering, Drew rose from his chair and grabbed his crutch. A few minutes later, he stood outside the courthouse.

A cab ferried Drew home. His SUV was parked in the driveway. Surprisingly, his subdivision consisting of concrete-and-steel condos had weathered the quake rather well.

Drew let himself inside his unit with his key and surveyed the minor damage. A few ceiling tiles lay on the kitchen floor. Smaller dishes had plummeted from the cabinets and lay shattered on the tile floor. These were repairs he could take care of himself.

He flipped a switch. No light, no electricity, no surprise.

Luckily, the sun was shining brightly through the windows. It might be the only happy sign of the day. No rain, no wind to speak of, and no shaking. After he had unpacked and taken a shower, he wanted to go over to Grace Riley's house and see if she was okay.

He was hoping she had heard from Mary.

Grace wasn't home. He'd left Little David in her care.

Where were they?

Not wanting to return to his empty condo needing a good cleaning, Drew decided to rent a motel room for a couple of days until he felt like dealing with the stuff cluttering his condo.

2

DREW CHECKED INTO THE Day's Inn located in the vicinity of the North Mall then drove over to the building on Highway 64 East, formerly occupied by Dover's Statues and Figurines. The owner, an artist, had passed a few years back. In absence of a will, or heirs, and the fact no one had purchased the property at a county tax sale, the city was glad to rent it to the Fernwood Police Department.

Not ideal for a temporary police operation, at least the abandoned building was a large enough space to accommodate their equipment and staff. With many mom-and-pop businesses shut down on court square, watching out for the bad guys was even more important. Drew turned off Highway 64 into the parking lot.

Dover's was surrounded by dirty black-and-white squad cars squatted like racoons around the two-story white concrete structure. Drew pulled his truck off in the grass, killed the engine and got out. The double-wide, commercial steel, door, stood open like an invitation. He picked his way over the gravel surface and hobbled inside, hoping that Sarah would not grill him about where he'd been for close to a week. He accessed the situation.

Unfortunately, not in the best of moods, Sheriff Boswell was yelling directions as desks were hauled through the garage door at the back entrance. Windows stood open to counter the heat. Temporary dividers had been erected down the right side of the building for make-shift offices. Battery-operated lights installed on a few walls dispelled the darkness in the twenty-foot-tall building.

Drew crutched over to Sarah and waited for her to finish yelling instructions. Eyeing him out of the corner of one eye, she faced him. "Where have you been all week, Detective Taylor?"

Not a good sign. Drew grimaced then replied, "Out of town," maintaining his balance on a shaky crutch.

"Well, I want details."

"If you're busy, Boss, we can talk another time."

"No, now!" Sarah pointed a finger at Drew then yelled at Officer Robert Fellows, "Hey, Bob! Get somebody to help haul that larger desk over by that window where the lighting is better!"

Drew stood like a statue, waiting for the next shoe to fall.

Sarah turned to Drew. "Sorry, trying to organize this mess."

"Wish I could help." Drew raised his crutch. "I wonder when our electricity will be up and running." Fatigue tugged at him after his long trip. And the day would likely get more stressful.

"Hopefully, by Monday," Sarah piped, her mind centered more on the furniture hauled by workmen through the backdoor.

"I see you have a food table set up." Drew's stomach growled.

"Yeah, have something to eat while I check the delivery truck out back." Sarah walked to the open garage door in the back.

Drew hobbled over to a ten-foot-long table covered in a beige vinyl cloth and loaded with plastic plates of sandwiches, compliments of Burger King. Coca Cola Company supplied the drinks in iced bins. Really hungry, he snagged a burger from the plastic tray and woofed it down while standing. Brushing crumbs from his hands, he snapped open a can of Coke and guzzled it.

"Sorry, about walking away from you like that," Sarah apologized as she approached Drew. "You were saying?"

"It can wait." He shrugged, swiping his hands on a paper napkin. "Food's good, did you try a sandwich?"

"Maybe later," Sarah piped, sweat peppering her furrowed brow. "We really need you back at work, Detective Taylor."

"I can see that." He nodded. "Anybody hurt in the quake?"

"Skeeter Jones," Sarah reported. "He went to the ER with a cracked ankle, crushed ribs, and minor cuts from falling ceiling tiles. Fell right through a hole that opened up in the second floor."

"Sorry to hear that," Drew said.

"We all suffered trauma, but that's another story."

Drew waited a beat then asked, "Have you seen Mary?"

"No. Hey, Georgie!" Sarah was distracted. "Open some more windows. This heat is really getting to me," she barked.

"About Mary. . .? Drew's question was unanswered.

"Goodness, we're in a mess." Sarah turned to Drew. "I don't know what's going on with you, Detective, but I'll give you a raise if you come back to work. As you might guess, crime is on the rise."

He nodded that he understood, but she didn't. He was in no emotional shape to work cases. Rather than tell the sheriff no, he copped a reason: "I need to find my wife first and see if she's on board with me working again. Plus, I have to clean up my condo so it's livable. I only stopped by to see what was happening."

"Now you've seen." The oomph went out of Sarah.

"You should know I talked to Priscilla Dunn earlier today."

Sarah shook her head. "That girl's a piece of work."

More than you know, Drew thought but didn't say.

"Where were you all week?" Sarah inevitably asked again.

"I can't talk about it right now," Drew replied. "But we'll discuss what I've learned when things around here settle down."

"Related to a case?" Sarah's eyebrows arched to attention.

"I can't say yet."

Drew observed the frantic activity around them. Sarah should know that Priscilla Dunn had forwarded Sullivan's stolen murder evidence to her uncle in Canada then rerouted it to parts unknown. Maybe the FBI should be notified. He intended to hunt down Caroline Sullivan, even if it was the last thing he did on earth.

For now, he needed to concentrate on finding Mary.

"Okay," Sarah said. "Go do what's necessary, then come back and we'll talk. I want to know what secrets you're keeping."

Drew left Dover's and drove over to Cory Lindsey's house. It was a sight to behold. The front porch had caved in but the house still stood. He walked around the right side of the property and approached the back door, feeling strangely like an outsider.

Peering through the kitchen window, he spied Cory standing by the gas stove cooking something in a large pot.

Same ole, same ole, life continues on for the living.

Drew tapped on the window and Cory crossed the kitchen to unlock the back door. "Up to some company?" he asked.

"Absolutely, come inside," Cory mouthed. "My pot of ham hock with white dried beans will be ready soon. Alexi is craving some good ol' cornbread and collard greens, too."

"Smells delicious." Drew stepped inside the kitchen. "But isn't it a little hot outdoors to be heating up the house?"

"Oh, I have a backup generator," Cory said.

"What's with Alexi's craving?" Drew asked.

Cory laughed. "She just found out she's pregnant," he piped. "I'm pretty excited. My first kid and all, you know."

"I can see that, man!" Drew slapped Cory on the back. "Congratulations!" The timing seemed off, considering the brief number of years left on earth. *Every man to his own* . . .

Cory took a moment to scrutinize his friend. "What's going on, Drew? You don't seem genuinely enthused over my news."

"I am," Drew replied, "it's just I'm bogged down over some unresolved issues." He didn't want to plow into his relationship with Mary or his recent findings in Canada. A failed mission.

"Been home yet?" Cory asked, sampling the bean soup.

"Yeah," he shrugged, "Place needs some cleaning up. Have you seen my wife?" That was the real reason Drew had come.

Cory parked his wooden spoon. "You two haven't talked?"

Drew frowned, troubled even more.

"She was here yesterday," Cory said. "She picked up your SUV and said she was going home. Didn't you see her?"

"No. Were you home when the quake struck?"

"No, we left Fernwood," Cory explained. "Mary came and got us. She found Elijah in California and he told her to go home, something bad was about to happen in West Tennessee."

Drew stared at Cory, no comment.

"Mary woke us up shortly after midnight before the quake struck. She insisted we leave town with her and Little David.

Something terrible was about to happen in West Tennessee. We resisted at first, but she finally convinced us. I drove."

"Where did you go?" Drew asked.

"Nashville. We stayed with Tom Rave. He told us you spent night with him before catching a flight to Canada," Cory said.

Drew nodded. "Yeah, I did."

"What was that trip about, buddy?"

"Just chasing down a lead for an unsolved case."

Cory turned off the gas eye and took a seat at the bar. Ready to get off his bum leg, Drew parked his crutch and joined Cory.

"The trip did not go well," Drew revealed.

"How so?"

Drew questioned if he should discuss his trip with Cory since he hadn't yet told Sheriff Boswell about his discovery.

"You know I'm good at secrets," Cory said.

"I know." He shrugged. "I'm at my wit's end."

Cory noted the despondency in Drew's voice. "That's a cynical remark if I've ever heard one, friend. It's not like you."

Drew frowned. "Life turns on a dime."

"Okay, know that I'm here if you need to talk."

"Thanks." Drew grinned.

"It's too warm in the house, I'd better turn down the AC." The control dial was on the wall. "Want something cold to drink?"

"A glass of cold water will suffice," Drew replied.

They were still seated at the bar when Alexi trotted in the kitchen with Miracle balanced on one hip. "Hi, Drew."

"I heard congrats are in order, Alexi." The mama was wearing one of Cory's large tee shirts. "You better teach Miracle how to use her legs before you make room for a baby."

"I'm already expanding." She blew a riotous cinnamon curl off her long forehead. "If this heat doesn't let up, we'll die."

"No, it's hormones kicking in." Cory hugged his young wife and patted her abdomen. "You're going to birth a normal child."

"Or two," she piped. "I'm a prime target for twins."

3

Monday, July 12

The Vatican

THE CONCLAVE TO ELECT a pope had been in process for six days. Usually, the participants were chosen from cardinal-electors. In this case, a lottery had selected the seventy qualified candidates.

Black smoke had gone up the Sistine Chapel's chimney twice and the voting ballots burned. Delegates could not agree on a suitable candidate for pope. Angry and somewhat controlling, everyone wanted that job, believing they were the best choice.

With all the unrest and bickering among the constituents, Lazarus suggested that his brother, a world leader and not a Catholic, address the Conclave regarding a consensus.

Sunday had not been a day of rest. Lazarus had bickered with his brother over which one of the seventy participating in the Conclave was most qualified to effectively lead church affairs since an untold number of Catholics left Planet Earth on 12/24/25.

With a huge void in world leadership, many local church vacancies had been filled with less competent priests.

Another problem, the general population was so skewed in their views of how the church should operate, whoever was chosen might not have wide acceptance. If religion was to be tolerated, the largest congregation in the world needed people with leadership skills, all willing to cooperate with world government guidelines.

They agreed peace was required to counteract terrorism.

The twins finally arrived at an idea that would astound the members of the Conclave and place Lazarus in charge of Catholic affairs. No religious institution since Jesus Christ had more ethical influence over the general population. Diplomacy was required.

On Monday, following Catholic protocol, members of the Conclave repeated standard prayers, liturgies, and sang praise songs.

That done, Luceres stood before his anxious audience. Warmly smiling, he grasped the wooden lectern with both hands and perused the faces of the seventy participants.

"Thank you for inviting me to address this Conclave," he said. "I complement you for your patient indulgence in this important process of selecting a pope. The Catholic Church would be less influential in the world but for your fortitude. God is pleased."

Some applauded, sharing a few positive comments.

"In light of the monstrous disasters plaguing our planet, what you accomplish here today as a group is enormously important."

A loud applause struck a chord of pride in Luceres.

"It is your job to uplift congregations and encourage members to trust in a Higher Being. Especially since trials, plagues, and destruction have touched every family of every races."

He held up a hand to silence the clapping.

"It's a privilege indeed to meet with you today, so together we can envision a better future for the Catholic Church."

Empowered by his own words, Luceres continued.

"I understand how difficult this process has been." *Empathy always forges a consensus.* Luceres thought his speech was going well.

"What is *empathy*?" Andre whispered to his daddy.

"Shush, son! Pay attention to Uncle Luceres."

Andre frowned, not happy at being scolded. He turned around in his seat and looked at all the big people. He did not like them.

"There's a small boy in our midst," Luceres said. "My brother's son is with us today. Introduce Andre, Father Bacon."

Lazarus stood up with Andre and whispered for him to wave and toss imaginary kisses at the Catholics. In response, the Conclave members chuckled before a hand shot up.

"Yes, Bishop Boyd?" Luceres recognized Lydia, a Chicago-born American. Once, during an outbreak of small pox in London, England, they had served together on a committee. Dedicated to Catholic ministries, Lydia was cautiously obstinate at times. It would be fruitless to deny her the opportunity to air her remarks.

"Isn't your brother a celibate priest?" Lydia asked.

"Of course, he is *now*, Sister," Luceres replied. "As you well know, it is never a good idea to abort a child." He appealed to Catholic theology. "My brother has been absolved by a priest for his carnal mistake. At the time, he was not a priest. He's my brother, and I assure you no one is more devoted to the faith."

A few comments circled the audience.

Bishop Boyd was still standing, conflicted.

"Jesus Himself said, 'He who is guilty, cast the first stone.' Don't you think Lazarus deserves your forgiveness? He's an excellent father and presently raising Andre at the Vatican."

Not a peep, nor a protest, erupted over the remarks.

"Is that a problem, Lydia?" Luceres asked.

"I guess not." She relented and sat back down.

"As I was saying . . ." Luceres continued, "I appreciate your devout dedication to the Catholic Church. Since the birth of the Christian Church, Catholics have influenced society and taken good care of the poor and indigent. I compliment you and your forefathers for their dedication to that task. What happens today is even more important." He paused to allow introspective reflection.

"You know it is imperative that we select a pope. And quickly. Especially now. Our distressed world cries out for a religious leader with the ability to inspire faith and courageous behavior."

Heads affirmatively nodded at the statement.

"Furthermore, each of you have willingly accepted the job of electing a pope, a serious process. Are we all in agreement?"

Heads bobbed as discreet eyes met and moved on.

"No person that ever walked this earth has exhibited more of the Creator's characteristics than Jesus Christ," Luceres stated.

Hearts were crossed to signify Christ's death.

"Should we not acknowledge the few *other* good prophetic men who have also exhibited personal traits so astounding that religions were founded in their names? All faiths have worth, correct?"

The idea that all religions were equal sent the Catholics into a flurry of comments. "Are you referring to Islam and Buddhism?"

The question came from a priest in his seventies, seated in a pew near the back of the Sistine Chapel. "Yes," Luceres replied.

"Surely not, those are false religions!" several shouted.

"Cardinal Joseph and Bishop Culpepper, I appreciate your comments. You express a shared view of many Catholics. However, your argument is mute since the PEACE FIRST DECREE has been endorsed and widely accepted by all religious groups. Why revisit that non-issue now during this serious process?"

Embarrassed, the cardinal and bishop sat down.

"Excuse me, Dr. Ramnes?" Bishop Boyd intervened again.

"Yes, Lydia?" Luceres grew impatient at her interference.

Standing, she sputtered, "If you truly support a one-world religion, why are you helping us select a Catholic pope?"

"Thank you for asking." The electors were growing upset at the discussion. Luceres window of opportunity for consensus was short-lived. "Let me introduce to you my candidate for Pope."

Talk burst forth like a storm unleashed. "But we haven't cast our votes again!" Protests erupted in maddening fashion.

"Quiet, please! I understand your concerns, please bear with me while I present my case." The chapel whispered quietness.

"Father Bacon," Luceres addressed his twin. "Bring your young son to the podium so that everyone may clearly see him."

Lazarus hauled Andre up two steps and faced the electors.

"This is Andre, a most unusual gift from God."

The audience of seventy grew instantly still.

"This boy has uncanny abilities." Lazarus' gaze roamed the faces of the electors. "I don't recall the exact scripture in the Bible, but it has been said, 'a little child shall lead them.'"

That statement prompted discussion.

"Is there anyone in here who has a medical problem?"

The electors' eyes wandered the chapel before Bishop Jernigan from Ireland spoke up. "I have been crippled since birth."

"Would you step up on the podium and stand by me?" Luceres extended a hand. "Don't be frightened, this is no test."

A few people lightheartedly chuckled.

Bishop Jernigan hobbled to the front of the Sistine Chapel on crutches and stood at the base of the podium.

"Is the boy going to heal me?"

"Why don't we find out?"

Lazarus was so pumped he thought he might explode a few light bulbs. His brother was a genius. No one like him ever.

"Andre, this is Bishop Jernigan. He's a good man." Luceres smiled at the boy. "Will you reach out and touch him?"

Andre looked to Lazarus. "Is it okay with you, Daddy?"

An elderly nun on the front row chuckled.

"Bishop Jernigan needs your help," Lazarus explained. "He is crippled in one leg. That means he cannot walk normally."

A few nervous chuckled erupted, as if it were a joke.

"Okay, Daddy, if you say so." Andre timidly took a few steps toward the bishop then pointed a small finger. "Him?"

More laughter erupted as comments were shared.

"This is all very amusing," Bishop Boyd remarked. "What is the point of this demonstration? Andre isn't qualified to be pope."

"Lydia, my good friend. Why not let the majority decide if this boy is qualified for the office?" He motioned for her to sit down.

Not comfortable with the process, she sat down anyhow.

"Andre," Lazarus said, "reach out and touch Bishop Jernigan on his withered leg and say the words I taught you."

Andre bent over and touched the bishop's leg with one hand. "Be healed according to your faith in Jesus," he proudly stated.

Anxiously, with hope in his expression, Bishop Jernigan leaned forward and placed his wrinkled hand over the boy's small warm hand. "That was really very sweet, Andre. Thank you."

"I'm not through yet," Andre said. "Be still."

Many chuckled at the boy's cute antics.

"Be healed right now!" Andre looked up at Lazarus. "Did I do it good, Daddy? Is this man going to be all better now?"

"You did *great* son! Perfect!"

Anticipation was nearly palatable in the chapel. Everyone waited and watched Bishop Jernigan as he walked back to his seat.

"What's happening?" Jernigan felt the bones in his feet pop and his ankle lengthen. "I can't believe it, praise God!"

"What's going on, I can't see?" Necks stretched to see past the people blocking their view. "What did the boy do to him?"

Bishop Jernigan lithely leaped upon the stage, ecstatic over his healed leg. "Look! See for yourselves!" he shouted out at the audience. "I can wiggle my toes. And walk." He demonstrated.

The audience stood and loudly applauded.

Satisfied with Andre's performance, Luceres raised a hand to silence the applause. "Lazarus . . .?" he turned to his brother. "With your permission, ask Andre to demonstrate his other unusual gifts."

4

Jerusalem

MONDAY EVENING, RABBI Michael Thoene was in his apartment located in a forty-unit complex constructed after Jerusalem was decimated by an Iranian missile attack. Antiquated buildings in the city had fallen like dominoes in the wake of the terrorist attack.

Like other homes built on the outskirts of the city, Michael's house was in need of repairs before he and Ari could move back in.

Only the Tribulation Temple was left standing on the Mount of Olives in Jerusalem. A miracle in light of the destructive bombs.

Abram, later called Father Abraham, offered his son Isaac as a blood sacrifice to Jehovah God on this holy mount. Abram trusted God to protect the heir that would bless all nations, the first act of faith on behalf of Israel. Instead of allowing Abram to slay his son, God substituted an animal sacrifice in Isaac's place. His Son Jesus later was called the Lamb of God since He gave His life for sinners.

Many of Michael's cohorts had not yet accepted Jesus as the Messiah. Only with the Holy Spirit's help could anyone be saved.

It is what it is, he thought to himself.

After receiving his third dose of chemo earlier that day, Ari had gone to bed shortly after eight p.m. Cancer of the blood targeted his lymph nodes and weakened his immune system. The prognosis for his recovery from lymphoma was not good. The young teen suffered much. Michael was comforted he was sleeping soundly.

It had been a grueling work day for them both. Michael had met with a few bank managers about the overflow of funds pouring into their coffers from Christians all over the world. Many wanted to use the funds to rebuild Jerusalem. But there were not enough vaults in the city to hold all the gifted gold and silver.

Michael's thoughts collapsed. He was tired from thinking and hungry. He fixed himself a tuna sandwich and watched a news report out of Rome, Italy. The Conclave had been in process at the

Vatican for over a week and had finally ended. BREAKING NEWS flashed on the screen as the scene evolved to St. Peter's Square where a plume of white smoke rose out of the Sistine Chapel.

The camera zoomed in on a CNN reporter standing by the courtyard fountain. He pointed at the balcony. "As you can see from the rising white smoke, a new Pope has been selected. Momentarily, the recipient will be introduced to the hundreds of people anxiously waiting here at the Vatican. Excitement continues to mount as the moment grows closer."

The camera panned St. Peter's Square. Cardinals, bishops, priests and nuns, waited anxiously for the results. They were joined by other enthusiastic Catholics who had traveled some distances.

"About now," the reporter said, "our newly elected Pope is stepping through the Door of Tears where he will be taken to a dressing room and fitted with the appropriate white vestments and reemerge into the Sistine Chapel to receive the Fisherman's Ring."

More panning of the courtyard by several CNN cameramen occurred before their star reporter said, "After the new Pope gives his blessing upon the conclave participants, he will emerge from that balcony and address the people in St. Peter's Square."

Cameras zoomed in on the balcony.

"With seventy members of the Conclave vying for the office of pope," the reporter took a huge breath, "we can only imagine who won the vote." He stuck his microphone in the face of a startled nun. "Sister, who do you think has been selected?"

The prune-faced elderly nun boasted in a German tongue that she believed Bishop Lydia Boyd would make an excellent pope. It was high time that a woman had some say in the *Curio Romano*.

The nun's statement was quickly translated into several languages and broadcasted to the millions viewing the event. Hashtags and Tweets instantaneously circled the globe.

* * *

"Are you ready to greet your audience?" Lazarus asked Andre. "Don't be afraid, everyone loves you, adores you."

The boy wrapped in white stuck his thumb in his mouth.

"I'm too small to be a pope." He stamped his foot.

Lazarus laughed. "Your uncle and I will help you make decisions and fulfill your responsibilities. Don't get all stressed."

He mussed Andre's mop of black hair. "You'll be fine."

* * *

Luceres had been chosen to announce the name of the new Pope to the world. Not being a practicing Catholic, he read from a script. *"Annuntio vobis gaudium magnum! Habemus Papam!"*

Then he translated the Latin: "I announce to you a great joy! We have a pope!" Cheers erupted from the courtyard.

Lazarus appeared on the balcony carrying his young son dressed in a white tunic with a gold sash. His pontiff hat was too large for his head and sat askew. Andre waved at his constituents.

As if an alien ship had appeared, conversations in St. Peters Square ceased. Only the whisper of the wind marred the silence. The CNN reporter dropped his microphone and stood in awe.

Realizing his error, the reporter quickly scrambled to compose himself and go on the air. The camera was pointed at the balcony.

"Greet Pope Benedict the Twenty-first, the grandson of the previous pope who taken on Christmas Eve, 2026," Luceres announced, not surprised at the reaction of the audience. They did not know whether to clap or drop to their knees and pray for guidance. The CNN reporter began to describe the unfolding scene.

"Those who are present in St. Peter's Square, and viewing this event on their electronic devices, are witnessing a first," the CNN reporter shakily stated. "A small boy has been selected as Pope."

A tidbit of information on the new pope was fed into the earbud the reporter was wearing. "It's been said that 'A little child shall lead them.'" He looked at his lead cameraman.

"What?" the gal mouthed.

"Shut that thing off, I'm done here."

"What about the follow up?" she asked.

"Forget about it, I can't report what I don't understand." He walked to the nearest exit gate and left St. Peter's Square.

Michael Thoene turned off the television, puzzled over the Catholics' selection. There must be more behind the scene than meets the eye. For one thing, the phrase, "A little child shall lead them," came from Isaiah 11:6 and referred to a time during the millennial reign of Christ when children would not be afraid of ferocious animals. A time when peace ruled the earth.

Michael phoned Rabbi Yohann Waddi for his opinion.

"Yohann, Michael here. I hope I didn't wake you."

"Oh, no, I was just catching up on some reading."

"Do me a favor," Michael said, "turn on the television."

"What's going on? Are we about to be bombed again?"

"No." Michael waited a couple of minutes for Yohann to see what was taking place at the Vatican and offer a comment.

"Well, well . . ." Yohann said, shocked.

"What do you make of the new pope?"

"I'm dumbfounded, as you must be."

Michael inhaled deeply. "How can a boy rule over the affairs of the Catholic Church? Unless this is a ploy of world government to control the masses under the guise of religion."

"Exactly my sentiments," Yohann said. "Dr. Luceres Ramnes has found a way to influence the decisions of the *Curio Romano*."

"That being the case, isn't it uncanny that Pope Benedict the Twenty-first is the grandson of the recently departed pope?"

"Makes me think of the Deceiver," Yohann said. "The Bible says a False Prophet will support the Antichrist's reign."

"Scary thought, isn't it?" Michael sighed.

"Out of our hands, my friend." Yohann waited a beat, then, "How's Ari doing after his chemotherapy treatment?"

"He's sick and went to bed early," Michael replied. "I'm probably skipping the meeting scheduled for tomorrow morning."

"I understand your concern over Ari, but it is imperative you attend the meeting. You're our spokesperson, Michael."

"I know I am, but someone else can do that."

"What is more important than soliciting twelve thousand anointed Jews to respond to God's call to evangelism?"

"Whether I'm there or not, the event will come off."

"But you are focal to this movement," Yohann pointed out. "With record deaths around the world, people need to hear about the saving grace of Jesus. Messianic Jews trust your leadership."

"I am no Peter or Paul." Michael sighed. "If I come to the Temple, Ari will be with me. I want him covered in prayer."

"No problem." Yohann empathized with the situation. "But you know that we are not gods over our own lives. If Ari does not survive cancer, he will dwell in Heaven with other Christians."

Michael tensed at the idea of losing Ari.

"Never forget departed believers are always praying for those left behind," Yohann said. "But, hopefully, Ari will survive."

"I know the Bible!" Michael countered. "But letting go of my only son in death is too hard for me to bear. It's good that you have never suffered loss of a wife to cancer as I have."

"Let's not dote on death," Yohann said. "We must all work together to help many souls experience the Light of Salvation!"

Michael was too choked on emotion to respond.

"Come to the meeting tomorrow, Michael. We'll lay hands on Ari and pray for his healing. Besides, Mary Ralston is speaking.

"I didn't know that," Michael said, truly surprised.

"I emailed you this morning."

"Sorry, I haven't checked my messages today."

"She's bringing her adopted son. Little David, I believe."

"How old is the boy?" Michael inquired.

"Ten months, I've been told."

"Healthy, I hope," Michael said.

"Some allergy issues, but otherwise—will I see you tomorrow at the meeting?" Yohann asked. "We need you there."

5

Tuesday, July 13

Fernwood PD at Dover's

"I TOLD YOU SO!" Detective Georgie Adams exclaimed to Drew as she filled a Styrofoam cup from the coffee carafe then added ample cream with sugar. They were in Dover's compact kitchen and he was seated at the square vinyl-top table, deep in thought as he tapped the tips of his right-hand fingers on the morning paper.

"What? You're not speaking to me?" Georgie hawked.

Looking away, hanging onto sanity by a thread, Drew was in no mood to address whatever topic Georgie was about to throw at him. All he could think about was Mary. She had picked up his SUV at Cory's after their trip to Nashville and gone home, so Cory believed. If she had, she packed and left again. Why?

"I know you're a troubled man, Andrew Taylor," Georgie used diplomacy. "My advice to an ailing heart won't cost you a thing. I'm a good friend, have you forgotten?" Georgie recalled the rumors floating around that Drew and Mary were separated.

"This is not a good time, Georgie," Drew muttered, eyes downcast on the shiny vinyl table purchased third-hand.

"Your wife is out of the family picture, forget about her."

The scathing look Drew directed at Georgie would have chastised an ordinary person, but not the savvy female detective.

"What? You can't man up and face the truth?"

Drew half stood, eyes blazing at Georgie. "My marriage is not up for discussion, Detective! Mind your own business!"

Georgie threw up her hands. "I can't believe you!"

"Believe who?" Sarah entered the make-shift kitchen formerly used for storing cleaning items such as mops and vacuums.

Drew shrugged, sat down, and offered no response.

"Okay, you two, what is going on in here?" Sarah's charcoal eyes widened. "Don't tell me my *only* detectives are at odds."

"Don't blame me," Drew said. "I was reminiscing when this busybody. . ." he pointed at Georgie, "interrupted my solitude."

Georgie opened her mouth but nothing came out, a first.

"Come on, I wasn't born yesterday," Sarah sputtered. "Tell me what's got both of you in such a stitch." She grabbed a coffee.

"Wanna see a henpecked husband?" Georgie pointed a finger at Drew. "You're looking at one sick puppy, Sheriff."

Drew shifted uneasily in his chair, uncomfortable with the truth. He had bent over backwards to please Mary.

"Is this really necessary, Georgie?" Sarah sassily parked a hand on one hip, her plum-colored lips twisting with disgust.

"Who else has the gumption to make Drew see the truth?" Georgie quipped. "His *so-called* wife Mary has turned our Andrew into a first-class wimp!" She was on a mission to fire him up!

"That's quite enough, both of you!" Sarah snapped, hoping the sparring would not escalate and ruin their friendship.

"I don't think so." Georgie wasn't finished. "If Drew doesn't stop mooning over Mary, he'll be no use to the PD."

"She's way off base," Drew countered, standing to leave. He didn't need Georgie's verbal abuse or the job. He'd be fine.

"I agree with Drew. When has his personal life become your business?" Sarah got up close in Georgie's face. "Stop this."

Georgie took a step back, more determined than ever.

"You helped me when I was down, or did you forget, Sheriff? It is my business if *my* friend can't stand up for himself!"

"Georgie . . ." Sarah tried to remain the adult in the room. "This is not how to win or influence friends. Let it go, okay?"

Not deterred, Georgie sidestepped Sarah and pointed a finger at Drew. "Where's your spine, Taylor? Your will to overcome and survive? You gonna wallow in self-pity till the chicks come home?"

Sarah laughed, muttered, "It's 'till the cows come home.'"

"Same thing," Georgie mouthed.

Standing shakily using his one crutch, Drew blinked back tears he refused to release. Georgie was right, but he could not face the idea his marriage was over until he'd spoken to Mary. There must be a reasonable explanation. If only she would talk to him.

"I'm sorry, Drew," Sarah apologized. "Georgie didn't mean it. She has no right to tell you how to run your household."

Drew's lower lip quivered as he lifted a weak defensive hand. "No, she's right." His droopy brown eyes drifted to Georgie. "I need to find Mary and see if there is any hope for us."

"Finally, hot dog!" Georgie slapped her thigh. "Then we'll get our detective back, fully in gear, ready to work macho cases!"

Sarah shook her head. It was all pretense. She steadied herself with a hand on the back of a chair. "Don't judge Mary too quickly. She has a knack for trouble. Don't forget Sullivan is out there."

"Call her now," Georgie said.

"I've tried."

"Not one word since you went to Texas?" Sarah asked.

"Nope."

"Maybe she has a good reason. Don't sink the ship yet."

Georgie chuckled to herself. "Give me a break."

Ignoring the jab, Drew said, "I'm going to fill out a Missing Persons' report on Mary. I need to know if she's safe."

"Wait!" Sarah intervened. "Are you sure about this?"

"Yeah, I am." Drew dragged his useless leg across the room toward the open doorway. "You asked me to come back to work, so here I am." He ambled through the opening and headed across the huge wear-house-turned Fernwood Police Station.

Sarah snagged Georgie by the shirttail as she started after Drew. "Let him go, girl, he's in no mood to hear an apology from you right now." She pulled her friend back in the kitchen.

"How did you know?" Georgie spun around to face Sarah.

"Honey, I've been living in the same house with you for a year now. What's *not* to know about you?" Sarah returned.

Georgie shrugged. "I was a little hard on him."

"Uh-huh." Sarah smacked her lips.

"Do you think he'll forgive me?"

"Probably not for some time," Sarah replied.

"What should I do?"

"My best advice? Stay clear of him for a while."

"How long is awhile?"

"You'll know," Sarah said, "until he talks to you again."

"I hate it when you're right," Georgie mouthed.

* * *

Drew checked the work schedule thumb-tacked to a bulletin board by the front door. He penciled in his name where there were vacancies. By Monday, he'd be on the regular schedule, have a designated work area cordoned off with dividers, a desk with locked drawers for files, a land phone, and hopefully an ergonomic office chair that swiveled in all directions so he could park his lame leg on the lip of the desk. For the rest of the morning, he was off the job.

And for a good reason. He had an appointment with Dr. Susan Parrot for 11:00 a.m. He left Dover's and drove over to the Hardeman County Hospital, parked, and entered the building.

He was early as he rode the elevator to the fifth floor. After checking in with Dr. Parrot's office secretary, Liz, he sat down and waited for Dr. Susan Parrot to invite him into her office. Which happened sooner than he anticipated. "Detective Taylor?"

"Yes." The female psychiatrist sanctioned by the Fernwood PD to counsel their troubled officers invited him into her office and pointed a floral lounge. "Have a seat, Detective."

As homey as the lounge appeared, he chose the cushioned chair. He wasn't interested in comfort, just a little good advice.

"Good morning, Andrew," Susan said with confidence as she took a seat behind her desk. "Okay if we record our conversation?"

He nodded then yawned. "Sorry." Almost sighing, he wished he'd chosen the reclining lounge with the plush pillows.

Perceptively, she said, "You can still use the lounge if you like."

"No, I'm okay," he said, uncomfortable with her staring.

"Aren't you sleeping well?" she inquired, glancing down at her notes from his last visit. "Did you get your meds filled?"

"Meds work fine, but I'm pitifully troubled," he admitted.

She smiled. "I hope I can help you with that."

He nodded. "Yeah, maybe we can settle this today."

"That isn't how therapy works, Andrew. I need to see you on a regular basis, get to know you better. Not just when things turn nasty in your life." Her aquamarine eyes bore down on him.

He grinned. "Aw . . . so you read minds, too."

"On occasions," she teased. "Want to tell me about your day?"

Andrew Taylor was an attractive male. As strong as he appeared, Susan knew he was emotionally vulnerable. She should be careful not to judge his situation too soon. She smiled.

"How do you want to begin our discussion?" Susan asked.

"It's more about my wife." He stared into her beautiful face, suddenly prepared to bear his soul to her, possibly more.

Then he caught himself and shut off his lusty thought.

"Relationships are sometimes difficult." Susan had suffered failed relationships far too often. But like Andrew said, he was *pitifully troubled*. Not a good candidate for a romantic entanglement.

"I'm really glad you understand," Drew said, grateful he had the ear of someone who would not criticize or condemn him for his failures. With confidence, he launched into his latest drama with Mary, careful not to reveal specific details regarding his secret sting in Canada. "When I returned home, Mary was missing again."

"Missing, or possibly kidnapped? Or just out of sight without an explanation?" Susan suggested. "There are huge differences."

"I can understand why Mary took off to California to find the Two Witnesses," Drew told Susan. "She wanted to find out why the sinkholes were occurring around the world," he explained.

"But something else happened," Susan concluded.

"Yeah, we missed connecting on our cell phones." He paused then continued. "She phoned me once, but I did not want to divulge I was in Texas working on a lead to catch a serial killer."

"When she was ready to talk, you weren't," Susan said

He nodded. "Yeah, that time it was my fault."

"Best guess, where is Mary?" Susan asked.

"According to a friend," Drew shifted his weight in the chair to position his bum leg better, "Mary came home from California the day after I left for Canada. She warned Cory and his family to leave Fernwood, something disastrous was going to happen."

Susan blinked with understanding.

"Oh, the earthquake event? How did Mary know?"

"She has inside information with the Two Witnesses."

To that, Susan had no remark. This conversation was indeed strange. But she had to admit, Andrew Taylor interested her.

"Mary and Little David ended up going out of town with my friend and his family. I later learned they stayed with a mutual friend in Nashville. I'm glad they were safe during the quake."

"Looks like that story ended well," Susan said.

"My friend said she came back home to stay."

"But that wasn't the case," Susan said.

"No, and I have not heard from her."

"And that troubles you a lot," Susan concluded.

"Yeah, it does."

Susan was patient, listened carefully, took notes, and remained alert in her facial expressions as Drew painted the picture of a wife who was more centered on evangelism than being with him. They rarely talked to one another, except when they were engaged in sex.

Susan's cheeks glistened with red spots.

"Sorry if I embarrassed you, Counselor," Drew apologized.

"No, it's just that, well, sex is usually the first thing to wither in a failed marriage. Could it be that Mary loves you but is more devoted to Jesus?" She let the idea solidify in the compact room.

Drew was at a loss for words.

"Andrew, you can't compete with Mary's faith."

"So . . . what should I do?"

"Well, keep trying to call her. Check with her friends."

"I left four message and she's ignored them."

"Or you're calling the wrong number."

"Could be she has a new burner phone."

Susan tapped her pen on her desk. "As I recall, cell towers in West Tennessee are down. Did you consider she may have tried?"

"No, I guess not," Drew admitted. Staring a bit, he said, "So you think I've judged my wife too quickly?"

"If you love Mary, doesn't she deserve a chance to explain her absence?" Susan leaned forward to rest her forearms on her desk.

Drew nodded. Susan was right.

"I know you're angry on several levels, Andrew."

Drew cursed. "Darn straight, I am."

"You despise how life has turned out in the past—getting shot twice, then a stroke that left one leg lame. Added to that trauma, your wife has different goals than you. She's not as devoted to the marriage as you are." Susan opened up a can of worms for him to examine. He might get angry and just walk out. But she hoped he would think about his agreement with Mary before they married.

"Yeah, I don't come first, and that bugs me."

"Would you respect Mary more if she abandoned her mission to serve Christ in these fleeting days?" Susan asked.

"I guess not," he replied, unsure if that were true.

They talked another twenty minutes then Drew left the hospital. Outside, he turned on his cell phone and it worked.

6

Tuesday, July 13

Jerusalem

THE MEETING IN THE Temple Courtyard was scheduled for 10:00 a.m. for the purpose of assembling Messianic Jews called by God to evangelize the world on behalf of His Son, Jesus. In the seventh chapter of Revelation, an angel foretold the number of descendants of Jacob who would be called to the task. Whether women would be included in that number, Mary was uncertain.

Hadn't God chosen her as His advocate?

Yet, 144,000 Jews let loose on the planet preaching the Gospel of Jesus Christ was a huge undertaking. Who would respond with a hearty *"Here am I, Lord, send me"*?

Standing near the entrance of the Temple courtyard, Mary kept a sharp eye out for Rabbi Yohann Waddi as people gathered. After arriving in Jerusalem on July 8th, she had located a women's shelter operated by four nuns. A free hot shower and clean bed for her, plus a cradle for Little David, was greatly appreciated.

Once wealthy, with unlimited funds to spend, she had not once considered donating money to organizations of this kind. Now destitute, it had taken her last piece of expensive jewelry to afford the international flight over. Nevertheless, coming here was right.

Today, Mary stood among the throng of people with a plump baby boy cradled in her arms. To be honest, she was a little anxious but still hopeful. While enjoying the beautiful day God had arranged, a scholarly-looking man wearing the trappings of a Jewish rabbi approached Mary and faced her. "Can I help you?"

"Are you Mary Taylor?" the man inquired.

"Yes." She smiled. "Are you Rabbi Waddi?"

"No, my name is Michael Thoene," he replied.

Mary freed up a hand and shook the lean rabbi's hand.

"Yohann is dealing with last minute details, so he asked me to walk you to the front stage and help you get seated."

Mary stared into a pair of eyes as clear as blue crystals.

"Thank you, Rabbi, do you mind carrying my son David?"

"No problem."

Mary released her sleepy toddler into the strong arms of the handsome man. "It was a long flight over and David's weary."

"He's quite a little bundle to carry." Michael held the boy against one shoulder. "I have a son." He gently swayed the sleepy boy. "His name is Ari. He's fourteen. How old is your son?"

"He'll be one year old in October." Mary walked beside Michael toward the state. People graciously parted to allow them to pass. Some older children smiled and waved at Mary.

"Don't be surprised, your face has appeared on television often enough for people to recognize you," Michael remarked.

"I suppose rising from the dead gets people's attention."

Michael laughed. "Absolutely."

"Does Rabbi Waddi want me to talk about my experience?"

"Up to you, Mary." Michael followed her onto the stage. "Be seated and hold David while I see what's detaining Yohann."

Michael handed David to Mary then disappeared into the crowd. The number of believers gathered in the courtyard was larger than Mary anticipated. Unfortunately, skeptics would be present, too. They came out of curiosity, some to get a closer view of the Temple erected on the very site as King Solomon's Temple.

From Mary's perch on the stage, she had a bird's eye view of Jerusalem's new buildings rising out of the ground like glistening steel robots encased in glass. Smiling, she recalled the movie titled *The Terminator*. As a youth, the possibility of Judgment Day had seemed far-retched if not impossible. But *now* she knew the Battle of Armageddon was eminent. The thought was chilling.

Mary closed her eyes and began praying. She let out a slow breath then took another in. Let one out and took one in. It was a way to calm her nerves. As the sweet scent of jasmine teased her nostrils, she questioned if the odor siphoned from the floral pots lining two sides of the courtyard, or if the Holy Spirit was making His presence known. The Bible indicated God could smell the righteous prayers of His saints and it pleased Him.

Mary opened her eyes and felt a release. Little David was muttering and sucking on his thumb as she held him tightly. "You little bugger." He playfully giggled as she tickled his bare feet.

For July, there was less humidity in the air than an ordinary summer day in her hometown of Fernwood—which made her ponder why she and Drew kept missing each other. Feeling for her cell phone, she thought better of calling now. After the meeting, she promised herself to make an effort to reach her husband again.

The time she'd spent with Tom Rave in Nashville and Cory's family had been rewarding. Never apart, the newlyweds were so in love they beamed. Mary longed for that kind of relationship with Drew, but something, someone, or some mission always interfered.

She'd intended to drive straight home after dropping Cory and his family off at their house, but she'd gotten only as far as the front door of the condo when God clearly spoke: *Go to Jerusalem.*

"No," she'd almost blurted out aloud, "I can't."

Do not tarry, I have work for you.

In Mary's mind, she had questioned Jesus' directions. Moses had said to go home and save her family. Surely, he'd meant for her to save her marriage. But Christ's commission was clear. *Go!*

She'd let herself into the condo, dropped off their dirty clothes in the laundry, repacked and left for the airport. And here she was.

Repressing tears, Mary tried to put her troubled marriage out of her thoughts as she waited for the two rabbis to reappear.

What could she say to the audience that someone else couldn't say even better? Who was she to speak for God?

"Sister Taylor!" The half-Irish man with bowl-cut, burnt-orange hair, a tatty beard, and alert eyes the color and size of chestnuts, stepped on the stage and offered a plump hand.

"Rabbi Waddi." She shook his warm hand. "Where's Rabbi Thoene?" She glanced out over the increasing crowd.

"He went home to fetch Ari. The boy has been pretty sick, diagnosed with leukemia shortly after Jerusalem was bombed."

"Is Michael—I mean Rabbi Thoene—expecting me to pray for Ari's healing?" Mary inquired, nervous over her upcoming speech.

"He would never put you in that position."

She nodded. *Only God can heal.*

"No need to apologize for using first names, Mary," Yohann said. "Michael and I would not have it any other way."

Out of the corner of her eye, Mary spied an elderly woman mounting the stage. "Sister Taylor?"

"Yes."

"Let me hold your child while you speak."

"It's okay, let Sister Juliana help," Yohann said.

Mary made eye contact with the head nun for the local women's shelter for the abused. "That is very kind of you."

"David and I will sit on the first row, and if he gets cranky, I'll give him right back to you," Juliana said, eyes bright on Mary.

"It's a good idea," Yohann told Mary. "David will be fine and we need to talk briefly about your part in the program."

Little David settled into Sister Juliana's arms like he belonged there. She provided a plump shoulder on a warm body, stuck his pacifier in his mouth, and he began snuggling and sucking.

"I've never spoken before to so large a congregation," Mary shared with Yohann as they stood together behind the lectern.

"You've preached in churches across the United States, have you not?" he returned. "Just tell the folks out there how you feel about Jesus. I don't think you'll have any problem at all."

Mary smiled. "You make it sound so easy."

"It is, my child. God just wants His best for all of us."

7

Fernwood

DREW FINISHED HIS SESSION with Dr. Susan Parrot shortly before noon on Tuesday. Afterwards, he stopped by the condo for lunch. All that was left in his fridge was a carton of Chinese noodles swimming in stale oriental vegetables. He shoved the food in the microwave to heat and waited impatiently for the beep-beep.

Psychoanalyzing his mistakes with Susan had not brightened his day. His truck keys and cell phone were on the bar where he'd dropped them when he came inside. Should he call Mary?

While eating lunch, Drew blankly stared at his iPhone.

Susan thinks I should call her again.

But, if he did, and Mary ignored his call, it might throw him into a fit of depression. He recalled his breakdown in front of Little David. Feeling antsy when life ahead looked bleak, he was tempted to pop a can of beer, no two, and wallow in the buzz.

He stared down at his food, growing cold.

But if he didn't talk to Mary, he might never know for sure if she came home then left again. Susan's words slapped him in the face. *Are you jealous Mary loves Jesus more than you?*

The beautiful psychiatrist had him pegged, played him like a maestro on his fine-tuned violin. Every hidden note in her words pinged at him. Maybe he was self-centered and self-serving.

I'm not going back to work today, he decided. *I don't feel like answering questions about where I was last week or what I was doing there.*

That Priscilla Dunn was still in town after the damage she'd done to Caroline Sullivan's case irked Drew. He'd seen that subtle glimmer tucked away in her eyes. It said she knew he knew.

His hands were symbolically tied. Sarah required proof that Dunn stole the murder evidence before an arrest warrant was sanctioned. Eventually, Dunn would make a mistake.

What is Dunn's relationship to the serial killer?

Weary of his thoughts, Drew fell asleep in the den recliner and woke up mid-afternoon. He turned on the tube and surfed through the news channels. Nothing reported but devastation, death, and threats of plagues breaking out in West Tennessee if the government didn't get the water and sewage systems operating properly. He was about to switch off the TV and call Sarah when a special report from FOX interrupted the normal programming.

The camera panned the Tribulation Temple Courtyard in Jerusalem. Drew couldn't believe his eyes when he spied his wife standing at the podium giving her testimony. He turned up the sound to hear what Mary was telling her audience.

"I would be home right now with my husband and son if Jesus had not told me to come here," she spoke with emotion.

So that's why she left Fernwood.

"I believe there are people here who are sick and in need of healing." Mary's sparkling blue eyes panned the courtyard.

"Don't be shy. If you want me to pray for you, please come forward and kneel at the altar. Rabbis Waddi and Thoene will anoint you with holy oil as I pronounce a prayer over you."

The Jerusalem scene segued into the FOX studio.

"During the event this morning, fifty people received a healing. In addition, hundreds of Jews entered the courtyard, knelt before the altar, and committed to evangelizing the world for Jesus."

A clip of the crowd disbanding after the service was shown before the reporter continued his fair-and-balanced report.

"Christians are calling the station to report a total of 144,000 Jews from the twelve tribes of Israel will ultimately volunteer for missionary service. Tune in at six o'clock tonight for a full report."

Drew turned off the television, shaken. Mary would be home if Jesus had not instructed her to go to Jerusalem. She was only being obedient to Christ's instruction. Susan was right. He could not compete with her faith? But did she still love him?

He fell to his knees and wept over the situation.

From somewhere deep inside of Drew, words burst forth as he confessed to God his bent for sinning. How he'd so often chosen the path of unrighteousness and doubted his salvation. How he'd become bitter at life because his first wife Marie and their baby son had been snatched from earth during the Rapture.

"God, I pray you will restore my relationship with *You*. If it is *Your* will, I ask you to bring Mary and David safely home. Heal our marriage, and give me a chance to be the husband I should be."

He wept between thoughts coming so fast he was dizzy.

"I want to be obedient to your commandments, Lord. Please help my unbelief. Increase my faith in Your ability to deliver me from trials. Grant me the will to remove the Mark of Satan."

Drew was unaware of how long he'd prayed on his knees, weeping like a wounded child when he heard his phone ring. Blinking back tears, he read the caller I.D. and answered.

"Mary?" A flash of hope exploded in his spirit.

"Yes, it's me, Drew."

* * *

Sarah had agreed to meet with Drew at seven p.m. He'd insisted that they talk alone at her house, refusing to give his reason for the meeting. The sun was a bloody wound on the western horizon when he left the condo. Angry clouds assembled on the western horizon, threatening to usher in a windy rain front.

Memphians were distraught about the prospect of more water flooding their streets and flushing through the already overloaded sewer systems. People were still trying to salvage their belongings from collapsed buildings. City officials were discussing how to construct a new bridge between the New Great Divide—the gap created by the quake along the Mississippi Riverbed.

It would be a long time before West Tennessee residents returned to anything resembling a normal life. With these thoughts in his head, Drew parked his truck in Sarah's driveway and got out.

Sarah stood on the front porch landing. "Come in, Detective, I just made a pan of fresh cornbread to go with my beef roast."

She waved him though the front door.

"Thanks." He hobbled toward her using his crutch.

"Hope you brought a healthy appetite with you, Detective."

"I can smell the roast from here." He smiled at the prompting of his appetite. After speaking with Mary by phone, his mood had improved significantly. She wasn't sure how long she'd be in Jerusalem, but promised to come straight home afterwards.

"What's so secret we can't talk at Dover's?" Sarah asked.

Drew trailed the sheriff through the living and dining rooms into the kitchen. It was the first time he'd been inside her home. A plate of buttered sweet potatoes sat on the stove.

"You know how to win a man's heart, Boss." He glanced down the hallway. "Where's your roommate?"

"Out." She removed the heavy lid from an iron skillet then began slicing the cornbread with a butter knife. "After you phoned, I sent Georgie in search of a few difficult grocery items."

"What I have to say won't take long," he remarked.

"Okay, supper can wait." Sarah swiped her oily hands on her apron. "Let's go back in the living room and talk."

"As a side note, I spoke to Mary today. She's in Jerusalem on God's business," he said. "But she's coming home. We're fine."

Humph. "Tell that to Georgie," Sarah remarked as she sank into the comfortable padded rocker. "Have you forgiven her?"

"For browbeating me?" He sat down on the sofa and parked his crutch at the end. "I didn't like it, but I'll recover."

"I have to say you've done a one-eighty!"

It took Drew a couple seconds to digest Sarah's remark.

"Now that I know Mary's safe, I feel a lot better," he said.

"Okay . . ." Sarah leaned forward in the rocker, "what's so cotton-pickin' important that it can't be discussed at the station?"

"Priscilla Dunn."

Drew launched into his private sting carried out in Canada in an attempt to recover the murder evidence stolen from the station right out from under their noses. Sarah frowned but listened, not interrupting except to clarify a few points before chastising him for not having the proper police backup in place before going.

"I didn't get a look inside the boxes Dunn shipped but I know it was our evidence." Drew didn't waver on that point. "Dunn's neighbor, Annie Pope, told me she stowed three boxes for her."

"We need to talk to Annie," Sarah said.

"She's in her early nineties," Drew reported. "She has memory lapses—not sure how much she'll recall." He stared at Sarah. "Annie means well, but she might not make a good witness."

"But," Sarah interjected, "if we can verify the date Dunn parked those boxes at Annie Pope's apartment, we can establish a reasonable chain of criminal intent, though circumstantial."

"It will take a court order to obtain the rerouting shipping address from the FedEx office in East York, Canada," Drew said. "Maybe you can convince Greg Diamond to expedite the query."

Sarah leaned forward in the rocker, hands grasping the sides.

"You should've told me what you were going to do, Drew. Wherever that shipment landed, it's probably long gone by now," Sarah pointed out. "You know I don't approve of rogue tactics."

"I know," Drew said.

"You know, yet you did it."

He nodded. "I'm sorry I disappoint you."

"No, you're not." Sarah stared at her detective. "You'd do it again if it meant recapturing evidence against Caroline Sullivan."

Drew dropped his head. "Yeah, I guess I would."

"Look at me, Taylor!"

Drew's head shot up.

"Texas has first dibs on Caroline Sullivan. She murdered thirty-five officers from three branches of government when multiple bombs exploded inside Wanda Sullivan's house. VICAP has broadcasted her photograph, including her disguises, all over the United States and abroad. The FBI and CIA are involved."

"So, what? You want me to back off?"

"No, I want you to come back to work and let's investigate Priscilla Dunn by the book. We'll get the evidence back then we have more solid ground to prosecute her and Sullivan for their crimes. No more solo flights. Are we clear, Detective?"

"As a bell," he said.

"Clear about what?"

Sarah and Drew's heads simultaneously swung toward the intruder. "I didn't hear you come in, Georgie," Sarah said.

"Back door was open." The detective sat her sack of groceries on the dining table and stared at Drew. "Who uses Bombay oil? Is that even a product? Give me a break, Sarah!"

"I take it you didn't find the items on my grocery list."

"Gave up after I talked to the guy shelving products," Georgie confessed. "He glanced at my list and laughed."

Drew glared at Sarah, deft to comment when Georgie asked, "What's all this about Priscilla Dunn, Detective Taylor?"

"How much of our conversation did you hear?"

"Enough," Georgie replied, "fill me in on the details."

8

Wednesday, July 14

D.A. GREG DIAMOND TALKED to Judge Emit Longstreet and he signed a search warrant for both Priscilla Dunn and Annie Pope's apartments. Detective Georgie Adams rode shotgun with Sheriff Boswell. SWAT occupied the back seats. They were traveling in a Chevy Suburban, on their way over to the Lilly Hills Apartments.

"What's up with Drew?" Georgie asked as Sarah handled the black suburban with skill. SWAT officers dressed in black gear rode silently behind them. "Is he quitting for good?"

"I don't know." Sarah wagged her head. "He's got to sort out his relationship with Mary and get his head screwed on straight before he'll be any good at detective work again."

Georgie's nod said she agreed. "What that woman's done to Drew is a crying shame." She never trusted Mary.

"Let's not revisit that discussion," Sarah grumbled. "Hopefully," she centered on the sting, "Annie Pope can enlighten us regarding what was inside the boxes she stowed for Dunn."

"If she can remember." Georgie piped as Sarah pulled the Suburban up to the entrance of the apartment complex and let her and SWAT got out on the walk. They were to wait outside the office until Sarah talked to the apartment manager and cleared what was about to take place through legal channels.

Within ten minutes, Sarah was back.

"Okay, guys and gals, let make this effort count." She pulled a bullet-proof vest over her blue jacket and secured it.

"You think Dunn will give us some grief?" Skeeter asked.

"Too clever for that," Sarah replied.

The six of them took the side stairs up to the third flood and Sarah banged on Priscilla Dunn's apartment door. Receiving no response, she opened the door with a key the apartment manager provided. The place was cleaned out, dust particles afloat.

"She knew we'd be coming!" Georgie scoffed.

"Let's see what Annie Pope knows." Sarah stepped across the hall and rapped on the door. Receiving no response, she knocked again harder just to make sure no one was home before entering.

The door swung open. "Yes?"

An elderly woman holding a pad and pencil in one hand blocked their entry, surprised to see people wearing black gear.

"Fernwood Police Department," Sarah quickly announced then presented the woman with a search warrant.

"What's this?" The woman stared at the paper.

"Our permission to search the premises," Sarah replied. "Are you Annie Pope?" Sarah glanced into the living room.

"No, I'm not."

"We need to check this apartment for criminal evidence. Are you a relative of Miss Pope's?" Sarah inquired. "Where is she?"

The woman's hands flew to her face. "You don't know."

"Know what?" Sarah asked.

"Annie was killed when the quake struck," she informed the sheriff. "Didn't the apartment manager inform you of that?"

"No, he didn't. Sorry." Sarah glanced over at Georgie then back to the woman. "What are you doing in Annie's apartment?"

"I was sent by the Director of the Funeral Home."

"Your name?" Sarah asked.

"Cordell King."

"And why where you sent, Ms. King?"

"Since Miss Pope has no living relatives, she specified in her will that her apartment belongings were to be donated to the Salvation Army. I was making a checklist of the contents when you knocked on the door." Cordell trembled. "Am I in trouble?"

Sarah let out a profound sigh. "No, but my team still needs to go over the apartment," she said. "Can you come back later?"

"Sure." Grabbing her purse off a chair, Cordell gratefully skirted out of the apartment and ran toward the hall elevator.

"Okay, guys, do your thing," Sarah ordered.

Georgie started in the guest bedroom while Sarah raked through Annie Pope's bedroom and clothes closet. Bob and Jason Perkins—the newest rookie officer—tore the kitchen apart, looking in every nook and cranny for evidence that Priscilla Dunn had been in the apartment. The search took a less than an hour.

* * *

Dover's

Back to work at Sarah's request, Drew was unhappily seated at his assigned desk. At least there was a window view of the highway.

In no physical shape to accompany Sarah's SWAT and search Dunn's or Annie Pope's apartments, his dysfunctional leg ached worse than the headache blossoming in his skull. He wondered if the meds he took for sleep were responsible. Like a hangover.

He should talk to Dr. Susan Parrot before refilling the pills. Sleep was fine, but he needed a clear head the next morning.

Worry never left him. No use denying that he was upset that Mary decided to attend the commissioning service for the Messianic evangelists. Uncertain if she would be asked to speak, she had felt it was more important to remain in Jerusalem than come home.

What could he say? *Don't listen to God.*

He chuckled to himself. What would Susan Parrot think of his inability to express his feelings? And why should he even care?

In a funk mood, Drew mulled over his troubled marriage to Mary. For their relationship to work, one of them needed to become more submissive. Mary would not. It had to be him.

I'll have to have help to do that.

He stared deftly at the folder containing information he had accumulated over weeks on Priscilla Dunn's activities, mostly written notes he'd scribbled in the margins while in Canada.

Whatever he believed about the rogue cop was conjecture. It was inconceivable that not one shred of physical evidence tied Dunn to the stolen Murder Book, or the two evidence boxes that contained snapped photos and discovery items collected at the murder scenes of Tracy Diamond, Tonya Baker, and Kelly Peters.

Did anyone really know who Dunn was? Although a copy of her application with references had been forwarded by the station by email, had Sarah taken the time to recheck them? He knew she'd received a call from the Memphis Chief of Police forewarning her to keep an eye on the troubled officer. Only Sarah knew what Dunn had done to displease the Chief, and was not given a choice regarding the transfer sanctioned by the state police commissioner.

He removed Dunn's application from its folder and read through the names of the people she'd given as references.

John Fallon was at the top. His cell phone number was listed with a New York apartment address. *What the heck!*

Using the landline, Drew punched in Fallon's number. It rang four times before voicemail requested the caller to leave a name and number. "Andrew Taylor, give me a call, John. It's important."

Drew had not prefaced his name with his title, thinking if Fallon was a friend of Dunn's, he might not call back.

11:09 a.m. Morning was slipping by.

Going over Dunn's and Pope's apartments was taking longer than Drew anticipated. Maybe he should've gone with them.

No, if Priscilla Dunn was home, no way could he look at her face and tolerate the smug amusement he had witnessed on other occasions. She knew he'd failed to retrieve the murder evidence.

Fifteen minutes later, Drew's desk phone rang. He looked at the I.D. caller and saw it was a New York exchange.

"Yeah?" He pounced on the call.

"This is John Fallon. Did you just call?"

"Yes, I did Mr. Fallon. My name is Andrew Taylor. I'm a detective with the Fernwood, Tennessee Police Department," he explained. "May I ask you a few questions about Priscilla Dunn?"

"Who?"

Background noises indicated Fallon was driving in city traffic.

"Priscilla Dunn," Drew loudly repeated. "She's a recent transfer to our department. I saw where your name was on her original application." He looked at the date. "August, 2022."

He waited to see how Fallon would respond.

"Oh, yes," he said, "Priscilla and I used to be friends."

Red flags went up. *Use to be—as in not anymore?*

"How did you know Priscilla?" Drew moved forward.

"She lived in New York for over a year. That was before she went to the Academy. We hung out together at the YMCA," Fallon explained. "I didn't know she'd given me as a reference."

"No one ever called you?" Drew was surprised.

"I moved about the time Priscilla decided to be a cop."

Drew scrubbed his itchy beard. "Look, Mr. Fallon—"

"John, please."

"Look, John, I need to learn as much as I can about Priscilla," Drew said. "I was hoping you could enlighten me."

"It's been awhile," John said, sighing. "What can I tell you?"

"Does Priscilla have relatives in the New York area?"

"I heard her mention a cousin named Lloyd *something*," John recalled. "Actually, I didn't know Priscilla all that well."

Nobody knows her all that well, buddy, Drew thought then said, "Okay, if you think of anything else relating to Priscilla, will you call me at this number? She's a person of interest in a crime."

"Really? Actually, that doesn't surprise me."

Drew's pulse leaped. "What makes you say that?"

"She talked a big game but I never saw her ship come in," John said. "She's always dreamed of being rich or famous."

Haven't we all at times? Drew thought to himself.

"One more question, John. Did Priscilla ever mention the name Caroline Sullivan?" Drew inquired.

"Now the name *Caroline*, I know." John chuckled. "A wild chick in anybody's book. She dated Priscilla's first cousin, Brad *something*." He fell silent, trying to recall the guy's last name.

"Bradford Mansfield?" Drew ventured a guess.

"Big mean-looking dude with a giant chip on his shoulder, I recall," John offered. "Why? Are you looking for him, too?"

"No, Brad's deceased." Drew divulged no details of his death.

"Well, guys like Brad are bound to have a bad end."

You don't know the half of it, Drew thought.

"Okay, John, you've been very helpful. Call me on my cell phone if you think of anything else."

"Okay, gotta make some work calls now."

"Thanks for your time." Drew ended the call and glanced up. "How long have you been standing there, Detective Adams?"

"Long enough," she piped. "Who was on the phone?"

"Am I under investigation?"

"Don't get cute with me, Detective Taylor."

"Okay, I give up." Drew raised his hands in a show of surrender. "I spoke to a guy in New York named John Fallon." He reached for his crutch leaning against the divider.

"What's Fallon got to do with anything?"

"Priscilla Dunn gave him as a reference when she applied to work for the Memphis PD in 2022," Drew replied.

"How did you get hold of her application?"

"I borrowed it," Drew replied.

"You went through Sarah's file cabinet?"

Without answering, Drew locked the drawer to his files, mounted his crutch, and hobbled toward the front door.

"I'll find out anyhow!" Georgie called after him.

He waved her off, in no mood to explain his actions.

"Wait up." Georgie trailed after him. "Where are you going?"

"To get lunch, wanna tag along?"

"Then we're friends again."

"As long as you keep your opinion of Mary to yourself."

He would eventually tell her that Priscilla Dunn was Bradford Mansfield's cousin, so she knew Caroline Sullivan well.

"Then all is forgiven?" Georgie opened the front door.

"Well, not all, but I'm working on it."

They exited Dover's.

"Sarah asked me to fill you in on our morning sting at Dunn's and Annie Pope's apartment," Georgie said, crossing the graveled

parking lot with Drew. For a change, the weather was pleasant—
still sunny and hot, but not so humid.

"I'm all ears," he said.

"What are you hungry for?"

"Food," said Drew. "My pantry's a desert."

So, Mary's not home yet. Georgie surmised.

"I'm parked over there." Drew pointed a crutch at his truck
hunkered down under the shade of a large maple tree.

"Ride with me." Georgie eyed Drew. "Are you legally licensed
to drive yet?" She popped the Crown Victoria's locks.

"Applied, just need to take the driver's test," he reported as he
slid into the nylon passenger seat and set off sparks. Met by a wave
of heat, his gaze fell on a clear glass container of water with a
stringed teabag. "You make sun tea?"

"No, that's Bob's tea!" Georgie laughed. "We're taking his ride
since my vehicle is in the shop with transmission problems."

She ignited the Vic's powerful motor and turned the vehicle
around to face the highway. "How is Annie Pope?" Drew asked as
the engine idled while Georgie waited for the traffic to clear.

"Died in the quake, poor soul," Georgie replied. "According
to the coroner's report, a hanging brass-light fixture came loose and
bopped her on the head. She was already half there, anyhow."

"That's no way to treat the dead!" Drew teased.

"Stating a fact."

Noontime traffic had picked up. Georgie looked both ways
then took off down Highway 64 toward town. "A representative
of the Fernwood Funeral Home let us inside Annie's apartment.
She was making a list of Annie's donated items."

"Annie was a nice person." He recalled her perky personality.

"We tore the place apart and found no evidence that Priscilla
Dunn had ever been in Annie's apartment or stowed three boxes
for her." Georgie glanced over at Drew. "What?"

Should he tell Georgie about his visit with Annie before going
to Canada to collect the boxes? No, Sarah should tell her.

"What about Dunn's apartment?" he asked.

"Cleaned out," Georgie replied.

"She was always operating on borrowed time."

"What do you know that I don't?"

"Pizza okay with you?" It was a conversation for later.

"Pizza's fine." Georgie turned a corner and circled the courthouse. "Gloria's soda shop has reopened under a new management. No more burgers I'm afraid, but the antique bar is still serving milkshakes and all flavors of Jerry's ice cream."

"The Olde Soda Shoppe will never be the same without Gloria manning the bar," Drew remarked as they pulled into a parking space in front of Jennifer's Pizza Extravaganza.

"Tell me about John Fallon," Georgie said.

"Let's eat first then we'll go back to the station and find Sarah," he said. "You both need to hear what I have to say."

They exited the squad car on opposite sides and Georgie popped the automatic locks as Drew pushed open the front door and set off the familiar tinkling bells, as if Gloria was ringing them from Heaven's side. They found seats at a table near the back.

After ordering the pizza bar special with sweet tea, Drew asked Georgie if she had any idea where Dunn might have moved.

"If she has family, we should look at them first."

"Plus, she can't survive financially without a job."

Drew took a sip of Sun Tea, playfulness in his gaze.

"John Fallon. How does he fit in with Priscilla Dunn?"

"Let's eat," Drew said. "I don't want to ruin your appetite."

"It's already ruined," she piped.

9

DREW WAS SEATED IN Sarah's office on the second level of Dover's. The deceased owner, Franklin Dover, had accessed his office space via an electric lift like those found in the converted apartments of remodeled mid-town buildings in dying U.S. cities.

Dover's laminated desk faced a plate-glass window that overlooked the cavernous space below so Sarah could observe the ongoing work. Her back was to him as he approached.

Sheriff Boswell swiveled her chair around to face him.

"Detective Taylor. What can I do for you?"

The overlook into the space below felt like you were hanging off the side of a huge cliff. From this perch, Sarah could observe all the work going on below. Plus, a window AC attached to a window pumped 72 degrees Fahrenheit air to cool the office.

"Unbelievable!" Georgie quipped as she exited the lift and entered the office. "Our leader can't suffer heat with the rest of us?"

"Perks belong to the boss." Sarah eyed the detective.

"Nice cool view." Georgie peered into the vault below. "We can always count on your watchful eyes to keep us safe."

Sarah snickered. "No hanky-panky going on between you guys, I'll be watching over you like a guardian angel."

"No kiddin'!" Georgie plopped down in a metal chair with no padding and extended her lanky legs. Drew was already seated, his bum leg resting on a vacant chair while his crutch leaned against the putrid yellow wall. "This space needs serious redecorating."

"We won't be here that long, I hope," Sarah piped. "Is your leg still giving you serious grief?" she asked Drew.

"Nothing I can't handle," he said.

"Maybe you should talk to a surgeon, get a second opinion," Sarah suggested. "You don't have to live with constant pain."

"I'll give it some consideration." He stared down at the space below. They might've been sharing a booth at an opera house somewhere in Europe. "We have more worries, don't we?"

"Maybe it's a pinched nerve," Georgie speculated.

"I'm taking therapy for that," he responded.

Sarah looked at her detectives. "Why the ambush?"

"Drew has some news," Georgie answered.

"I don't need a translator!" Drew barked.

"I thought you guys kissed and made up," Sarah said.

"We did," Georgie said while Drew remained silent.

Sarah's dark eyes targeted Drew. "I suppose Georgie filled you in on our sting at the Lilly Hills Apartments."

"Yeah, too bad Annie Pope died in the quake," he said.

"Drew has a confession," Georgie impatiently offered.

Drew frowned at her then shifted his weight to accommodate his discomfort, unhappy that Georgie was pushing him.

"What is there to confess?" Sarah asked Drew.

"Tell her, Andrew!"

"I can speak for myself!" he yelled at Georgie.

"Would you two quit bickering?" Sarah slammed her fist on the desk. "Either tell me, Drew, or get out so I can work!"

"Sorry, Boss," Drew apologized. "I borrowed Dunn's job app from your file cabinet." He paused. "John Fallon was given as a reference when she applied to work for the Memphis PD."

"I'm listening." Sarah would not fuss at Drew for his improper behavior if he came up with something new to tie Dunn to the stolen murder evidence. "What did you learn?"

"I talked to Fallon," he replied. "He used to work out with Dunn at the gym—a year before she attended the Police Academy."

"So . . ." Sarah rolled her hand.

"He said Dunn regularly hung out with another couple."

"For goodness sake, Drew, just tell her!" Georgie exploded.

"You try my patience, Detective." Sarah glared at Georgie.

"Bradford Mansfield is Dunn's cousin, so she knew Caroline Sullivan," Drew continued. "Even back then, Mansfield was a bad dude, so Fallon wasn't surprised to learn he died."

"Not executed?" Sarah asked.

"Didn't go into all that," Drew replied, "but Fallon told me no one here ever contacted him about Dunn's reference."

"My bad," Sarah confessed.

Drew wasn't about to criticize his boss.

"Do you think Fallon's info is solid?" Sarah asked Drew. "Will he testify under deposition that Dunn knew Sullivan?"

"Probably, he seems like a solid guy who'd cooperate with our investigation. We should keep him in mind if Dunn is tried."

"So now we know Dunn has a past with Sullivan," Sarah remarked, feeling as though progress had favored them. "But we don't know why Dunn is risking her career to save Sullivan."

"Follow the money trail," Georgie remarked.

"You think Sullivan is paying Dunn for information?"

"Yeah, I do," Georgie answered Drew.

"Is that enough to get an arrest warrant?" Drew queried.

"No," Sarah replied, "but it's building a case against Dunn."

"I've already started a file." Drew held up his folder. "Maybe we should BOLO Dunn nationally?"

"She moved her personal belongings," Sarah said. "I want both of you to talk to the managers of every moving company within a hundred-mile radius." She paused. "Split the work."

* * *

Drew left Dover's a few minutes after two p.m. On his way over to Kennedy's Moving Company in Whiteville, Tennessee, he called ahead. The secretary told Drew the owner was spending the afternoon at his funeral home location and would not be back.

He thanked her and set his GPS to the new address.

The drive was brief. From the number of vehicles parked in front of Kennedy's Funeral Home, Drew assumed a service was in progress. Climbing out of his SUV, he mounted his crutch and made his way around the idling hearse preparing to lead a string of grievers to a burial site. The front door of the funeral home stood open like an invitation but was blocked by two elderly men wearing suits and smoking pipes that seriously polluted the atmosphere.

Drew coughed and stepped past the seniors into a vaulted foyer, plentiful in painted white wood molding and embossed antique wallpaper. The plush ruby carpet beneath his feet felt like resting on a cloud as he glanced around at the prestigious 18th-century home, a peaceful setting where the dead could rest.

The inside atmosphere was laden with fresh floral odors and lingering formaldehyde from embalmed bodies. Two rosters, one on each side of the foyer, displayed sign-in books for guests.

Drew presumed two funerals were in process behind the closed doors on opposite sides of the foyer. Uncertain how to find owner Bryan Kennedy, he ventured down the long-carpeted hallway until he came to a massive door marked OFFICE.

Drew lightly tapped on the door. It came open promptly, and a man dressed in a summer beige suit with a Peacock blue tie stood there. "What can I do for you?" he queried Drew.

"Mr. Kennedy?"

"Are you looking for Theodore or Bryan?"

"Bryan," Drew replied.

"He's at Cloy Johnson's gravesite, making sure everything is ready for occupancy. May I take a message for him?"

"Maybe you can help," Drew said. "Are you his brother?"

"No, I'm Teddy Kennedy, a first cousin," he replied. "We're extremely busy today. Could you come back another day?"

"No." Drew presented his detective badge.

"Detective Andrew Taylor," Teddy noted his name. "Are we in any legal trouble?" He pointed to a plush rose-colored wingback.

"Did you do anything wrong?" Drew decided not to sit.

Teddy smiled. "You jest?"

"Look," he said, "An officer with the Fernwood PD left without giving notice and moved out of her apartment a few days ago. I need to know if she used Bryan's moving company."

"He stores that information at his warehouse," Teddy informed Drew. "You'll need to ask him."

Drew snagged a business card from its holder on the desk and read the address and phone number. "Is Circle Road close by?"

"Yeah, south of Whiteville about two miles," Teddy replied. Pointing his finger west, he said, "Go right out of the parking lot and pass through town. You'll see a Wal-Mart on your left. Circle Road is the next left." He smiled. "It twists and turns a bit."

"Thank you for your time, Mr. Kennedy."

On his way to the warehouse, Drew phoned Bryan and relayed the information he required. Bryan said he'd call his foreman and have him look up the name. Drew thanked him.

10

Fernwood

BY THE TIME DREW was home on Wednesday, the sun was on its knees, surrounded by a thin purple haze. Drew switched off the engine, grumbling to himself as he recalled Bryan Kennedy's report that Priscilla Dunn had not hired his moving company. In fact, Kennedy's records indicated no one with a Fernwood address had hired their services in three weeks. Discouraged, he let himself inside his condo and sensed a hint of perfume permeating the air.

What's this? He turned on the kitchen lights and spied a mass of blond curls hanging over the back of his sofa.

Dr. Susan Parrot stood up, turned around, and faced Drew.

"Hi, Andrew, hope you don't mind an uninvited visitor."

"How did you get in?" He parked his keys on the hook and walked into the den, laser-brown eyes hard on his guest.

"Grace Riley was here and let me in."

He stood loosely on his good foot, dumbfounded.

"Oh, yeah, I forgot Grace was coming by to pick up a book she left behind last week," Drew recalled then tossed his billfold and pocket change on the counter. "Have you been waiting long?"

"No, you missed your 5:00 session with me."

"So, I did." Drew shrugged, longing for a pull on a cold beer. "I went out of town on police business. Why are you here?"

"You're my responsibility. I care about what happens to you."

Drew could not help but grin at his intruder.

"Are you always this personal with your clients?"

Susan glanced away. "You're right, I should not have come." She grabbed her bag and started for the door.

"Wait!" Drew snagged her by the arm. "That was rude. Are you hungry? Why don't I order something delivered?"

Susan looked into his eyes. "Are you sure?"

He saw tears in her eyes poised to flow.

"This isn't about me, is it?" he asked.

"No." She was trembling.

"Okay, we can talk a bit," he said. "I'll call Chu's and order an oriental dish for two, if that's satisfactory with you."

She nodded, clasped her hands and walked back into the den where she sat down on the sofa again. "I just needed a friend."

"Do you drink?" he queried.

"Yes, sometimes." Her gaze fixed on him.

"Okay then. After we have a glass of wine, you can tell me what's bothering you." He was uncertain how to feel about her being in his condo. However, he welcomed the company.

"White or red?" he asked.

"What?" Susan appeared distracted.

"Wine," Drew said.

"Either is fine."

He filled two glasses with a Chablis, handed one to Susan and eased down in a chair positioned in front of the window.

Susan took a sip. "It's good."

"It's a California wine I order by the case."

"Thanks for not kicking me out," she said.

"You want to tell me what's going on? Not that I'm qualified to counsel." He actually smiled.

"Did you order our food yet?"

"No, I'll do that now."

He sat his wine glass on the side table and removed his cell phone from his belt. While he called Chu's, Susan sipped on her wine, staring out the window at the descending darkness.

"Okay, where were we?" He picked up his goblet.

Susan's global seaworthy eyes fell on Drew. "I didn't know where else to go," she said. "I don't make friends easily."

"We aren't exactly friends, Dr. Parrot."

"Please call me Susan."

He nodded, puzzled by her friendliness.

"I'm certain someone was outside my apartment watching me when I got home from the office around six today."

Drew perked up at the news. "Who do you think it was?"

"Possibly Ben, or one of his friends," she replied.

"Who's Ben?"

"My ex-boyfriend," Susan answered. "Ben's a cop for the Seattle, Washington PD. I left there to get away from him."

Drew listened with caution, said nothing.

"At first, Ben was a perfect gentleman."

"I'm not your therapist," Drew pointed out.

"I know, but I need to explain. Okay?"

He nodded his consent to continue.

"Like I said, at first we were fine. Then he became adamant that I have sex with him." Her gaze enveloped Drew.

"In a dating relationship, that's common today." Drew sighed. "I assume you denied him that privilege."

"Yes, because I'm a Christian." She took another sip of wine. "I suppose I should not even be drinking alcohol." She set the glass aside and defensively folded her arms about her waist.

"Did Ben threaten you, Susan?"

She made eye contact. "Yes, he said if he couldn't have me, no one would. That was when I decided to leave Seattle. After four months, I really believed all of that was behind me."

"Wait. Do you think your life is in danger?"

Susan's eyes bubbled with tears. "I don't know, maybe."

His detective mind took over, outweighing caution. "I need more information, Susan, in order to evaluate your situation."

"The night before I left Seattle, Ben showed up at my door skunk drunk. He threatened to expose me for dating a man I'd counseled. He said he'd make sure I lost my license to practice."

"I take it Ben was one of your patients," he said.

"Yes, that's how we met."

Drew winced. "I can understand a guy falling for you, Susan. You are beautiful and desirable." He'd said too much.

"I didn't come here to seduce you, Drew." Susan stiffened.

"Sorry, I wasn't implying that."

"I came to see if you'd follow me over to my apartment and determine if I'm being watched or just plain paranoid."

"Sure, I can do that. First, let's eat something."

They watched a movie until Chu's driver delivered the food. The oriental vegetables with the sweet-and-sour chicken were sumptuous. Afterwards, they shared fortunes inside their cookies.

"Mine says I will have a long life," Susan said.

"Mine says, beware of trouble."

"That's not true." Susan jerked the slip of paper from Drew's hand and read it. *A new romance is on the horizon.*

"When is your wife coming home?" she asked.

"I don't know."

The silence became increasingly uncomfortable.

"Are you ready to leave?"

"Yes," she replied. "But there's another matter."

"What?"

"You missed a counseling session," she said. "I want you to call my office tomorrow and reschedule an appointment."

"Do you think that's wise, now that we're friends?"

"I'm okay with the arrangement, if you are," she said.

They cleaned up the kitchen and Drew followed Susan to her apartment complex. Parked across the street, he watched for any suspicious activity for another hour. When her lights were out, and he was certain she was safe, he drove home and went to bed.

11

Thursday, July 15

Jerusalem

MARY WAS IN A hotel room with the famous Two Witnesses, a meeting she'd prayed for, but made her feel displaced from reality.

Wearing a sackcloth toga and scruffy leather-strapped sandals, Moses appeared exactly like the actor who played him in the 1950s' movie, *Exodus*. Enjoying the present, he munched on a leftover piece of toast slathered with marmalade from Mary's breakfast tray.

"I wished you'd warn me before you show up," she said.

"Didn't God tell you we were coming?" Elijah asked.

"I guess I wasn't listening close enough."

Moses chuckled. "That's a sure way to land you in trouble."

"I don't want to talk about me." Mary was seated on the edge of her bed, nervous as to why they were there.

"Okay . . ." Moses' deeply-set onyx eyes ominously slid on Elijah, then to Mary. "What do you want to talk about?"

"What's happening to earth," she replied, releasing a held breath. "Don't pretend you don't know what's going on."

Elijah chuckled as he playfully eyed Moses. "That's what the Father likes about that girl, direct and to the point."

"That doesn't answer my question," Mary said. "Are you two causing the worldwide earthquakes and sinkholes or simply here to protect people?" She glanced at her cell phone for the time.

"Do you have to be somewhere?" Moses asked.

"No, but Michael and Yohann will be here shortly to pick me up. We're going over to the Bank of Jerusalem to make some financial arrangements for the traveling evangelists."

"The 144,000, you mean," Elijah clarified.

"Yes, but back to my question . . ." Mary needed answers. "Please help me understand what's happening to Mother Earth."

"Easy, the planet is submitting to Father God."

"Moses, please don't confuse me more, okay?"

"To be precise, it's both things."

Mary jerked her head at Elijah, the practical prophet. Moses was the tease. You had to get past Moses' personality to obtain a straight answer. Elijah, on the other hand, was intellectual and powerful in his speech. "How can it possibly be both?" she asked.

"God granted us the power to create disasters and protect people. He believes that hardships sharpen a person's character."

Moses scratched his long beard.

"It's simple, don't you see?" Elijah asked.

"Easy for you." Mary contemplated his answer. "You need to help people realize that life will never be normal again."

"Right!" Moses exclaimed. "Jesus never promised that living a holy life would be easy. It's narrow and treacherous and few will enter Heaven. But if people trust Jesus to save them, the benefits of Heaven on earth will roll alongside their persecutions."

Mary recalled Romans 5:3 when Paul the Apostle said the same thing: *"We also rejoice in our sufferings, because we know that suffering produces perseverance, perseverance, character; and character, hope."*

"Paul was a smart man," Elijah uttered, as if reading Mary's thoughts. "He knew all about suffering while he claimed the distant hope of an eternal life in Heaven uncluttered by persecutions."

"With the help of the Holy Spirit, Paul had the Mind of Christ. He knew the Torah like the back of his hand, yet embraced the concept of grace as seen through the Father's eyes," Moses said.

"But," Elijah qualified, "like the eleven apostles of Jesus', Paul suffered dramatically and died a horrible physical death."

What is their underlying message for me? Mary pondered.

The personality contrast between Moses the law-giver and Elijah the prophet was confusing, yet phenomenal. Gazing into the eyes of Moses was like peeking through black holes in the deep recesses of the universe. Elijah's eyes, a shimmering blue, reminded Mary of a mist hovering over a crystal sea. Together, with the help of the Holy Spirit, the Witnesses spoke as one voice.

"How Paul died is speculation," Mary noted. "Some think the Romans boiled him in oil." Her gaze skittered between them.

"It was his path," Elijah simply stated.

Loud knocking on the door brought Mary out of her speculation as to how Paul met his death. "Excuse me, guys."

She opened the door and peered at the two rabbis. Michael and Yohann waited for an invitation to come inside.

"Your timing is perfect," she said.

"Sorry we're late, I—" Yohann stopped mid-sentence when he spied the Witnesses. "My, my, I didn't know *they* would be here." He quizzically glared at Mary. "Did you know?"

"I was as surprised as you are," Mary replied.

Michael looked at Moses and Elijah, larger than life. "Should we leave? Are we interrupting something private?"

"Is it okay for them to be here?" Mary queried Moses.

The Two stood loosely and shrugged.

"I guess not," Mary said, "come in."

"What's happening here?" Yohann whispered to Mary.

"Not a clue," she replied, closing the door. "They have a habit of appearing out of thin air and scaring the wits out of people."

"This is an awesome moment," Michael quipped in awe.

"Don't think of making a sacrificial offering to us," Moses said. "Peter, John, and James, already tried that and it didn't go well."

Jesus transfiguration on the mount, Mary recalled then said, "Guys? Meet my friends, Rabbis Michael Thoene and Yohann Waddi."

"Good morning, Mary's friends," they said in unison.

"Michael and Yohann probably have questions for you."

* * *

Fernwood

It had been a harrowing week for West Tennessee residents. On top of the damage created by the quaking earth, torrential rains had flooded neighborhoods already under repair and washed out the foundations of the newer ones under construction. Companies hired by the county commissioner to repair the police station came back with a report that the building was inhabitable and needed total replacement. Sheriff Sarah Boswell was beside herself when she received a copy of the insurance report. A project of that magnitude required appropriated public tax dollars, and a ballot vote would not be taken until the county election in August of 2028.

Even if the bill passed, the police department would need to occupy the vacated premises of Dover's Concrete Statues and Figurines for possibly another year. Hardeman County could apply for federal funds for the project, but with all the damage done in West Tennessee, the Fernwood PD would not be first on any list.

Sarah broke the news to Georgie, who had a total hissy over the report. But that was only partially why she was upset. After chasing a rabbit down a hole in Henderson, Tennessee, Georgie had driven over to Jackson and interviewed the managers of two popular moving companies. Neither had moved Priscilla Dunn.

After a ratty day, Georgie sat in her truck and downloaded the phone numbers of every West Tennessee moving company listed. During the drive back to Fernwood, she'd called all six companies and hit a blank wall. *Conclusion?* Dunn had rented a U-Haul.

* * *

Georgie beat Sarah to bed after the ten o'clock news. The clock ticked beside her bed. Wide awake, sleep impossible, she traipsed down the hall into the kitchen barefoot for a mid-night snack. After scouring the fridge and pantry for food, it appeared Sarah had not grocery shopped in a while. But tucked behind the out-of-date clabbered buttermilk rested a small carton of yogurt

Strawberry, my favorite! Georgie grabbed it like a scavenger, tore off the cap, and spooned generous portions into her mouth.

"What are you doing up?" Sarah pattered into the kitchen in her noisy Wal-Mart flip-flops, yawning and stretching her arms.

Georgie spun around and pointed a finger. "Heavens to Betsy, Sheriff, you scared the britches off me!"

Sarah sassily parked a hand on one hip.

"The Grinch stole your sleep, too?"

"Yeah." Georgie dug into the carton of yogurt with her big spoon as Sarah bent over and gazed into the empty fridge.

"Anything left worth eating?"

"*Nada.* I got the last of the edibles." Georgie snorted when Sarah's frilly panties peeked from beneath her short housecoat.

"What?" Sarah erected her skinny black frame. "You had the nerve to devour my last carton of strawberry yogurt?"

"Yeah, is that a problem?" Georgie scraped out the last of the yogurt and licked the spoon clean. "Obviously, you didn't grocery shop this week." She tossed the carton in the trashcan.

Sarah pointed a finger. "It was your week to do that."

"Nuh-uh, you didn't put it on the wall calendar," Georgie retaliated. "I'm your guest, remember? Are you kicking me out?"

"No." Sarah collapsed at the kitchen bar, ragged out. "I'm so tired of thinking about Caroline Sullivan and how Priscilla Dunn pulled the wool over our eyes, I could wring somebody's neck."

"Not mine, I hope. Is God punishing us?"

"Seems to me evil is winning this round," Sarah piped.

Georgie leaned over the breakfast bar. "Maybe it's time we close Sullivan's case. I'd like to catch a decent night's sleep."

Sarah countered, "Me, too, Detective. But it would be nice to have a win occasionally. Finding Priscilla Dunn is our best chance of capturing Sullivan again and sending her butt to prison."

"Maybe we can cut a deal with Dunn."

"We don't have any idea where she is," Sarah said. "Besides, when were you ever into bargaining with a criminal?"

"I know my limitations."

"That's good to know," Sarah quipped.

"Oh, one other thing—forget about talking to moving companies, Dunn rented a U-Haul and moved herself."

"Which little bird told you this?" Sarah asked.

"Makes sense, since no moving company Drew and I contacted has paperwork on her. We need to think out of the box."

"Don't even mention the word box!" Sarah exclaimed.

"At that depressing thought, I'm going to bed."

"See you in the morning," Sarah said. "Sweet dreams."

"In your nightmares," Georgie quipped and left the kitchen.

Sarah chuckled, turned out the lights, then trudged down the hall into her bedroom and shut the door. *What a day!*

12

Friday, July 16

Jerusalem

MOSES AND ELIJAH WOULD be at the Commissioning Service for the 144,000 Messianic evangelists on Saturday. The event would be held in the Jezreel Valley, and Elijah had promised favorable weather. Mary had no doubt it would be. She'd been napping in her hotel room when Lazarus phoned. "What are you doing?"

"I took a nap, why?"

"Did you see the TV special on our new pope?"

"No," she'd replied. "I've been pretty busy."

"You missed a great event."

"How is Andre faring?"

"Beautifully," Lazarus bragged. "In fact, he's like Brer Rabbit taking to a briar patch. The Catholic Dioceses has never seen anyone like him." He paused. "You should be proud, Mary."

"This is your brother's doing. It won't work. Catholics will see though the ruse and realize they have been bamboozled."

"Our son is known by the world as Pope Benedict XXI. As I said, you should be very proud. Don't say anything to upset him."

"I would never cause Andre stress."

"I'm pleased to hear that."

"But I'm not blind or deaf, Lazarus. I know Papa somehow manipulated the Conclave process. He's using our son as a pawn in some shady world-government scam. At that thought, Mary trembled like the last leaf clinging to a dead branch in a hurricane.

"You worry too much, Mary."

"Not enough, because I should have seen this coming," she fussed. "Andre is not qualified to be a pope and you know it!" she spouted. "As soon as possible, I'm coming to get my son and take him home to America! And don't you dare try and stop me!"

The silence hung like icicles between them.

"That's not possible, Mary," Lazarus countered. "Andre is not legally yours anymore. The World Court has granted me legal guardianship over the Pope. You have no more say in the matter."

"What? How can you be so cruel?" Mary screamed. "I'm Andre's mother and you know how much I love him. Please don't do this to my son. He's too young. It's child abuse."

Abuse . . . ? Lazarus hadn't seen it that way.

"Okay, calm down, Mary. If you promise not to make waves, I'll arrange a visit," he negotiated. "But one negative remark to Andre and you'll be cut out of his life forever. Am I clear?"

"From your mouth to my ear," she replied.

After the disturbing call ended, Mary informed Rabbi Michael Thoene by phone that she would be leaving Jerusalem immediately following the commissioning service on Saturday. He agreed that under the circumstances her place was in Rome with her son.

After the call, she broke down and wept.

Oh, God, what are you thinking? Life has not turned out like I imagined? Talk to me. Tell me what to do. I'm so sad.

Mary sat on the bed in the hotel room, staring at her cell phone. Little David had been napping for hours. She was afraid he was catching a cold virus. She should not drag him around like this.

It's time to call my husband and repair our marriage.

Mary called Drew's iPhone number and received a disconnect message. Answers whizzed before Mary. Did this mean he was cutting her out of his life? Then decided he'd probably changed his number after the quake or was using a prepaid phone.

* * *

Back in Fernwood

Drew stared at his new prepaid cell phone and debated over whether to call Mary again. He'd texted her his new number last night. Did he really want to subject himself to more uncertainty?

Fully devoted to evangelizing the world for Jesus, she would never be the wife he needed. They were at opposite ends of the spectrum. She was light, and he was what? Just another dark spec in the universe? The thought was depressing. He needed to talk to Susan Parrot. She was helping him make the right choices.

But he'd have to be careful around her. Susan's sexuality would tempt any red-blooded male pumped up on hormones.

Do I want a relationship with Susan?

Maybe it was time to cut Mary loose and encourage her to do whatever she thinks God wants. He was her stumbling block. They could annul their marriage and go their separate ways. Divorce didn't have to be a nasty affair. They might end up as friends.

One test left: *Do we love enough to make the required sacrifices?*

Afraid of how Mary would answer the question, Drew decided not to call her. Then his phone rang. "Mary?" he answered.

"No, it's Susan. Since you haven't called my office to set up a new appointment, I set one up for you," she said.

"I'm sorry, I've had other things on my mind."

"It's okay, I understand. Is five o'clock today suitable?"

"I see no reason why I can't come." Part of the day would need to be spent in calling U-Haul companies.

"Good, I'll put you down on my calendar."

"Susan?"

"Yes?"

"Do you want to have supper with me afterwards?"

Her silence said she was thinking about it.

"Yes, but I think we'd better dine outside of Fernwood. I don't want people to see us together socially."

"That's not a problem. We'll drive over to Jackson. I know a great steak place." Was he thinking they could spend the night?

What about your promise to remove the Mark?

"Did you say something?" he asked Susan.

"No, what do you mean?"

You promised you would remove the Mark.

Drew trembled at the words in his head.

"Are you still there, Drew?" Susan queried.

"Yes." His skittering heart was beating out of his chest. *Did God just speak to me?*

"Drew, what's wrong?" Susan asked.

"Do you believe the Holy Spirit speaks to a person—in words, I mean?" This would be a first for Drew.

"I believe He influences our thoughts."

No, Drew sighed, *I heard the words.*

"Susan. Maybe it's not a good idea for us to have dinner after my session." He knew opportunity could lead to infidelity.

"Did I say something wrong, Andrew?"

"No, Susan, you've said everything right. And to be honest, I'm attracted to you," Drew admitted. "But I'm still married."

The phone abruptly disconnected.

"Way to go, Detective Taylor." He shrugged at his inept behavior as his phone rang. "I'm sorry," he said.

"For what? It's me."

"Mary." He was shocked at her uncanny timing.

"Your line was busy, who were you talking to?"

"A business associate," he replied.

"I was praying you would answer your phone."

"You spoke loud and clear, Mary."

"What do you mean?" she queried.

"Never mind, what's going on in your territory?"

"If you mean Jerusalem, quite a lot," she replied. "I spoke at the temple service earlier this week and hundreds of devout Jews dedicated their lives to Christian evangelism," Mary said.

"I saw the news report on TV," Drew said.

"Within twenty-four hours after the ceremony," Mary continued, "Michael received thousands of email responses from other Messianic Jews, all wanting to sign up for the job."

"Who's Michael?" Had he already been replaced?

"Rabbi Michael Thoene," Mary said. "A friend."

Drew offered no comment. Susan was a friend.

"It's a very exciting time in Jewish history," Mary said. "I wish you could be here for the Commissioning Service scheduled for Saturday afternoon. 144,000 Jews will be commissioned to go out in the world and preach the Gospel of Jesus Christ."

"Christians claim it's a prophecy fulfilled," Drew said.

"Moses and Elijah will be there," she added. "Saturday is going to be a beautiful day, spectacular, like no other in modern time."

"How can you know that?" Drew asked.

"Elijah predicted it and he's never wrong."

The airways fell silent.

"Are you still there, Drew? Did I lose you?"

You have no idea, he thought to himself.

"You'll come home after that?"

"No, I'm flying to Rome to see Andre."

"What about Little David?"

"He's with me, of course."

"Of course," Drew muttered. "I heard about Andre—or rather I saw on television that he's been confirmed as the Catholic Pope."

"That's the reason I'm going to see him."

"Isn't Andre a little young to tackle that job?"

"Don't get me started, Drew. That's why I have to go. Lazarus applied for legal custody of our son through the World Court."

"I guess that means the Evil Twins will be dictating their will to the Catholic Church," Drew predicted. "Poor kid."

"Andre is a good boy." Mary denied tears. "He will do the right thing." She prayed that was true. The Witnesses had foretold that Andre was troubled and his path would prove difficult.

"After that, you'll come home," Drew repeated.

"Yes, unless Jesus directs me otherwise."

Her words settled into Drew's spirit like poison.

"Mary, I can't live like this anymore. I know you're doing good work for the Kingdom of God, but we are married and I need you home with me." He was at his wits end. "You have to choose?"

"Between you and Jesus?"

"Yes, I'm not doing well here by myself," he said.

"I'm sorry, but God's work comes first, Drew."

"I think it's time we annul our marriage."

Mary was shocked. "Drew, I still love you."

"Love is not enough."

Wounded in her spirit, Mary didn't know how to respond to Drew's petition. *Jesus, this is so hard.*

"You won't fight me on this, will you?"

"Not if you're sure that's what you want," she said.

From the beginning of their relationship, Drew had known that her first love was serving Christ. That would never change.

"I'll be in contact," he said and ended the call.

13

Jerusalem

FRIDAY EVENING, MICHAEL THOENE invited Mary and Little David over to his house. He wanted her to join him in a prayer walk through the city following their evening meal. Ari would sit Little David, so Mary saw no reason to refuse his invitation.

Besides, after the breakup with Drew, she was lonely.

Unaccustomed to Jewish cuisine, Mary found Michael's housekeeper's cooking first rate, a baked fish with a vegetable medley, served with unleavened bread doused in honey for dessert.

Afterwards, they enjoyed a glass of fruity wine in the living room and shared details of their lives. While Mary grieved over her failed marriage, Michael was obviously still suffering from his wife's untimely death from cancer. Around eight o'clock, Little David fell asleep in Mary's lap. "I guess it's time for our prayer-walk."

Michael nodded then placed the toddler amid a bundle of colorful blankets on the floor where Ari could keep watch on him. The video playing softly over the television set depicted the childhood years of Jesus Christ growing up under the leadership of Joseph, a carpenter. Mostly fiction, the storyline delighted Ari from the expression on his smiling face. "They'll be fine," he said.

Outdoors on the horizon, the moon glowed like a Halloween pumpkin as wispy clouds played hide-and-seek with the orb.

"See, there!" Michael pointed out the Big Dipper to Mary as they speculated how a bright star led the Wise Men to the Bethlehem stable where they offered gifts and worshipped Jesus.

The gentle rabbi possessed a comforting spirit.

"So, if I may be so bold to ask . . ." Michael stared at Mary, "why isn't Andrew here with you?" As they walked past the Bank of Jerusalem, the Temple on the Mount came into full view.

"Our relationship is complicated, Michael." Mary clenched her hands without realizing it. "Our priorities are at odds."

"I'm sorry to hear that, Mary, but whatever you tell me stays between us," Michael said. "I promise I'm a good listener."

She smiled at him. "Are you sure you're up to some drama?"

"Yes, if it helps you sort out your feelings."

Mary nodded. "After my first husband Lucas was taken in the Rapture, I realized what he said about the Bible was true."

"You repented." Michael shook his head. "Many of us can identify with that, Mary, it's God's way of getting our attention."

"Up until that point in my life I was a spoiled brat."

He stopped walking. "I find that difficult to believe since you're not at all like that now." He examined her expression.

"I didn't have a wholesome childhood," she recalled. "My father, a respected politician, sexually abused me after my mother left us to become a star in the California movie industry."

Mary began walking again beside Michael, wondering if he'd despise her after he knew about her sordid past and poor choices.

"Go on," he encouraged Mary.

"Well, the abuse started out with caresses then evolved into touching. By the time I was ten, we were—you know." Mary gulped back tears. "It made me feel, so, so dirty."

"You don't need to tell me all of this, dear."

"For you to understand me and why my marriage to Drew is complicated, I feel like you do!" Mary sputtered.

Michael was silent as they walked the block.

"We met Lucas at a local coffee shop in Fernwood, Tennessee. I worked there the summer before my senior year in high school. We had an immediate attraction. He was in town because his adoptive father, Texas Ralston, was being tried for murder."

"Another story too long to share," Michael presumed.

"Yes. It was puppy love, I suppose," Mary admitted. "But when Lucas learned about my abusive situation at home, he went to bat for me," she said. "He wanted me to expose my father."

"But you didn't?" Michael's bushy eyebrows arched.

"No, I was too embarrassed, but then Luceres intervened."

"Are you referring to Dr. Ramnes, the suspect Antichrist?"

"Yes, for some reason he became involved with situation, and convinced my father to grant him legal custody of me."

"For a purpose you still don't understand," he surmised.

"Exactly!" Mary said. "I moved to Europe with him and he paid for my private-academy education. After I graduated, I came to the states to attend Harvard University. That's where Lucas and I reconnected." She didn't think it wise to tell him about aborting Lazarus' baby. "I had my own bank account and later the Mark."

"The symbol signifying Satan." Michael profoundly sighed.

"I wasn't a Christian back then, so I never considered there was anything wrong or sinful about using the banking chip."

"Number 666. The Bible calls it the Mark of Satan. Without it no person can buy or sell," Michael recalled biblical scripture.

Mary stopped walking and stared at Michael.

"What is it, dear?"

"Remind me why I'm telling you all of this?"

Grasping Mary's hand, they began walking.

"It's because you are a beautiful, passionate woman for Christ," he noted. "Nothing you tell me will change my opinion."

Mary finished her story, how she removed her banking chip, changed her looks and name, and left Cambridge, Massachusetts.

"When I made my way home to Fernwood in early 2026, Drew—a rooky cop then—stopped me for speeding."

Michael laughed. "How romantic!"

"I recognized Drew as my former classmate in junior high. He looked different, more mature, and very handsome. When he realized I was Mary Sellers, he gave me a warning and let me go."

"Of course, he did!" Michael chuckled. "Who wouldn't?"

"We got together, talked about old times, and eventually fell in love. Unfortunately, I was continually pulled between my old sinful habits and the new ones evolving. It took death to make Jesus real to me. Strangely, I was resurrected on a coroner's slab."

"No wonder you feel . . . isolated."

"Maybe that's it, Michael. I haven't found anyone who can identify with what I've experienced. Last year, in November, Drew was shot twice by a serial killer and nearly died. After a stroke, his left leg was affected. He uses a crutch now to help him walk." Mary choked up on tears. "He needed me more than ever after that."

"You said it. What does that tell you, Mary?"

Mary gasped. "Do you think I married Drew out of pity?"

"That's not a question I can discern."

"Well, it doesn't matter now, the straw has broken the camel's back." It was an expression Mary had heard all of her life.

"Why are you giving up so quickly on your marriage?"

"It's not me," Mary said. "Drew's out of patience with my sudden trips. I do love him, and he's a good father to David, but must I always choose between satisfying him and obeying Jesus?"

Michael understood. Since he'd accepted Christ as the long-awaited Messiah, his work for the cause took precedence.

Mary realized they had reached the Temple Gate.

"Shall we go in and pray?" He caught her eye.

"Yes." She grasped his hand.

* * *

Fernwood

A couple minutes before five p.m., Drew entered Hardeman County Hospital. In light of his breakup with Mary, he decided to keep the appointment set by Dr. Susan Parrot. Taking the elevator up to the fifth floor, he was buzzed inside the office.

Her secretary had already left for the day.

Drew stood motionless, staring at the closed door to Susan's office. When it came open, he did the first thing on his mind. He swept her into a tight embrace then kissed her passionately on the mouth. At first, she shoved him at arm's length.

Then stunned, Susan instantly responded to his advances. Time was lost for several minutes. Coming up for air a minute later, she whispered in his ear, "Is this a proper counselor response?"

"It's so improper I'm dying to get you in a compromising position." His emotions were exploding in all directions.

"I have a lounge that is perfect for that," she said.

There was no turning back when he witnessed Susan stripping off her clothes. He had only seconds to escape making a huge mistake. No doubt what he was about to do was wrong in so many ways. Dismissing his conscience, he let the moment rule and take him down to zero before catapulting him to infinity. The release of his pent-up emotions and repressed anger faded with the thrill.

Thirty minutes later, lust satisfied, they began dressing. Guilt came rushing in but Drew blamed Mary for neglecting him.

"That was amazing." Susan giggled like a teen as she swiped her sweaty forehead with a tissue and glared at Drew.

"You're not sorry, are you?" she asked.

"No, no, you are amazing." Drew kissed her on the nose.

"Do you still want to counsel with me?" she asked.

"I already did that," he admitted with a sly grin. "But if you want another round of my counseling . . ." he kissed her.

"No, not here at the office." She put on her pumps.

"By the way, you are quite the lover."

She shook out her long blond hair, licked her lips, then laughed. "I have a partner who knows how to satisfy a woman."

Embarrassed over Susan's comment, Drew slowly came off his sexual high and leaned against the locked door.

"Susan?" he softly whispered.

She filed away the last folder that was on her desk and locked the metal cabinet then gazed at him. "Yes, Love?"

"Do you have regrets about . . .?"

"None," she confidently replied. "Do you?"

"No, I'm filing annulment papers on Monday."

"Did your wife agree to ending your marriage?"

"She won't contest it," he said. "I'll soon be a free man."

"You can move in with me," Susan said.

"I have my own place," he reasoned. "Let's take it slow."

Susan gasped. "I'd hate to see when you take it fast."

She was so beautiful and desirous, Drew wanted to strip off her clothes and repeat their last performance. He could understand why she drove her ex-boyfriend crazy. He was suddenly frightened this was some kind of psychological test, then dismissed the idea.

"Did you notice anyone lurking outside your apartment again last night?" he inquired, popping a piece of gum in his mouth.

"No, are we still driving over to Jackson to dine?"

"Sure."

Susan gathered her things to leave.

"You know, we can go back to my place and order in," she suggested. "It will give us more privacy. Your call, Detective."

Lust was tucked in Susan's gaze driving him wild again. "That's not even a fair choice." He winked and they exited the office.

14

Saturday, July 17

Jezreel Valley

AS PREDICTED BY ELIJAH, it was a cloudless Saturday afternoon with a jeweled sun set in the midst of a cobalt-blue canopy. The breeze was notably cooler and summer plants were in full bloom.

Lying south of Jerusalem, Mount Tabor could be seen from the fertile valley of Jezreel that encompassed three-hundred-and eighty square kilometers. The valley was a paradise of lush green plots of wheat, fields of cotton, myriads of sunflowers, and scattered fish ponds. "Jezreel" means "God Sows" in Hebrew.

What better place to commission 144,000 Messianic Jews?

Here, on this slice of land where Mary stood, the Messianic Jewish volunteers would receive their commissioning to go forth into the world and preach Christ's gospel. This plot of soil was the southern portion of the fertile valley called *Megiddo*. Here, Gideon led an Israelite army against the Midianites and won. King Saul also defeated the Philistines in this valley. And here Mary knew that the final Battle of Armageddon between good and evil would be fought.

To save the day, Jesus would end the battle by stepping down on the Mount of Olives in Jerusalem, split it in two, and establish a thousand-year reign over the earth. History becoming prophecy.

On this radiant mid-July day, thousands of visitors were arriving in the valley from all directions, utilizing GPS to identify the exact commissioning site. In addition to the Jewish volunteers who came forward during the temple service, the remainder of the 144,000 had registered online. Leave the logistics to God.

This was a unique day, a rare event in history. It was a true privilege to be present and witness this long-awaited prophetic event recorded in the Revelation by the Disciple John in 96 A.D.

Only one worry nagged Mary: her failure to be a good wife to Drew. If they stayed married, Jesus would have to work out the logistics. Their bond of physical love had fallen short. *Agape* love, the kind God extended to people, was unbreakable. *Mine is.*

Another concern of Mary's, Michael's son Ari had not been healed of leukemia during Tuesday's Temple service. Yet, not once had either of them complained. She respected Michael's willingness to accept God's will for his son. But if it were Little David, or Andre, God forbid, would she so faithfully accept their ill fate?

On the other hand, this was the End Times.

No one could predict what hardships Christians would endure during the next four years. Perhaps those who died sooner rather than later might be the lucky ones. Souls in Heaven would join forces with Jesus and pray for the suffering of the Tribulation saints.

As Mary observed the gathering throng of visitors, she prayed that Drew would not digress into his former sinful ways, like he had after his wife Maria and his son left Planet Earth. The banking chip embedded in his left wrist suggested he trusted in money more than in Jesus' ability to deliver him through hardships. Mary was quickly learning that blessings come alongside terrible persecutions.

She gazed at the horizon in awe. The 144,000 evangelists marched toward her as one heavenly army into the Jezreel Valley. Forming rows of one-hundreds, they approached the enormous stage erected fifty feet away, anxious to receive their anointing.

Hundreds of thousands of witnesses, family and friends, the drive-by media, and naysayers, stood on the sidelines watching. It took an hour for everyone to be in place and the ceremony to begin.

Using a battery-operated microphone, Michael instructed his audience to be quiet. After a beautiful opening prayer, he instructed the evangelists to repeat a pledge of allegiance after him.

"I promise to obey Jesus, my Lord and Savior," Michael paused for their response. "I declare to the inhabitants of earth the Lord desires to save souls." Their response, then, "I pledge to preach the Gospel of Jesus Christ wherever I am led and never fear evil."

In united voices, their edict reached Heaven.

"As God is my witness, and Jesus my Savior, I commit my life to this holy task of delivering God's message of love and grace."

The echo of thousands of unified male voices resonated in the surrounding hills. Some spectators were on their knees, weeping.

"Please kneel, Chosen Ones, while Mary prays and dispenses holy oil from the Temple into the atmosphere, signifying the anointing of the Holy Spirit, the Third Person of the Holy Trinity."

Honored to be part of the service, Mary stepped on stage.

The evangelists knelt and bowed their heads.

Mary poured a vial of olive oil into the atmosphere until there was none left. Using the microphone, she quoted Matthew 28: 18-20. "Therefore, go and make disciples of all nations, baptizing them in the name of the Father and of the Son and of the Holy Spirit, teaching them to obey everything I have commanded you. And surely, I am with you always, to the very end of the age."

As Mary stepped down, Moses mounted the stage.

Holding out his wooden staff, the Old Testament prophet said: "And now soldiers of Christ, receive in the Holy Spirit's gifts!"

The breeze immediately ceased. Fields of wheat and corn fell limp as if praying. Birds in the blue sky paused in flight. A profound hush hovered over the Jezreel Valley. In response, hundreds of thousands of spectators could not catch their breaths.

Whoosh!

Mary trembled at the sound as Little David whimpered. The mighty wind was so loud she had to cover his ears. High in the sky, she spied a flaming tornado forming over the 144,000 evangelists. Instantly, the solid flame separated into a myriad of fiery tongues that shot down and slapped the 144,000 Jews on their foreheads.

In response, the evangelists were suddenly swept off their feet and catapulted backwards some twenty feet, slain in the spirit as if dead. Then it was over, and the wind began to gently blow again.

"What just happened, Elijah?" Mary gasped, hugging Little David to her bosom to comfort his whimpering. "Are they okay?"

"Isn't it obvious, Mary? They have been sealed."

The evangelists began to stand up and point at one another. Phone cameras went off to validate the event. Television network anchorpersons began reporting the event to the world's audience.

"What are the evangelists doing?" Mary queried.

"They are pointing at the seal of the Lamb," Moses replied.

Mary stepped off the stage and approached one of the Jewish evangelists. Clearly, there was a mark on his forehead. She closed the gap between them to get a better view. It was a tiny cross.

"I think God is going to win this battle." Moses chuckled.

Elijah wagged his head. "It's been a fine day."

15

Mid-day in Fernwood

SKEETER HOBBLED ON CRUTCHES into Dover's makeshift kitchen. During the quake, he'd fallen through the second-floor at the police station and cracked an ankle and hurt his rib cage.

"How're you doing, pal, we missed you," Bob uttered.

"Still in pain, but I'm moving better."

"Good to have you back. Been a zoo around here."

"Yeah? Hospital ain't no place to hang out, either," Skeeter yawed. "Guess I know how Drew feels, gittin' around on these blame things." He pointed a crutch. "Any coffee left?"

"Stay put, I'll fix you a cup." Bob ambled over to the counter and grabbed a mug from the stacked clean dishes.

"Did you see the news report coming out of Israel?"

"No, what's up?" Bob munched on a jellied donut.

"Got an extra donut over there for me?" Skeeter belted out as Bob delivered a welcome mug of strong Columbian coffee.

"All kinds—chocolate, strawberry, gooey filled."

"Bring over the box and I'll pick."

"Do I git a tip?" Bob hustled back over to the counter and returned with the box. Skeeter slugged down a glazed donut.

"Good, ain't they?" Bob said. "Boss got 'im for us."

"Beats hospital food by a mile." Skeeter helped himself to another donut, discarding any dietary requirements.

"Tell me about the news report out of Israel." Bob joined his buddy at the table. "What's so innerestin' about it?"

"Well, them 144,000 Messianic Jews got themselves sealed." Skeeter stared at Bob, guzzling coffee to wash down the donut.

"They did *what*?" Bob dug a finger in one ear.

"They got sealed!" Skeeter loudly repeated.

"Looks to me like you got more 'n your leg damaged." What Skeeter said made no sense at all. Bob studied on it.

"Well, it does to me. A bunch of Jews were out in the desert and got slain in the Spirit—CNN showed them falling out."

"*Slain?* Is that some kind of French word?"

Skeeter chuckled. "Guess God got mad at them Jews and punched out their lights. Only they got up and didn't seem hurt."

Drew stood in the doorway to the kitchen, listening to the ridiculous conversation between the two zany cops. Bob spotted him standing there and waved him in the kitchen.

"Come on in, sit a spell, Drew."

"Don't mind if I do." He hobbled over to the table.

"Ever heard of someone slain in the Spirit?"

"It's sort 'a like *dying*." Bob ventured an opinion.

Slain? "Yeah, I heard of it," Drew said. "Happens to a body when the Holy Spirit comes on so strong, people faint."

"I wuz right. God got mad at those Jews," Skeeter piped.

"On the contrary, God empowered them for mission work."

"What kind of mission work?" Bob sobered at the idea.

"Do you remember in the New Testament, when the Disciple Peter held the very first church meeting in Jerusalem?" Drew didn't wait for an answer. "Well, people came from all over the Middle East to attend. Most couldn't understand what the others were saying. When Peter began to preach Jesus' message of salvation, the Holy Spirit took care of the language problem."

"What do you mean?" Skeeter asked.

"The Holy Spirit fell on the congregation like tongues of fire, so everyone could understand what was being said."

"Guess that qualifies as a miracle." Skeeter grinned.

"I never read about that in the Bible," Bob confessed. "Maybe when I git home tonight, I'll take a good look."

"You never went to Sunday School?" Drew was surprised.

Bob wagged his head. "Ma and Pa worked on Sundays."

"I did!" Skeeter raised a crutch. "But I don't remember reading or hearing about all that. Maybe I wasn't listening."

"After that," Drew expounded, "the church grew quickly all over the populated world. Faithful Christians sold all they had and gave it to the poor, thinking Jesus was coming back soon."

Even after two centuries, some still watched the sky.

"That's so cool," Bob remarked.

"Where is that story found in the Bible?" Skeeter asked.

"Check out the Book of Acts in the New Testament," Drew said. "It tells how God sent His Holy Spirit into the world."

Skeeter scratched his head. "What puzzles me about the whole thing is how the wind quit blowing in that valley."

"Revelation, the seventh chapter," Sarah remarked as she stepped into the kitchen with Georgie trailing. "There were four angels standing at the four corners of the earth and they—"

"But the earth is round," Skeeter interrupted.

"Well, buddy, maybe God knows something we don't." It was as good an answer as any. "FOX News is reporting that the wind ceased all over the Middle East for a full sixty seconds," Sarah said.

"Fair and balanced," Bob said with a chuckle.

"Is that impossible?" Georgie cranked up the cappuccino machine and filled a metal carafe with tap water. "I mean," she glanced at Sarah, "wouldn't birds fall out of the air without wind?"

"That answer is above my pay grade," Sarah piped.

"Whole thing seems pretty weird." Georgie filled the drip cup with strong Pilon coffee, hooked it to the cappuccino machine, then tapped the ON button. "Just saying . . ." she looked at Sarah.

"Look, guys." Sarah splayed her hands. "All we need to know is that a Bible prophecy just became reality. I know it's hard to do, but maybe it's time we all removed our banking Marks."

"You can't be serious!" Bob exclaimed.

"How will I pay my rent?" Skeeter spouted.

"Are you gonna fire us if we don't?" Georgie sputtered.

"No, I'm not," Sarah replied. "I actually have no idea how I would survive without access to money." She mused. "But, if we don't obey the command of Jesus, we might miss Heaven when Jesus returns again. I worry about how I'll be judged."

Sarah stared at her officers. "Just saying . . ."

"It'll take a lot of faith to do that." Georgie sighed.

Shaking his head, Skeeter speechlessly glared at Bob.

Drew was painfully silent on the matter. He had failed on many levels. Plus entered into an adulterous relationship with a woman he barely knew. Did that mean he was eternally lost?

"Well, team, while you chew on all that, I'm going back to work." Sarah fixed her a cup of Joe and took it with her.

* * *

Later Saturday in Tel Aviv

Mary's flight out of Israel was scheduled for six p.m. Michael drove her and Little David to the terminal entrance then placed ten gold coins in her hand to cover their expenses going forward.

When Mary protested, Michael reminded her that she was in ministry, too. The donated funds residing in the Bank of Jerusalem were meant to cover those kinds of expenses. Eyes bubbling tears, she uttered a choking "Thank you" and took the coins.

Ari removed Mary's bags from the back of Michael's Volvo and set them on the sidewalk. "I'll miss you, Ms. Mary."

She hugged the teen. "Keep a daily journal of your experiences with God, Ari. When you get discouraged, read what you wrote."

"Does that work for you?" he asked.

"Yes. Jesus is our healer, our sustainer, our peace on earth that surpasses all human knowledge," she passionately replied.

Ari said, "I'm not afraid to die." He looked at his father.

"Dying is living again," Mary offered. "Believe me, entrance into heaven is a glorious experience. I've been there and back."

Unhappy at the thought of his son dying, Michael leaned against the passenger door as the Volvo's motor idled.

"We need to go, Ari," he said. "We're in a no-parking zone." To Mary, "Please come back and visit us soon."

"I will." Mary grew even more emotional at parting.

"Well, I guess this is goodbye." Michael loosely hugged Mary.

"Thank you so much for your hospitality."

"The feeling is mutual." He felt overwhelmed. "You have been such a blessing to me and Ari. Please be safe."

"You, too." Mary wished Drew was half the Christian Michael was. "I'll let you knew when we land in Rome," she added.

Michael blushed as he recalled how much he missed his wife. When around Mary, he realized how important a wife's role was in the life of a family. But it would be a huge mistake for either of them to form an emotional attachment in the last days. Time was winding down at warp speed and there was still much to do.

"Until we meet again. . ."

Mary turned around once and waved goodbye at two of her favorite people and walked with David into the terminal.

After renting a cart, she placed him in the seat carrier then loaded their two bags in the front basket.

"Ready to visit your big brother, little buddy?"

David joyfully muttered something she didn't understand.

It was a long walk to Gate 30 in Concourse 2, but Mary didn't mind since she used the time to contemplate her uncertain future with Drew. People scurried about the airport like they were going somewhere important. Did they know their most important destination is Heaven? She prayed that lost souls would soon hear the Gospel message and receive salvation through God's grace.

Trials were forecast in the Bible. How would people react when they broke out in skin boils? Or when locusts invaded their homes? Repent and confess Jesus as Lord, or curse God?

On autopilot, she reached their gate alongside one-hundred and sixty-five other passengers. Everyone took a turn boarding the large plane and found seats. Mary held David as the plane lifted.

16

Rome, Italy

LAZARUS WAS STANDING outside the terminal when he spotted Mary with Little David. He waved them over to the curb.

"Welcome to Rome." He gave Mary a friendly hug.

"Take David, he's breaking my arms." She hoisted her son at Lazarus as the driver placed their bags in the trunk of the limousine.

"Did you see the guy helping me?" Mary asked, suspicious of who sent him when he disappeared before she could thank him.

"No, why?" Lazarus frowned.

"Never mind, he was a good Samaritan, I suppose."

"By the way, Mary, you look radiant—like a bird set free!"

Lazarus opened the passenger door for Mary and waited for her to be seated in the limousine before handing over Little David.

Turning remarkable blue eyes on him, she stated, "I have been set free by God's Spirit, Lazarus. What about you?"

He chuckled. "I won't touch that one."

"Where is Andre?"

"Asleep for the night when I left for the airport," Lazarus replied. "His sitter will bring him over to your apartment in the morning for a visit." His olive eyes oddly eclipsed.

"You rented another apartment for us?" Mary blinked.

"No, it's the same one you had back when," he replied.

The driver waited for Lazarus to signal for him to pull out in the hectic traffic. When a traffic cop blew his whistle at them for loitering, the Iraqi revved the engine and spun off the curb.

"Where is David's car seat?" Lazarus inquired.

"I left it behind in Tel Aviv. Too cumbersome to bring along," she replied. "Michael's going to keep it for me."

"Who's Michael?" Lazarus glared at Mary.

"Rabbi Michael Thoene," she replied. "He was in charge of the commissioning events. Did you watch the services on TV?"

"I was a bit busy," Lazarus muttered with a shrug.

"Go ahead and ask your question," Mary said.

"What?"

"Why isn't Drew with me?"

He chuckled. "You are no mind-reader, my dear."

Tears threatened to flow. Angst over her past wouldn't help. "How is my son coping with his new assignment?" she asked.

"Perfect in all ways," Lazarus said. "He loves his job. It's like a game to him. I wish other people were so pliable."

"What you mean is, so easily *manipulated.*"

"Let's don't get into a contest of words, it isn't productive."

"No, I guess not. But you did promise me that Andre would not be party to anything sinister." She needed reassurance. "Don't corrupt our son's innocence." Her fists clenched at the thought.

"I'll see to it that Andre only does good deeds."

"Thank you." Mary released a tight breath.

Lazarus gave the driver the address to the high-rise apartment complex and instructed him to take them directly there.

"Isn't it a waste of funds to keep an empty apartment?"

"I knew you'd come to Rome again," he said. "I sometimes hang out there with Andre, when life at the Vatican gets difficult."

"With you, life is always difficult." She glanced away.

"You should thank me for keeping up the rent. Don't forget you're broke. Without my help, you'd be begging on the streets."

Mary repressed tears. "You've been gracious to me."

"Thank you. Finally, a compliment."

"I still think you could spend the Vatican's money better than maintaining an apartment hardly ever used. I'm not staying long."

"Surely you jest, Mary. The coffers at the Vatican are literally unlimited," he replied. "I can pay for anything I need, or want."

Mary couldn't help but chuckle. Those who rejected Christ and had the Mark seemed to be blessed while Christians struggled just to make it through one day. "Different strokes . . ."

"Yeah, by choice."

Little David began to gnaw on his fingers.

"David's hungry. I need to feed this little guy." Mary dug a jar of apple sauce out of the diaper bag and unscrewed the lid.

"We're close to the apartment, fifteen minutes tops."

"I'll be careful and not spill on your fancy limousine."

David welcomed the fruit but kept trying to take the plastic spoon away from Mary. "Hold on, David." He spit at her.

"Here let me help." Lazarus removed a bib from David's diaper bag and tied it around his neck. "There, little guy."

Mary smiled at Lazarus. "You make a good dad."

"I hope so, I'm trying."

"Just remember, Lazarus, you always have a choice between doing the right thing and submitting to forces of evil." Mary bit her lip while contemplating another question she was dying to ask.

"Go ahead and lay it on me." Lazarus glared at the only woman he ever loved. "I won't lie to you."

"Has Andre demonstrated any *special* gifts?"

"Not here." Lazarus thumbed over his shoulder at the driver. "Let's get you and David settled in at the apartment and I'll tell you everything that happened during that crazy conclave."

The apartment looked exactly the same. David was wide awake so Mary sat him on the floor to play with a set of plastic keys.

"Lazarus, watch David for me, I'll be back in a moment."

She used the facilities in the master bath. Coming out, she spied the open door to the wall-to-wall closer. Her expensive clothes still hung there on racks. Almost angry, she gathered them in her arms, carried them into the living room, and dumped them on the floor in front of Lazarus. "Really? You kept these?"

"Why not? There're still in style. And they belong to you."

"Don't you realize that I'll never *ever* wear these outlandishly expensive clothes?" Furs and glittering evening wear did not fit into Mary's profile of fasting and prayer and suffering for Christ.

"Whatever . . ." he said. "Take a breath and chill out."

"You're right." Her nerves were stretched tight.

"We'll give them away to needy people," he said.

Mary giggled. "I doubt they'll have anywhere festive to wear them." The homeless preferred rainproof boxes over fur coats.

The conversation was going nowhere positive.

"Are you hungry? I am," Lazarus said.

"Yes, but it's too late to eat." She glanced at the wall clock. 11:12 p.m. "I need to get David settled down for the night." She locked eyes with him. "You should go home now."

"I thought you wanted to hear about Andre's gifts."

"I do." Mary lazily yawned. "Let's talk about it tomorrow when I have a fresh mind and can process your information."

"Okay, I'll go now." He turned to leave.

"Wait. Is there food in the fridge for breakfast?"

He spun around. "Of course, there is. Fully stocked, my lady. You know I always plan ahead." He waited for another question.

Mary nodded. "Thanks." Weariness nearly toppled her as she walked him to the door. Lazarus had a good heart, was thoughtful in many ways, but unfortunately corrupted by his older twin.

"Boy, that really was a double-edged sword."

"Okay, we're back to my rules again! No. Mind. Reading. Or I'm out of here tomorrow!" She snapped her fingers.

"I think that's my cue to leave."

Mary closed the door and locked it.

Tomorrow . . .

17

Sunday, July 18

Tennessee

LIKE MOST SUNDAYS, DOVER'S was booked to capacity with juvenile offenders, mostly young teens arrested the night before for fighting, illegal drug use, or loitering in a public place. With no lockup space at the site and the county jail not operational, suspects were hauled off daily in an armored bus to either Birmingham, Alabama or Nashville's city jails to await court arraignment.

It was Drew's time to drive the bus, complete with a sidekick armed with a weapon to ensure a peaceful transfer of the accused. Currently, eight juveniles rode in the back of the bus. Officer Bob rode shotgun, like the old westerners driving stagecoaches.

Saturday night's shenanigans could be chalked up to the youths' poor choices. Two offenders were identified as budding hardcore criminals unless they somehow changed the course of their lives. One of them was a model student who regularly sold marijuana to children. His politically influential father somehow managed to get his son's charges dropped every time he was picked up by the police. He was back in the criminal justice system again.

In one isolated case, a sixteen-year-old girl had been arrested for prostitution. Drew knew the fifteen-year-old girl. Her parents died in the quake and her home was destroyed. With no relatives to fall back on, she was simply trying to survive. Drew believed, with counseling, Lily still had a chance at a decent life.

But it all came down to choices. It was bad enough that some adults were addicted to either prescription or illegal drugs. Now children as young as ten were targeted by handlers peddling lethal substances of all kinds. Introduced to marijuana first, legalized in most states, youths tended to graduate to more potent substances.

With the breakdown of the family unit in America, illegal drug trafficking was increasing. Christians—for the most part law-abiding citizens—had departed the planet during the Rapture and left behind people with less scruples and moral convictions. Drew hated to sound cynical, but life on Planet Earth was not going to improve before Jesus returned to earth as Lord and King.

Meanwhile, radical Islamic groups and Christians were at odds as to how people should live and think and worship. While world leaders proclaimed peace among the nations, acts of murder, hatred, envy, and other nasty emotions infiltrated society.

Now that the 144,000 Messianic Jews had gone out into the weeds of the world to proclaim Jesus' kingship, Drew didn't see how a major war between Islam and Christianity could be avoided.

Halfway to Nashville, Drew phoned Tom Rave and asked if he'd have a late lunch with him. Tom agreed to meet him downtown at *Gillie's*, a restaurant famous for its barbeque and steaks. It also had a salad bar beyond belief, Tom had promised.

Drew pulled the bus up to the front of the jail and got out. Two officers came out to herd the offenders into the courtroom.

Drew parked the bus and went inside. Parents of the noisy arrested youths had congregated in the hallway with their lawyers. Drew was pleased to see that the Nashville City Jail clerks were organized as they checked in the offenders. Drew signed his name to the receipt form for his delivery and pocketed it.

It wasn't his job to view the legal process.

Leaving the armored bus parked in the Nashville police lot, Drew took an UBER over to Gillie's. Tom was already there and seated at a table when he arrived. "Thanks for meeting me."

"Good to see you again, man." Tom half lifted from his seat and shook Drew's hand. They both sat down.

"The traffic was maddening." Drew perused a menu.

"Did you find a parking spot nearby?"

"I Ubered over," Drew replied.

"Smart move." Tom grinned then said, "I took the liberty to order both of us sweet tea. I hope that was okay."

"Don't see anything wrong with that!" Plenty of other things were wrong in Drew's life but sweet tea was a no-brainer.

"The barbeque is excellent," Tom pointed out. "But if you're really hungry, order the shank steak with peppered potatoes and prepare for a surprise." He studied the dessert menu for later.

Drew laid down his menu and looked at Tom. "I owe you an apology for not calling when I returned from Canada."

"No need to explain, my friend."

"It's just that my mind was elsewhere."

"I imagine," Tom remarked. "Are you doing any better?"

"Oh, my leg. As well as can be expected, considering."

"Considering what?" Tom probed.

"Considering I still suffer pain on a daily basis." Drew chose not to mention his ongoing drama with his absentee wife.

"I'm sorry you're dealing with that injury," Tom empathized. "Guess having your family home and safe is a huge comfort."

Chagrined, he locked his gaze on Tom. "First, Mary went to Israel with David," he said. "Now she's in Rome at the Vatican."

"Last time I saw Mary was the day after the big quake. She left my house with Cory and his family headed back to Fernwood."

Tom waved at a waitress.

"Plans change." *What an understatement!*

Their waitress arrived with her electronic menu pad to take their orders. "Put our meals on my tab," Drew told the gal.

"Are you ready to order, sir?"

"Did you decide, Tom?" Drew asked.

"The barbeque special." He folded his menu.

"Same for me," Drew said and set the menu aside.

When the waitress was out of earshot, Tom asked, "Are you going to tell me what's going on with you and Mary?"

"We keep missing each other," Drew replied. "She'd call and it wasn't a good time for me to talk. I'd call back later and she was busy—this went on for more than a week," he explained.

"What prompted Mary to leave home again?"

Drew sighed. "God told her to go to Jerusalem."

"I see." Tom's gaze drifted a bit, lips folded in his mouth.

"No! You don't *see!*" Drew exploded and banged the table with his fist. The pent-up rage over his marital situation could no longer be contained. For a second, he thought he might stroke out.

"Calm down, man," Tom warned.

Breathing hard, he said, "I don't know if I even see."

"Take it easy, okay?" Tom grasped Drew's arm. "It's not like you to react like this in public, what's really going on?"

Embarrassed, Drew glanced around the restaurant to see how much attention he'd drawn, then made eye contact with Tom.

"I messed up, man." He blinked tears. "Really messed up."

Tom sat back. "Oh. What did you do, friend?"

"I broke my marriage vow."

Tom shook his head. "Infidelity?"

Drew nodded, so ashamed.

"Does Mary know?"

With bleary eyes, he said: "The question is: does she care?"

Tom glared at the smart detective, not knowing what else to say. Not knowing how to advise him. Only God could help him.

18

Rome, Italy

JOSEPH, LAZARUS' SECRETARY arrived at the apartment shortly before nine a.m. Sunday morning. Mary hugged Andre and thanked Joseph for bringing him over. There was still time to take the boys to a church service, but not a Catholic Cathedral. Fearful Andre might be recognized, she'd purchased new clothes for him in Tel Aviv. Andre looked adorable, just like a little man in his shorts and plaid jacket. He toddled around the apartment, babbling words Mary could not decipher as any language. But he was happy.

"Andre? What are you saying?"

"Oh, it's just something my father taught me."

"Lazarus?" Mary was curious.

"No, no, my other daddy." Andre babbled another sentence. "It's a chant, Mama, to help me become more powerful."

What? She watched him dance around the living room.

"Stop dancing, Andre." Mary scooped him off the floor. "You don't have another daddy. Papa Lazarus is your daddy."

Andre stuck his thumb in his mouth and mumbled.

"Take your hand out of your mouth, son. Tell me what you were saying. Who is this other daddy?" she demanded.

"He's big." Andre's olive eyes rolled in thought. "Sometimes he's beautiful and wears long beads around his neck, all the way to the tip of his toes. He likes to sing. He's really cool, Mama."

"Andre . . ." Mary's heart stuttered so hard she feared losing consciousness. "When do you see this *other* papa?"

"I see him when I'm asleep." Andre pointed to the air. "He's up there. He talks to me. He's so cool, Mama."

So cool . . . Mary guessed that was all she would get out of an almost three-year-old without putting disturbing thoughts in his head. She would address his fantasy problem with Lazarus.

"I need to get David up and dressed," she told Andre. "Why don't you play with these Legos?" She dumped them on the floor.

"I'm not dressed for church." Andre stamped his foot.

"You look just fine, like a little man."

"I don't care, Mama, I'm supposed to wear my pope's dress."

"Not today, Andre," Mary said.

"People are supposed to see me and curtsy."

Mary suppressed a grin. "That's for another day. Why don't you build me a lovely castle?" She sat him on the floor.

He picked up a Lego. "I can do that for you, Mama."

Hurrying to dress herself and Little David, Mary found Andre still at work on his creative castle. He'd constructed an elaborate building with a surrounding mote. "Son, this is beautiful."

Spying David seated on the sofa, Andre abandoned his work and raced across the room and dragged him to the floor. The ten-month-old began bawling. Andre laughed and danced around.

"That was a bad thing to do, Andre!" Mary grabbed him by the arm and pulled him to the side. "You've hurt your brother."

"He's not my *real* brother!" Andre stamped his foot.

"We are family, Andre. Tell David you're sorry."

"I'm not sorry, I'm the Pope."

"Not when you're with me, Andre." Mary parked hands on her hips. "I'm your mother and you will do as I say. Is that clear?"

The toddler looked up and frowned. "That's mean, Mama."

"It's the way it is. Children obey their parents."

* * *

Mary found a Presbyterian church listed in the online phone directory. The weather was pleasant in Rome so they walked, her hand in Andre's while she pushed David's stroller with the other.

"I don't think my daddy likes church very much," Andre whispered as they walked up the steps to the church portico.

"What makes you think that?" Mary queried. "Your daddy is a Catholic priest. He loves the church, and he loves Jesus."

"I can't say why." Andre looked up at Mary.

She knelt and straightened his bow tie. "Son, you can tell me anything and I promise it won't make me angry."

"No, I can't say. Daddy said not to say."

Which daddy is that? Mary wondered.

"Okay, let's find a Sunday School class for you and a nursery for David, so Mama can go to big church." Mary led Andre by the hand inside the 16th century vaulted church foyer and paused.

In front of her, two massive carved wooden doors to the sanctuary yawned open. At the end of the ruby-red carpeted aisle an altar glowed with dozens of stout flaming candles. Beautiful mosaic tapestries were artfully displayed on the fourteen-foot-high ornate walls and the angelic white figurines rested in the alcoves.

Glittering cut-glass chandeliers ran the length of the sanctuary, hanging over the two sets of fifty pews divided by the aisle. As if to bless the congregation, a hue of rainbow colors filtered through dozens of oblong stained-glass windows as sweet classical music siphoned from the harp of a skilled musician from an unseen perch.

Prominently positioned in an alcove behind the pulpit on a stage was a statue of Jesus holding a child in His lap: symbolic of God's love for all His children. Mary spied the minister working his way toward them as he paused to greet his members.

"Father Lawrence. We're so glad you came today."

"Thank you, we're just visiting." Mary smiled.

"We get that a lot in Rome." He looked at the children.

The Presbyterian clergy wore a white robe with a draping purple sash roped around his neck. His flock of white hair had been freed by a hair dryer, and his warm seasoned smile seemed to glitter.

The touch of his warm hand on Mary's made her feel safe.

"Is there a class where my two-year-old son can attend?" she inquired. "And Little David will need to stay in the nursery."

"We have both, Ms. . . .?"

"Mary Taylor," she replied.

"Hello, little guy." The minister bent over to greet Andre. "Do you love Jesus?" He handed him a peppermint.

Andre stripped away the candy wrapper and popped the mint into his mouth. "Answer the minister, Andre," Mary prodded.

He looked up and said, "Everybody knows Jesus is real, Father. But is He the Son of God? That's the tricky question."

Andre clung to Mary's leg with one arm.

"I'm sorry, Father Lawrence." She squeezed Andre's arm.

"No problem," he chuckled, making light of the remark.

Still, Andre's statement was disturbing to Mary.

* * *

After the service, Mary returned to the apartment with the two boys. Lazarus was waiting in the foyer. "Where have you been?"

"We went to church, Daddy." Andre leaped into his arms. "I got a mint from the Father and I colored a paper." He shoved his picture of Jesus riding a donkey into Jerusalem at Lazarus.

"That's nice, son." Lazarus' gaze was on Mary. "We should have lunch now, if that's okay. What sounds appetizing?"

"Can we have hotdogs at the public park?" Andre asked.

Mary nervously giggled. "I swear, Lazarus, you've ruined our son forever." Her meaning included more than just hotdogs.

"Just trying to be a good papa," he qualified.

"Okay, I need to take the boys upstairs first and get us all changed into more suitable clothes and comfortable shoes."

Mary glared at Lazarus.

"What?"

"Are you going to wait here or come up?"

"I'll go up with you." He pushed David in his stroller into the elevator. Mary followed with Andre, who pushed the button to the right floor. "What makes you think I ruined Andre, Mary?"

"We'll talk about it later. Little ears, you know."

Lazarus sat on the sofa and caught up on the Sunday news on television while Mary changed Andre into a pair of shorts, a tee, and tennis shoes. Back in the living room, she sat him on the sofa.

"I love you, Daddy," Andrew looked up at Lazarus.

Which daddy does he love more? Mary wondered.

19

Monday, July 19

Fernwood

GEORGIE'S FIFTH CALL TO a truck-rental agency hit payload. Smarty pants had paid in silver using her mother's married name. The guy identifying himself as "Peanuts" reported that Mrs. Sandra Orrin had not given an exact location where she'd return the van.

"Did Sandra give you an approximate date?"

"No, but she turned it in yesterday," Peanuts replied.

"Is that protocol for your company?"

"No, but Sandra showed me her badge so I trusted her."

So, did I, once. Georgie thanked Peanuts, ended the call, and trotted across the warehouse. The lift carried her up to Sarah's high-rise office. "Got a sec?" Georgie queried the busy sheriff.

Talking on the phone, Sarah waved Georgie to a chair. Hot to trot to deliver her good news, it took all the willpower Georgie had not to stand up and whoop, *Woo-wahhh!* Like she'd just won the Tennessee Lottery. Sarah must have noted her exhilaration.

"What?" Sarah ended the call and glared at her detective. "You look like the fox that stole the sheep out of the pen."

"You have no idea!" Georgie slapped her thigh. "I found the company that rented Dunn a moving van last week."

Sarah snagged a pen. "Give me the return address."

"Mrs. Orrin/a.k.a. Priscilla Dunn did not give one up front, but she returned the van yesterday according to Peanuts."

"Who has a name like Peanuts?"

"A little guy, I suppose," Georgie replied. "Possibly midget genes—why are we even talking about this?"

"We need to know where her furniture landed."

"I agree, but I wanted to run it past you before taking the inquiry further," Georgie said. "It really doesn't matter where Dunn turned in the truck, she won't be there."

Sarah groaned. "I hate to say it but you're right."

"Do we have grounds to put out an APB on our thief?" Georgie cracked her knuckles, a ritual when she was about to nail the coffin on a case. She would not be at the losing end again.

"I'll run it by the D.A."

Georgie nodded. "Otherwise we'll never find her."

"I'm not Santa Claus!" Sarah piped.

"Personally, I think Dunn is blackmailing her former friend Sullivan with the confiscated murder evidence," Georgie offered a plausible motive. "It's the only thing that makes sense."

Sarah tapped her pen on a pad, contemplating their next move.

"Why commit an illegal act and risk losing your job if the endgame isn't lucrative?" Georgie cracked her knuckles again.

"Stop that cracking thing, you're getting on my nerves."

Georgie wrung out her hands. "Sorry."

"Say I agree with you," Sarah muttered. "Sullivan always seems to have her hand in a piggy bank, even when it's not hers."

"Want me to talk to the D.A.?" Georgie asked.

"No, I'll walk over to the courthouse and tell Greg what you found out from Peanuts. The Intel Drew collected in Canada from Dunn's uncle, plus his discussion with John Fallon in New York connecting her to Sullivan, should be enough to get a warrant."

"Meanwhile, what do you want me to do?"

"Sit tight."

Cracking her knuckles again, Georgie grimaced at waiting.

"Okay, on second thought," Sarah changed her mind, "why don't you call Barry Longstreet's attorney and ask him to contact Barry's parents about pleading out his hit-and-run case."

Georgie's eyes widened with surprise. "Wow, never thought I'd hear those words coming out of your mouth!" She knew how close Sarah was to Gloria Gordon. They shared mega-history.

"No place safe to put him now," Sarah said. "Nashville City Jail is no place for a kid like Barry. Let's get him off the books."

"I'd prefer the DA does that," Georgie countered. "I don't feel qualified to insert my two cents into the case." She was bitter about Gloria's death and how nonchalant Barry had reacted.

"Okay, I understand. You and Gloria were great friends, too." Sarah nodded her head. "That's two things I need to address with Greg. Hopefully, Judge Lightfoot will be relieved to put Barry's misstep behind and he'll sign the Arrest Warrant."

* * *

Drew was seated at his desk when his cell phone vibrated and danced. He looked at the caller I.D. It was Susan Parrot.

"Oh, hi, Susan," he said, reluctant to call her when he returned from Nashville after confessing to Tom Rave his adulterous sin.

"Why didn't you call me last night?"

Why did he suddenly feel intimidated?

"My error," he answered. "Sorry."

"I made a delicious supper for us and you didn't show."

"Excuse me?" Drew's forehead furrowed as he leaned forward over his desk and lowered his voice. "I don't recall you inviting me, or *me* telling *you* I was coming over for supper."

He heard heavy breathing.

"Susan, unless you let me know your plans in advance don't count on me reading your mind. Understand?"

More stressed breathing. "I thought you cared about me, Drew. I thought we had a connection. Was I mistaken?"

"You are my counselor, Susan. And you've helped me."

Susan haughtily laughed. "I've been more than that to you, Drew. We both know that. Who came onto *whom* first?"

Drew tamped down his escalating anger.

"What? Have you forgotten about Friday already?"

"Susan . . ." Drew chose his next words carefully. "This is not a discussion we should have over the phone. And certainly not while I'm at work," he added, hoping she heard clearly.

"You're right, Andrew. Six o'clock tonight?"

"What?"

"My place, I'll make us supper."

Drew felt trapped but saw no way to avoid seeing her again.

"You're not going to stand me up again, are you?"

"Six o'clock," Drew muttered then ended the call.

"What was all *that* about?"

Drew warily glanced up. "I didn't see you standing there."

"That sounded pretty intense. Was Mary on the phone?" Georgie pulled up a straight chair and straddled it backwards.

"It's none of your business." Drew trembled at his dilemma. *Should I stay or should I go?* A crazy commercial surfaced.

"Okay, have it your way." Georgie shrugged. "I thought you should know Sarah's on her way over to see Greg Diamond about pleading out Barry Longstreet's hit-and-run case."

Drew sat up straight. "When was that decided?"

"Best decisions are made on the spur of the moment."

Humph, he huffed, "That sounds remarkably unprofessional."

"Make fun if you will, Detective," Georgie returned. "The Intel you collected in Canada from Priscilla Dunn's uncle, in conjunction with what John Fallon in New York told you about her association with Sullivan, should be enough for an arrest warrant."

When Drew didn't acknowledge her conclusion, Georgie added, "Hey! Dunn's our ticket to finding Caroline Sullivan."

Still mute, Drew glared at the dull surface of his desk.

"Earth to Drew!" Georgie piped. "Are you with us?"

"Huh?" He suddenly woke up to the moment.

"Did you hear one word I said about Dunn?"

Drew sighed. "I have other things on my mind."

"More important than closing a case?"

His innocuous expression was disturbing.

"What's up, friend?" she queried.

"It's personal, Georgie."

"Everything with you lately is personal." Georgie's lips quavered. "I like personal, so why don't you share."

Drew pushed back in his chair and grabbed his crutch.

"You're just gonna jump up and run?" she asked.

"Sorry, Detective Adams, but I'm not having this discussion with you." He shoved several file folders in the bottom drawer of his desk and locked it. "I need some air. *Alone.* Catch you later."

"Wait! Don't go off and do anything stupid."

He waved Georgie off. She watched the troubled soul hobble across the warehouse and out the front door.

Man! That was weird!

20

DREW WENT HOME FOR lunch. He needed to think about how to handle his situation with Susan. It was time to put an end to their impossible affair. For heaven's sake, she was his counselor! He should man-up. Besides, Tom Rave had convinced him to give his marriage more time. It wasn't like Mary had cheated on him.

Like he'd done with her, was implied.

It was admirable Mary was serving God, Tom had pointed out. God was always open to confession and forgiveness.

Do the right thing, Tom had insisted.

He agreed that Tom was right, but Mary's negligence as a wife had wielded its bitter effects on his floundering heart. He'd been less than dedicated to the cause of Christ, thinking only of his physical needs. Hadn't he promised God to remove his Mark?

If Mary decided to come home, Drew's place was by her side—wherever and whatever that meant. But what was he to do about Susan? She could cause him serious grief if Sarah learned of his sexual indiscretion. Susan had him in a vise. His thoughts ebbed even lower as depression and frustration made their inroad.

Lately, he'd been making all the wrong choices.

With his stomach acids screaming, Drew devoured a ham and cheese sandwich and washed it down with sweet tea. By the time he'd finished eating, he had formulated an exit plan with Susan.

Feeling a bit optimistic, Drew recalled that Jonathan Belk was the youngest son of his mother's former best friend, Cynthia.

Even though Drew's parents were deceased, Cynthia Belk had continued to send him Christmas cards every year. The last one he'd received was in 2026. Mrs. Belk said that her son Jon had attended the Knoxville Police Academy the previous fall and was hired on by the Seattle Police Department in January, 2027.

It was a gamble, but Drew hoped that Jon could enlighten him about Susan's ex-boyfriend, Ben. In the next few minutes, he thumbed through an online telephone directory for 2026 and found Mrs. Belk's Memphis number. He called her old landline.

Receiving no answer, Drew logged on his laptop and called up the Memphis City Phone Directory. Her name, address, and land phone were listed. Since the return address given on Drew's Christmas cards were the same, he assumed she was still living.

The land line rang four times. About to hit END on his phone, a raspy female voice chirped "hello."

"Hi," Drew quickly said back, only to get a voicemail: *Leave your name and a message and I'll call you back.* After doing so, he dripped a pot of fresh coffee and waited for a return call. It came before an hour was up. "Did you call?" a pleasant female voice asked.

"Yes, I'm Andrew Taylor. Katrina Taylor's son"

"Why, Andrew, I haven't spoken to you since your mother passed—how long ago was that? Oh, yes. 2023. She was a dear friend, yes, she was. So, Drew . . . how are you doing?"

"Fine," he said. They chatted about the devastating quake that struck Memphis. Cynthia had just returned home. Until yesterday, she was staying with her first cousin in Birmingham, Alabama.

After expressing his regret over her loss, Drew addressed why he'd phoned. "If it's okay with you, Mrs. Belk, I'd like to get in touch with your son, Jon. I'm a detective with the Fernwood P.D."

"Congratulations! Jon works in law-enforcement, too."

"Yes, I know. I need his help with a personal matter."

"I'm sure he'd be pleased to hear from you," she said.

"Too long since we've spoken," Drew said.

"Do you have a pen and paper?"

"Right here," Drew replied.

Cynthia repeated Jon's cell number.

"Thank you, I appreciate your help, Mrs. Belk."

"No problem, but Jon's pretty busy, you know. The new kid on the block—gets all the night shifts. You know what that's like."

"We all put in our time, Mrs. Belk, but it's worth it."

"You can usually catch Jon home after nine p.m. on Wednesday's. That's his one day to enjoy daylight." Cynthia laughed. "Gee, Andrew, it sure is good to hear your voice."

"You, too," he said. "Are you in good health, Mrs. Belk?"

"Actually, I've been poorly as of late."

"Hope you feel better soon." Drew didn't want to get into her health drama. "If you're ever in Memphis again, let me know. I'd like to visit with you." It was an offer he meant to keep.

"I'd love that Andrew. Tell my son hello for me."

"Thanks for Jon's number, Mrs. Belk," Drew said, anxious to talk to the Seattle cop and see if he knew Susan's ex—Drew suddenly realized Susan had never mentioned Ben's last name.

The call ended and Drew stewed over how to finagle Susan's former lover's last name out of her without arousing suspicion. Maybe the ex-boyfriend wasn't such a bad dude as Susan painted him. Maybe he'd been seduced into the relationship as he had.

Don't blame her, I jumped her bones first. Drew groaned as he sipped on the black Columbian. *Who came onto whom first?*

It was common for law-enforcement personnel to receive psychiatric counseling for emotional problems. Cops were infamous for abusing their spouses. In Drew's case, it was the other way around. Susan knew how to make that kind of hurt go away.

* * *

Back at Dover's by 2 p.m., the afternoon passed quickly as Drew wrapped up some minor cases and sent the files over to the DA's office for review. With no secure place to lock up offenders, it was better to plead out their cases, fine the perpetrators, or require community service duty. Life today was about moving on.

Five o'clock rolled around and Drew called it a work day. He drove home, showered, and plotted how to get on Susan's good side without revealing his true motives. On his way over to her apartment, he purchased a dozen red roses from the florist.

Susan let him inside the apartment. She was casually dressed in a pair of tight, bright-green khaki shorts and a floral tank top that scooped low in the bodice. Her salon tan gave off a velvety sheen in the dim indoor lighting. She was truly alluring.

Keep your mind on your plan, Drew reminded himself. But once having sampled cookies from the jar, it was hard to stop.

Susan stood on her tiptoes and kissed Drew on the lips. "I'm so glad you're here," she whispered in his ear in a raspy voice.

"Me, too." He handed her the bouquet of roses.

"These are exquisite!" Susan exclaimed. "Come in and make yourself comfortable in the den while I put these in water."

Said the spider to the fly . . . Drew hauled in a breath, said a prayer for restraint, and found his way into the living room, passing Susan's bedroom on his right where they had spent quality time.

He attempted to put the image of Susan's naked body out of his thoughts. *Tough.* He spied her coming through the archway with two glasses of red wine. "It's nice to relax," she said.

Almost impossible, he thought then said, "Thanks."

Drew tasted the Merlot and offered Susan a toast.

"How do you like it?"

"It's smooth, never thought I'd like a dry wine."

"The cookbook said it complimented my menu choice."

Susan sat down on the sofa beside Drew and set her glass on the coffee table then secured his arm around her waist.

"Doesn't this feel right, Drew?"

He blinked, trying not to stiffen. "I guess."

Too intense, was what came to mind.

"Weren't we made for each other?" She took his glass.

"About last Friday . . ." he nervously uttered.

Shush. She touched limber fingers to his lips. "Whatever guilt you are experiencing will pass, Drew. Don't think too much."

The counselor should know, he reasoned.

"Our meeting was the beginning of something wonderful," Susan said. "I've never felt this way about anyone."

Really? He studied Susan. *What about Ben?*

Not the least put off by his lack of response, the light in Susan's starry blue eyes said she believed in fairytales. Slowly removing her hands, Drew reached for his wine glass. This was not going well.

"Tough day, Detective?" Susan frowned. "I know all this is new, but give your feelings for me some time to mellow."

He took a sip of the wine, said nothing.

"I know how to make your tension disappear."

I bet you do, he thought as she snuggled closer.

It was time to go, but he couldn't. Not until he had what he came for, Ben's last name. God's Prophet Daniel had run away from the sexual advances of his Babylonian master's wife. She had ripped away Daniel's cloak and exposed his nakedness. If he didn't handle his acquittal with Susan properly, he could be exposed, too.

Lose his job and maybe Mary, too.

"I sense you pulling away from me, Drew," Susan said.

"No, just thinking," he professed. "Have you noticed anyone hanging around outside your apartment that looks suspicious?"

"Last night? No." Susan rolled her eyes. "I think you scared away any night prowlers. Thank you for saving me."

Is that what I've done? Who's going to save me?

"I hope it wasn't Ben," Drew planted the seed. "Did you tell me his last name?" He tried to sound casual, spontaneous.

Come on Susan, cooperate.

"Why, is it important?" she queried.

He shrugged. "I suppose not, just curious."

"Ben can't hurt us now."

"Now?" Drew felt a rush of confusion.

"Now that we're together," Susan clarified.

Is that what we are? He questioned.

"I thought I'd call Seattle and see if Ben's on vacation," Drew explained. "If not, we can definitely rule him out as a stalker."

As Susan glared at Drew, he gulped the wine, trying to hide his nervousness. With clasped hands, she glanced away.

"What do you think?" he asked. "Want me to check?"

"Sawyer," Susan decided. "Benjamin Sawyer."

He nodded, relaxed a bit and drank some more wine.

"Please don't mention my name when you call."

"Oh, I won't," Drew assured her.

It was another lie. One just seemed to lead to another. Sort of like that cookie jar. "It will make both of us feel better."

"I already feel good." Susan smiled. "Oh, the buzzer to the oven just went off. I think our baked lasagna is ready."

"Shall we dine?" Drew stood and offered her his hand.

The table was exquisitely set with gold-rimmed china over a beige linen tablecloth. "I'm using my mother's best china," Susan explained the formality. "The pattern is rare and expensive, so I only use it on special occasions." She paused. "Like tonight."

Drew managed a smile. "You always surprise me, Susan."

Now that was not a lie.

Drew managed to get through supper and a movie before he complained of a headache and excused himself for the evening.

"You're not mad at me, are you?" Susan stood at the door, appearing anxious. "I thought you'd be pleased with supper."

"No, I'm not mad. It's just been a lousy day. We've been working on a troubling case. Forgive me for disappointing you."

They kissed lightly and Drew left.

21

Tuesday, July 20

The Vatican

MARY WAS SEATED WITH Lazarus in the Vatican apartment attached to the same building that housed the Sistine Chapel. These were the official quarters for their son Andre, Pope Benedict XXI.

"I may never get used to the idea that Andre is the Catholic Pope." Mary hailed from the antique green-velvet sofa centuries old. "How did you convince the Conclave to select him?"

"It was my brother's idea."

"Of course, it was." Mary resisted an anger that threatened to tear out her heart and shred it to pieces. "But you are in charge of Andre, right? And you will do everything within your power to protect him? Correct?" If Lazarus didn't answer responsibly, she was taking him back to court and fight him for custody.

Lazarus sat in an ornate rocker that probably belonged to an ancient king. "Why do you assume Andre is misguided?"

"Rules of engagement," she said.

"Sorry, sometimes I can't help reading your thoughts."

She sighed. "It's an innate weakness."

"Most people think my gift is unique," he countered.

"Most people don't know you like I do."

"Touché!" He chuckled.

"I take it your controlling brother utilized his gifts during the Conclave to assure the desired results." It wasn't a question.

Lazarus laughed harder. "My goodness, you find practically everything universal distasteful." He respected her intelligence.

"Reading the thoughts of others in order to manipulate them is plain rude. People have a God-given right to their privacy."

"Okay," Lazarus remarked, "I surrender, this conversation is getting us nowhere and creating stress. Let's just agree to disagree."

Mary jerked a breath. "Okay, you're right."

Andre was in the next room sleeping. She despised seeing him used by his Uncle Luceres to reinforce world-government dictates. Maybe there was nothing she could do to change Andre's destiny.

"Would you like some hot tea?" Lazarus cordially asked.

"Yes, that would be nice." She was cold and trembling over the disturbing revelation. Only God, only Jesus, could save Andre.

Mary needed to learn all she could about Andre's gifts and return to the apartment by 11 p.m. as she'd promised David's sitter.

She tried to relax while Lazarus prepared their tea. He was back in five minutes and handed her a china cup.

"I added honey and lemon, just like you like it."

He smiled at a small victory.

"Thank you." She took a sip of the strong Chinese blend. "Will this make me fall asleep?" she queried then yawned.

"It has a relaxing quality, but I'll see that you get back to the apartment safely," he said. "You need to calm down."

You are so right, but her words were private.

"Are you ready to learn about our son's abilities?"

"Yes, but first I need to tell you something."

"My dear, you have my undivided attention."

"I overheard Andre mumbling something weird," Mary recalled. "I asked him what he was saying."

Intrigued, Lazarus crooked his head to one side.

"He said it was a chant his father taught him."

Lazarus' forehead furrowed with curiosity.

"He said it wasn't you who taught him, it was his *other* daddy."

Lazarus ceased rocking. "That doesn't make any sense."

"I didn't think so, either. Is Andre delusional at times?"

"I'm sure it's a game of sorts," Lazarus replied.

"Well, I don't think filling our son's head with grandiose fantasies of importance is helping him," she said.

"What do you want me to do, Mary?"

"Talk to Luceres, he has an answer for everything."

Lazarus set the rocker into motion again.

"You're angry at me," Mary noted.

He closed his eyes. "Disappointed. My brother treated you mighty fine when you were in trouble, don't forget."

"I wish I could take back all of it," she said.

His eyes popped open and he ceased rocking. "You say you have joy in Jesus, yet there seems no way to make you happy."

Mary shrugged. "You can't buy happiness. Certainly, wealth and prestige aren't my priorities anymore."

Lazarus sighed. "How did we get in this conversation?"

Mary didn't know.

"What?"

"Tell me about Andre's gifts then I need to leave."

"We don't know how Andre does it."

"Does what?" Mary's heart quickened. "Just say it!"

"Astral Projection." He splayed his hands.

"I don't understand."

"We believe Andre's spirit wanders while he dreams."

"Clarify, uh, wander," Mary stammered, trying to decipher Lazarus' remark while praying to God it wasn't true.

"How can I explain this?" Lazarus pondered. "Oh, do you recall having lunch with a stranger, a young man in Zurich?"

"Sure, I'll never forget that odd encounter."

"You told me the guy accepted your invitation for lunch, sat at your table in a restaurant, and had a conversation with you during a lunch you paid for." He looked deeply into her sea of blue eyes.

"Yes, I remember him, go on."

"After the guy left, you tried to pay for two lunches, but the cash register employee told you he saw no one with you."

"That's true." Mary recollected.

"You told the dude at the cash register that you ordered food for two, so who ate it?" He looked at Mary. "Am I correct?"

She nodded in consent.

"He said that you ate all the food yourself."

"I remember, but what does that have to do with Andre?"

"We think your visitor was Andre, wandering in his spirit. He possibly used a form of hypnosis to involve you in his vision."

"Do you know how crazy that sounds?"

"I do. Andre's gift is beyond comprehension."

"What? That's preposterous!" Mary bolted from her chair and began pacing the room. *Is that possible, dear God?*

"Sit down, Mary, and hear me out!"

Releasing a breath, she collapsed on the sofa.

"Something also happened to me," he said.

"When? You've never mentioned it before."

"I did not want to sound crazy," he said. The idea of a wandering spirit is bizarre." He actually chuckled. "A boy was in your hospital room when you were dying in the Jerusalem hospital."

"Andre came to see me?" This was a new revelation.

"Yes, despite his weird gift, it's evident that our son loves you very much. He's drawn to you like fire to paper."

"We're Andre's parents, we're supposed to protect him."

"I don't think we're up for that challenge, Mary. Andre is light-years ahead of us in intellect and psychic performance."

"Do you realize how irrational that sounds?" Mary exclaimed. "Our son will be three soon. He's—" she had a terrible thought.

"Yes, Andre's the baby dropped off on the church steps here in Rome. Andre purposely found by me, to get to you."

"No, that can't be true!" Mary's hands flew to her lips.

Lazarus said nothing.

"I gave him up right after the Rapture," she said.

"Somehow, he found his way to the nurse in Madrid Spain, and eventually into your care again. Andre loves you very much, Mary."

She trembled, frightened at her son's gifting.

"I know. Personally, Andre's abilities scare even me."

Tears bubbled in her eyes.

"You haven't heard the worst of it," he said.

Mary squeezed her eyes and groaned in her spirit.

"Dennis, Dr. Albert Swartzenberg's lab assistant, witnessed the new born slithering like a snake out of the hospital birthing room."

Mary opened her mouth but no words came out.

"Andre has shown remarkable psychic abilities involving hypnosis since he took his first breaths," Lazarus said.

"Okay, say it's all true," Mary uttered. "Does God have some grandiose purpose for our son?"

"I don't presume to know God's mind," he said. "But I'm doing my best to direct Andre's gifts for the good of mankind. I am a good father, though I was never good husband material."

"It's his *other* daddy I'm worried about," Mary said.

"What do you mean?" Lazarus queried.

"Is it possible that Satan intends to use Andre for evil purposes? The fallen angel despises God and wants to receive the worship of humankind," Mary theorized.

"You've lost me there, Mary."

"We must find a way to help our son resist evil."

"That's the silliest idea I've heard in a while!"

"It's what I believe."

"Listen to yourself, Mary. Your fanatical religious beliefs are off the charts. Nobody's coming to save the world—Jesus or al Mahdi. Face the facts: we humans must do that for ourselves."

"You're so wrong, Lazarus, blinded by sin."

"Sin is relative."

"Sin is disobedience to Almighty God."

Lazarus sneered. "I just hope your prayers keep those circling the earth at bay. We don't need more interference."

"What are you talking about?" Mary spouted.

"The aliens," he replied. "They're watching us."

Mary actually laughed. "If there are aliens in space, like you believe, they are demons. Revelation speaks of their attack."

"See what I mean."

"I need to go now and get some rest."

22

Back in Fernwood

TUESDAY, DREW HAD THE early work shift. He logged out at three p.m. and left Dover's, making a beeline for home. After guzzling down a large glass of sweet tea, he phoned the number Mrs. Belk had given him. In Seattle, Washington—two hours earlier than in Fernwood—the satellite connection rang five times.

Drew was beginning to think Jon had shut off his phone, either sleeping or working. Then a deep male voice answered the ring.

"Yeah . . .?"

"Is this Jon Belk?"

"Yeah."

"I don't know if you remember me, Jon, but our moms were best of friends," Drew said. "Cynthia gave me your number."

"Oh. How was she feeling when you spoke to her?"

"Isn't that something you should ask her?"

Immediately, Drew knew he'd misspoken.

"I don't need a stranger lecturing me, dude."

"Andrew Taylor." This was no way to solicit Jon's help in locating Benjamin Sawyer, Susan's ex-boyfriend.

"Oh, yeah, Andrew," Jon recalled.

"Sorry," Drew apologized. "Your mom said to say hello."

No response at the other end was troubling.

"Look Jon," Drew tried to smooth over his remarks, "your relationship with your mother is none of my business."

"You got that right!" Jon piped.

"She obviously misses you." Drew inhaled a deep breath. "The reason I'm calling is to ask for your help."

"Doing what?"

"I'm looking for a cop you may know. Benjamin Sawyer. A woman who recently moved to my town said he worked for the Seattle Police Department. Have you heard of Ben?"

"Which department does the dude work in?" Jon asked.

"Ben was hired on last fall, that's all I know."

"Why do you need to find him?" Jon inquired.

"His ex-girlfriend thinks he's been watching her apartment. She asked me to find out if he's still in Seattle," Drew explained.

"Why doesn't she just call him?" Jon asked.

"She's scared," Drew replied. "Look, if you can help me out here, I'd sure appreciate it, Jon. I'm a detective with the police department in Fernwood, Tennessee. I just want to talk to Ben."

"Okay, I'll ask around and get back to you."

"Thanks, Jon. Maybe I can return the favor one day."

"Gotta go now, my other line's ringing."

The phone disconnect was abrupt, but Drew thought he'd succeeded thus far. When he'd spoken to Ben, he'd know if Susan was telling the truth, or if Ben was the victim, as was his case.

Although adultery wasn't punishable by law, rape was. Add to that Susan's threats to expose him if he didn't continue the relationship broadened the spectrum of malfeasance.

Drew's cell phone dinged a minute later. Although he didn't recognize the I.D. caller, he answered anyhow. "Yes?"

"Is this Detective Andrew Taylor?"

"Yes, it is."

"I just received a disturbing call from a young woman who says you abused her." The unidentified caller fell silent.

"Come again?" Drew questioned if he'd heard correctly.

"My name is Clark Evans. I work in the I.A.D., the Internal Affairs Department," he revealed. "Got a minute?"

"Someone's filing a formal complaint against me?"

"Not exactly," Evans said. "The woman hasn't given her name or filled out a written complaint," he explained.

"What exactly did this woman tell you, Mr. Evans?"

"It's Sergeant Evans," the caller clarified.

"I'm still waiting for you to tell me the nature of the complaint, Sergeant?" Drew was in no mood to flirt with the idea of who made the call, certain it had to be Dr. Susan Parrot.

"I prefer not to discuss the nature of the complaint over the phone," Evans formally stated. "Can you to come down to my office this afternoon? I'll be here until six."

"Sure. I know the address."

"See you shortly then, Detective Taylor."

Drew ended the call and dialed Susan Parrot's private cell number. When he didn't get an answer, he left a message: "When you get this message, Susan, please call me, we need to talk."

Then he stewed over what she'd told Sergeant Evans.

After showering, Drew changed into casual clothes and headed off to I.A.D. The complaints' department that handled internal police complaints was located on the second floor of the First Federal Union Bank building. He took the elevator up.

After wandering down a long hallway, he found I.A.D.'s name on a door then knocked. "Come on in" was the response.

Drew pushed open the door and was about to say something to Evans when his cell phone dinged. "Do you mind?"

Evans waved him off. "Take your call then we'll talk."

Drew stepped back in the hall and made sure no one was around before he addressed Susan. "What are you doing to me?" He lashed out from anger, shaking with growing rage.

"I just thought you needed a reminder that nobody walks away from me without suffering the consequences," she said.

"Susan. We made love. It was magnificent," he said.

"Then I'll drop the matter and we'll move on with our lives. What do you say, Andrew? Isn't that the best possible choice?"

Drew beat a fist against the wall and put a dent in it.

"Susan, I can't discuss our relationship now. I'm at the complaints' department about to speak to Sergeant Evans."

"Okay, but be careful not to incriminate yourself," she warned. "Evans doesn't have my name, so if I let the matter drop and never file a formal complaint, the matter is over."

Drew bit his tongue but had to say it. "Thank you, Susan."

"Supper tonight at my place, is seven good for you?"

"I'll be there." He ended the call and silently cursed.

Sergeant Evans was seated at his desk sorting file folders. "Can I get you something to drink? Coffee or a cola?"

"I'm fine." Drew parked his crutch against the beige wall then collapsed in the guest chair in front of Evan's desk.

"I presume you have some idea who made this complaint?"

Drew nodded he did. "What's the nature of the complaint?"

"I'm not legally qualified to judge if you're guilty of what the woman said you did." Evans clarified his position of authority. "This query is a courtesy to you." He settled back in his chair.

Drew cringed and reminded himself: *Don't say too much.*

Evans gaze fell on Drew's crutch. "How are you handling your disability?" He stared. "I heard you took a bullet to the head that caused a stroke and crippled you. I'm sorry you have suffered for the cause of justice. But you're also lucky to be working."

"Sheriff Boswell has been more than fair with me."

"Look . . ." Evans leaned his forearms on his desk. "I just want to get to the bottom of this complaint and see that justice is applied, regardless who is at fault. You, or her, if that's the case."

"If justice is what you're after, I shouldn't be sitting here," Drew cautiously said. "I did not commit a crime against anyone."

"Okay, I get it. Maybe the sex was consensual." Evans spun around in his office chair and poured himself a cup of black coffee from the carafe. "I'd still like to hear your side of the story."

Drew blinked with clarity. He was in trouble, squeezed between a vindictive spurned lover and an I.A.D. savvy prosecutor skilled in detecting indiscretions committed by police employees.

This was his opportunity to come clean and tell the truth. Tom Rave's words "Do the right thing" rang true in his heart.

"So . . ." Evans entwined his fingers, "I'm listening."

Drew bit the bullet and said, "The woman who spoke to you is my appointed counselor." He jerked a breath. "She gave all the right signals she was interested in me, and now she's threatening to punish me if I back off from our adulterous relationship."

"Okay if I tape your testimony, Detective Taylor?"

Drew replied with an affirmative nod.

The taping session lasted for thirty-three minutes, with Drew explaining his reasons for feeling distressed over his relationship with Mary, and how Sheriff Boswell had recommended he talk to a therapist before annulling his marriage. He was caught in a vise.

"Dr. Susan Parrot was the only game in town," Drew explained. "I trusted her with my private thoughts."

Evans frowned then cut off the recorder.

"Do you have proof to back up your statement?" Evans scooted his chair away from the desk. "Did you initiate the affair?"

Evans posed several disturbing questions. Drew had kissed Susan first. She hadn't begged him to make love to her but after breaking up with Mary, he had sex with her in her office.

"You realize, Taylor, that it's your word against Dr. Parrot's." Evan's eyelids rapidly blinked. "In my experience with court trials, the judge usually rules in favor of the weaker sex."

"Trust me . . ." Drew huffed, "Susan is no weakling."

To that, the sergeant had no response.

"She's squeezing the life out of me and I don't know what else to do but submit," Drew elaborated. "I've been duped."

Evans chuckled. "I can see you are seriously screwed."

"Yeah, the handwriting is on the wall." Drew sighed.

"Point taken," Evans conceded. "Now, do you know of anyone willing to testify on your behalf regarding the nature of Dr. Parrot's sexual exploits involving her male patients?"

"I'm working on it," Drew replied. "Susan broke up with a Seattle Cop named Benjamin Sawyer. I'm tracking him down now."

"Okay." Evans closed his folder on Drew. "We're done here for the day, Detective. Let me know what you find out."

"Just so you know," Drew added one more thing, "that was Susan calling on my cell before we talked. She'll skip filing formal charges as long as I have supper with her tonight."

Humph. Evans considered Drew's dilemma.

"Should I comply with her request?"

"I usually don't recommend contact with the accuser at this point in my investigation, but I think keeping the communication channels open with Dr. Parrot works in your favor."

"What do you mean?"

Evans removed what looked like a button from his top desk drawer and showed it to Drew. "It's a recording device."

"Is it legal for me to wear a wire?"

"Let's just say we're gathering evidence. After you see Susan tonight, we'll listen back and evaluate if your recorded conversation reveals anything useful," Evans explained.

"In a court trial, you mean."

"Yes."

"What do you want me to do?" Drew inquired.

"Nothing specific, just act normal. Let Susan do the talking."

Drew released a breath. "Thanks for believing me, Sergeant Evans. I love my wife and want to reconcile our differences."

"Well, Detective, I sure hope you can do that. Mary has a good reputation among Christians. I'd hate to see her get hurt."

"She's the best." Drew felt even more like a heel.

Will Mary ever forgive me? He contemplated as he hobbled out of Evan's office and approached the elevator. This was a hellish nightmare he'd brought on himself through a very poor choice.

23

SUSAN ANSWERED THE DOOR wearing a flimsy pink housecoat that skirted her ankles over lingerie that left little to challenge the imagination. Drew leaned over and kissed her lightly on the lips.

"How are you?" He tried to sound casual.

"I'm great! Life is perfect!" Susan flitted over to the kitchen bar and grabbed two glasses of Merlot. "I thought we could have a drink, relax a bit, then spend time in bed before we dine."

Drew blinked. *What do I do now?* Sergeant Evans was listening to every word that was said. *Oh brother . . .*

"What do you think?" She smiled sweetly.

Me? Drew grabbed the wine goblet from her hand and drained it, inadvertently burping. "Sorry." He swiped his wet chin with the back of his hand. "It's been a long grueling day."

"More reason for me to relieve your stress." Susan rubbed Drew's shoulders. "Would you like another glass of wine?"

"Sure." Drew held out the goblet, his hand trembling.

"Your hand—what's wrong, Drew?"

"Nothing you should worry about."

Susan filled his glass. Putting some distance between them, he said, "I'm weak from hungry, what did you fix for supper?"

"Well, eating wasn't my first choice." Susan chuckled, already a bit tipsy. "But I can't let my man go hungry, can I?"

Her man . . . Drew knew he was in real trouble.

"My mother said the best way to a man's heart is through his stomach." She sweetly smiled. "I never found that to be true."

"Well, maybe just a snack, if you're not ready to eat yet."

"Of course." Susan grabbed Drew's arm and guided him to the sofa, straddled him, and began feeding him salty peanuts.

He gently set her aside on the sofa.

"Too fast . . .?" Susan peered at Drew.

"A little," he admitted. "I just need more time."

"I don't need more time. You have to know I adore you."

"Susan, we've only known one another for a couple of months," he countered. "Until last Friday, you were my counselor."

"I'm still your counselor."

"No, I think our—what we did changed all that."

Susan's expression grew somber. "What are you getting at, Drew? Are you accusing me of being unprofessional?"

The acid pumping in Drew's stomach said he was about to throw up. "Excuse me, but I need to borrow your restroom."

Placing a closed door between him and Susan felt like a sanctuary. He flushed the commode twice while trying to decide if he should continue trying to incriminate Susan or just run like a scared rabbit. He was no match for a female with piranha instincts.

"Hey, did you hear that? I hope so." Drew whispered to Sergeant Evans. "I'm not sure I can take this any further."

It wasn't a two-way message system, so Drew flushed the commode again, washed his hands then returned to the living room.

"Sorry, Susan, my stomach's upset today."

"Maybe you should see a doctor. You eat a lot of take-out and we all know it's sometimes tainted. You may need an antibiotic."

"Yeah, you're right." He stared at Susan. "Before we have supper, can we talk about why you called Sergeant Evans?"

"What's there to discuss?" Susan played with the hem of her frilly robe. "Did Evans phone and tell you what I said?"

"Yeah, he did." Drew glanced out the window and spied the sun dipping below the horizon, dragging light with it.

"You're hurt. I should not have reacted so harshly." Susan pulled Drew closer. "Can we start over? Will you forgive me?"

There, Susan's admitted she welcomes my affections.

"But when you kissed me, Drew, I believed you were ready to move on from your troubled marriage," Susan added.

Drew's forehead furrowed. *Susan just told Evans that I initiated the affair. Not good for me, and now I'm tricking her into a confession.*

"Don't look so worried," she said. "Nothing's going to happen unless I formally charge you for sexual abuse."

Dear God, I'm never going to get out of this without grief.

"So, what are you thinking, Drew?"

"I'm thinking, your statement sounds awfully like a threat. We stay together or else. . . am I right?" he queried.

She stiffened. "I just don't like being used."

"We made love, Susan. *Once*," he clarified. "I didn't know I'd signed a long-term contract with punitive damages if I decided to end the relationship. How am I supposed to feel?"

"Oh . . . that's terribly harsh," Susan made a face. "And it was three times, did you forget? Once while we were at my office on Friday, and twice after we came back here, at my apartment."

Susan stared at Drew, waiting for his response.

That was something Evans didn't need to know.

Susan threw up her hands and paced the room. "I don't like talking about this. It gets us nowhere. Can't we just dine and let bygones be bygones. I know you care about me. Forget about your wayward wife and let's move on with our lives. Okay?"

"And if I refuse?"

She stopped pacing. "Then, it's a whole new ballgame."

Drew was on his feet, forgetting about his lame leg.

"Susan, that's not fair! If you file charges against me for sexual abuse, I'll lose my job and probably never get another one in law enforcement." He felt a stab of pain in his lame leg.

"That's not what I want to happen, Andrew."

Not to mention the end of my marriage to Mary.

"Drew, sweetheart . . ." Susan's blue eyes enlarged as she clasped his hands. "None of that is going to happen as long as we're together. All you need to do is trust me."

Trust? Drew had played Susan's game about as long as he could stomach. It wasn't in him to lie down and submit.

"The problem is, Susan, I don't trust you," he said.

"What?" Her eyes bubbled with tears. "I can't believe you're saying that when we've meant so much to each other."

"Just let me go. Okay?"

"I can't. I won't!"

Drew grabbed his crutch and shook it at Susan. "Is that what you told Ben when he realized how unstable you are?"

"What did you say?" Susan's face washed out white.

"Tell the truth, Susan! You didn't break off with Ben, did you? He walked away because you're insane. Isn't that right?"

She blinked with comprehension.

"Aren't you going to offer a defense, Dr. Parrot?"

Gulping down her wine, Susan angrily threw it at the brick fireplace. With a loud burst, it shattered into a thousand glitters on the hearth. A woman's wrath is a bullet to behold.

"My, my, Andrew, you've really thought this through." She traipsed into the kitchen and used a pair of potholders to remove a vegetable casserole from the oven. "Are you still hungry?"

Drew swallowed bile and wilted. *She's impossible.*

Hands crossed over ample breasts, Susan came halfway into the den and asked, "Why don't you just say you're sorry, and let's have a pleasant evening. You're not going to win this one."

Drew blinked with the knowledge that Susan would never let him go without a fight. "Please. Let me go. I made a mistake."

"I can't do that!" Susan stubbornly exclaimed. "I don't handle rejection well. Nobody walks away from me without suffering."

"Is that why you became a shrink?" Drew grabbed at straws.

"Supper is getting cold."

"Did your daddy abuse you, or leave you and your mom to fend for yourselves while you were a child? Is that it?"

Seconds later, Susan's nightgown dropped to the floor.

Unequipped emotionally, Drew didn't realize he'd let go of his wine glass until it shattered on the carpet. Relying on his crutch, he hurriedly hobbled toward the door, praying for God's help.

"You'll be back, wait and see!" she called after him.

* * *

The moonlit night had turned suddenly dark with storm clouds. Following jagged streaks of lightning, sharp cracks of thunder exploded in the sky. Back at his condo, Drew pulled the curtains to shut out the storm and made sure his doors were locked.

Feeling like a little boy scared of monsters as darkness closed around him, he suffered remorse for becoming involved with his counselor. He plundered the fridge for a can of beer. After his fourth, he had a buzz that failed to drive away the monsters.

For what he's done, God would surely punish him. He deserved no forgiveness. He deserved to die. He stared at his un in its holster. A better man would have the guts to pull the trigger.

His cell rang and he reached for it. "Sergeant Evans?"

"No, it's Mary. Who's Sergeant Evans?"

Drew started crying. "I really messed up, baby. Come home."

"That's why I called, Drew. Little David and I are about to board a flight out of Rome to Atlanta, Georgia. Counting our layover time, I'll see you in approximately fourteen hours."

"We need to talk now, Mary. I'm in real trouble."

"Drew, I'm boarding the plane. Can we talk about this when I get home?" The background noises were enormous.

"Don't hang up, Mary."

The background noises grew louder.

"Mary? Don't believe anything you hear about me until I have a chance to explain. Someone may be filing a misdemeanor against me for sexual abuse," he hollered. "It's not true."

But the phone connection had already ended.

The phone rang again. "Mary?"

"No, it's Sergeant Evans.

"I messed up, didn't I?" he muttered.

"While your encounter with Susan is fresh on your mind, write down everything you remember," Evans said.

"I'm pretty bummed out right now," he said.

"From what I heard, I'm pretty sure you'll be facing a sexual complaint within twenty-four hours. A woman scorned in love is a tough adversary. You should get prepared for a battle."

Drew dropped the phone and threw up.

24

Wednesday, July 21

Baghdad, Iraq

LUCERES WAS SEATED AT his desk in his high-rise Baghdad office complex when someone tapped on his office door. "Come in," he called out, presuming it was his African secretary delivering the breakfast tray he'd ordered from the café down the street.

The door came open and there stood Ahmed Ramallah, a dark-skinned Arab with midnight eyes glinting in the bright morning sunlight. "What a nice surprise!" Luceres abandoned his chair and walked over to embrace his former Harvard University roommate.

Ahmed gave his usual cheek-to-cheek hugs.

"Did we have an appointment?" Luceres asked, holding Ahmed at arm's length, puzzling over the Muslim's thoughts.

"You know we didn't." The Arab stepped into the spacious office and closed the door behind him. "Shall we sit?"

"How did you get past security downstairs?"

"The Special Forces guy might have a headache but he'll get over it," Ahmed reported. "Plus, I said you'd make time for me."

"Always so aggressive." Luceres mused. "But, of course, I always welcome a loyal friend into my abode."

"Are we still that?" Ahmed's bushy eyebrows arched. A question mark lingered on his face. "Loyal friends?"

"I should hope so." Luceres smiled politely. "What brings you to Baghdad? Last I heard you were in South America."

"So, you do keep tabs on me?" Ahmed was pleased. "While I'm out doing work for Allah, you've managed to milk the world government's coffers to carve out a luxurious lifestyle." He took a seat without an invitation. "I won't take up much of your time."

"I'm always amazed how Western you sound." Luceres trotted over to his desk and sat down in his comfortable swivel rocker.

Tilting his head to one side, Luceres assessed Ahmed's motives for coming. Wearing traditional Muslim attire, he was a formidable leader with opinions that carried weight in the Middle East.

"I know you've read my thoughts," Ahmed said. "I only hope you appreciate how important this meeting is to me."

"Your motives offer me little comfort." Luceres erected his body and tugged at the hem of his tailored jacket. "Have I done something so offensive it warrants this unannounced meeting?"

"Not specifically. I'm here to see that you keep your word."

"What word is that?" Luceres queried, already privy to the Muslim's thoughts but interested in how the conversation would play out. There was always *wiggle room*, as politicians often say.

"In our last meeting, you promised me possession of the Jerusalem Temple when it was completed. Or did you forget?"

"I don't forget anything Ahmed." He locked olive eyes with the Muslim. "Did you forget I qualified my offer?"

"Let's not have a pissing contest!" Ahmed barked.

"I'm on your side," Luceres said.

"It doesn't feel like it," Ahmed countered. "I saw a television clip where hundreds of Messianic Jews gathered on the Temple Mount, too many to get inside the Temple Courtyard. Many volunteered as missionaries to preach the Gospel of Jesus Christ."

"That was unexpected," Luceres stated.

Ahmed scoffed, "Christians have yet to learn that violence is the best method to convince people they should obey the Ten Commandments. Even Muslims accept the Pentateuch."

"Must you always be so dramatic, Ahmed?"

"I do what it takes to get my points across."

Feeding a bad habit, irritated over the way their conversation was headed, Luceres opened a box of expensive Moravian Cigars.

"Would you like a smoke, Ahmed?" He lit the weed.

"You dare corrupt me! I'm disciplined, faithful to the Qur'an."

Luceres blew out smoke. "Except when you drink."

"I no longer use alcoholic beverages. I am pure of heart."

Luceres blew out a ring of smoke then coughed. "Are you pure in heart when you murder innocent people in the name of Allah?"

"Those things will kill you, friend."

"I worry more about you doing that. Could we call a truce?"

"My friend," Ahmed wasn't through, "you've become far too comfortable and pampered to do what it takes to rule the world."

Luceres angrily kicked back in his swiveling office chair. "Are you attempting to irritate me, Ahmed? Well, it's working."

"Read it any way you choose." He glanced away.

"You realize I could call my guards and have you arrested for threatening me. Not to mention your involvement with beheading that Christian leader—what was his name?"

"Ghost." Ahmed focused glistening black eyes on Luceres. "I told you I did not kill him, but I applaud whoever did."

"That's good, because you would not wear prison garb well."

"Well, well, a bit of humor!" Ahmed breathed deeply then uttered, "Keep your promise to me, Luceres. Do the honorable thing. Keep your word. Return the Temple Mount to my people."

"It's not the right time."

"Say the word and my soldiers will march on Jerusalem and take it from those stupid Jews!" Ahmed exploded. "The site belongs to us. Father Abraham gave it to his first-born son."

"Yes, I know all that. His bastard son, Ishmael."

"You dare blaspheme my heritage!" Ahmed pounded a fist on the coffee table. "You are no friend of Muslims."

"I am tolerant of religion, you know that!"

"It's not enough, I want possession of the Mount."

"Convince me why you must have it this moment."

"It's urgent I convince my people that I am *al Mahdi*."

"You intend to establish a world-wide Caliphate and rule from a Muslim temple build on the Mount," Luceres discerned.

"Muhammad has decreed it," Ahmed said.

"Will you also rule over my Committee of Ten?"

"You can handle the government's financial business, but Islam will unite all people under Allah. He is the one true God."

"Surely, you are not so naïve to believe other religions will roll over and play dead? I have a better plan. My brother and I have been working hard to sway the Catholics to our point of view."

"And what view is that?" Ahmed asked.

"Peace will only be achieved when people embrace the same God," Luceres said. "I don't care which religion is adopted."

"So, you'd accept Islam as the international religion?"

"Yes, but don't expect me to follow your silly rules. My nephew is a heaven-sent child. He will back you up."

"And who is this marvelous boy?"

"Andre Bacon, my brother's son."

"Your brother's bastard boy?" Ahmed shook his head. "The toddler can't be more than three years old!"

"Actually, he's still two going on one hundred, if you count his superb intellect. The child is a prodigy like earth has never seen."

"And he will worship me, as *al Mahdi*?"

"I doubt that," Luceres replied. "But the Catholics won't fight you. And the Committee of Ten will condone your deity."

"What about Protestants?"

"Rather than kill, re-educate them."

"This is a promise."

"Yes, I keep my word."

"You'd better." Ahmed stood up to leave.

"It's all about timing, my friend," Luceres said. "That's what I've been trying to tell you. I never break a promise. You will sit in a temple of your choice as *al Mahdi*, be assured. But not yet."

"I won't wait much longer," Ahmed said.

The leather soles of Luceres' shoes slapped the floor as he stood up. "Isn't creating lasting peace worth waiting for?"

"It is declared in the Qur'an that *al Mahdi* will rule the world as the uncontested Caliphate. I'm simply fulfilling that prophecy."

"I'm not going to change my mind, Ahmed. The answer is still no. You will not have my support if you attack Jerusalem."

"Know this, my *excellent* friend, while I wait for you to fulfill your promise, thousands of Messianic Jews will be running around the planet proclaiming Jesus Christ as Savior of the world!"

"Everything you hear on TV is not always true."

"These evangelists claim they are anointed by the Holy Spirit to perform miracles like the Old Testament prophets," Ahmed said. "They will convince people that by faith Jesus will save their souls."

"So, it's *al Mahdi* against Jesus." Luceres had no faith in anyone but himself. Success was the result of careful planning.

A tap came at the door. "Yes?" Luceres responded.

"It's Demetrius, Sir. Shall I serve breakfast?"

"Open the door for my secretary, Ahmed. Join me for breakfast and we'll discuss a compromise suitable to both of us."

Ahmed obeyed then leaned against the sunny yellow wall.

Demetrius stared at the Arab as he crossed the office with a sterling silver tray loaded with a carafe of strong Arabian coffee, condiments, fruit-filled pastries, and breakfast croissants. He set the tray on the glittering steel-and-glass sidebar and looked at Luceres.

"Anything else I can get you, Sir?"

"No, Demetrius," Luceres replied. "Please hold my calls while my friend and I dine and reminisce over old times."

25

Fernwood

DREW SUFFERED FROM A serious hangover Wednesday morning.
Dealing with Susan's threats had him in a quandary. It felt like his
survival hung by threads of lies. It was a terrible place to linger.

Having finished breakfast seconds before, someone knocked
on his door. Through the peephole, he spied Sheriff Sarah Boswell
and Officer Bob Fellows. Nothing to do but open the door.

"Hi, guys." *Was there egg on his face?* He belched. "Sorry."

"Good morning, Drew," Sarah spoke. "May we come in?"

"Door's open, everything okay at the station?"

Not answering his question, Sarah stepped into the condo and
glanced around. Bob slouched a few steps behind her.

"Is there anybody here besides you?" Sarah queried.

"No," Drew replied, his face itching from the need of a shave.
"Sorry I didn't make it into work, but I felt too sick to come in."

"That's not why we're here," Sarah said, glancing around the
messy kitchen with dishes piled in the sink and mud on the floor.

"Okay then, why are you here?" Drew queried.

Sarah frowned. "Sorry, Detective Taylor, but I'm here to arrest
you." She began reading Drew his Miranda Rights.

"But I haven't done anything wrong!" he protested.

Bob snickered. It was the same for everyone.

"I'll need to handcuff you. Sorry."

"Sarah, you know me. I don't deserve this."

"Tell it to the judge, it's not my call."

Drew offered both wrists, too stunned to argue. Evidently,
Dr. Susan Parrot had a busy night punishing him.

"At least tell me what I'm charged with?" Drew uttered.

"You already know." Sarah tossed Drew a look then nudged
him toward the door. "Sorry, I'm just doing my job."

"What's the charge?" Drew asked.

"Sergeant Clark Evans delivered the paperwork to the D.A. late last night. Dr. Susan Parrot has filed a rape charge against you."

Ashamed, Drew dropped his gaze to the floor. "It's not what you think, Boss." It took mega restraint to keep his cool.

"It never is," Sarah piped. "You still have to face a judge."

"How soon?" His puppy-brown eyes reflected sorrow.

"Four p.m. this afternoon. Lucky for you, I called in a favor from Judge Emit Longstreet. His son Barry was released from the Nashville City Jail earlier this morning and will do six months of community service there," she said. "Emit owes me big time."

Drew nodded. "Thank you."

"You'll need to hire a lawyer."

"What about my badge and weapon?"

"Bob, fetch Drew's things off the bar and bring them with you." Sarah nudged Drew toward the door. "You first."

A wave of summer heat hit him in the face like a furnace as he stepped outdoors. The arrest felt awkward. He'd done it to others many times. Sarah placed her hand on Drew's head and eased him in the back of the squad car when a Ford sedan pulled in the driveway. Sarah squinted at the driver through the bright sunlight.

Mary Ralston opened the backdoor and got out of the car and approached Sarah. "What's happening here?" She spied Drew in the backseat of the squad car. "Why is my husband wearing cuffs?"

"Drew is under arrest," Sarah informed Mary as she slammed the backdoor. "And no, you cannot talk to him right now."

"When then?" The driver revved the sedan's motor.

"Come over to Dover's after you get settled in." Sarah opened the front door and slid behind the wheel. Bob was already inside.

"Wait? What is the charge, Sheriff Boswell?" Mary asked.

"Miss? Get your kid! I have to be somewhere," the female UBER driver hollered out the window, waving Mary over.

"We'll talk about it when you get to Dover's," Sarah told Mary. "Better tend to your child. We have to go now."

As the Crown Victoria backed out of the driveway, Mary ran after it and placed her palms against the window. Peering through the glass, she mouthed *I love you* as the squad car pulled away.

"Miss, I have another pickup, come get your kid."

"Hold your horses, I'm on my way."

Mary instructed the driver to set their bags on the front steps while she gathered Little David in her arms. She thanked the woman and paid her with one of Michael Thoene's gold coins.

"Let's go inside, little guy, and get you settled in."

Mary left their two bags sitting on the porch landing while she carried David inside the condo. "Looks the same, partner."

But it wasn't. Drew wasn't there. The kitchen hadn't been cleaned in days. Whatever he'd done while she was away was serious or he wouldn't be under arrest. She'd have to deal with it.

After placing David on the den carpet where he could crawl around, Mary retrieved their bags from the porch and locked the door once she was back inside. It was chilly inside the condo.

Mary discovered the AC unit registered sixty decrees. After adjusting the thermostat to a comfortable temp, she returned to the den where she spied Little David pulling up on the sofa.

"Great job, little boy, but you stink. Let's get you cleaned up."

Mary hoisted David off the floor and carried him into the hall bath. As the bathtub filled with warm water, she stripped off his clothes and tossed in a yellow rubber ducky and a plastic sailboat.

Soon as David climbed in, he began splashing the water.

Seated on the potty lid, Mary watched him play. When David mumbled "Da-da" it nearly broke her heart.

"I know, little guy, I'm worried about Papa Drew, too."

Dover's, she recalled Sarah saying. *What is that?*

After David's bubbly soak, Mary dried and dressed him in fresh clothes then hauled him off to the kitchen where she placed him in his highchair and fed him a jar of oatmeal mixed with fruit.

He was hungry and guzzled down the food.

Afterwards, she sponged his messy face and squatty hands with a wet rag and put him to bed. Handing him a Sippy cup of apple juice, she hoped he'd finish all of it and fall asleep for a nap.

"There, you're on your own for a bit."

She closed the bedroom door and began to stress over Drew's arrest. Alone and shaken, she allowed herself to cry.

"Lord, none of us are perfect. Please help him."

Feeling some better after communing with God, Mary removed her sweaty clothes and stepped into the shower stall. Amply lathering her hair with fragrant shampoo, she turned the nozzle to a full spray of hot water to cleanse the soap from her tired body. Even more, turbulent thoughts wearied her.

Who is Andre's *other* daddy? Would he obey an evil spirit or his real daddy? Lazarus was not spiritually equipped to battle Satan.

Once Mary had showered and dressed for the day, she felt more ready to deal with Drew's legal problem. For the first time she noticed his clothes strewn about the bedroom floor. The bed wasn't made and the pillowcases stank from spilled booze.

He's been drinking. A lot while I was gone.

Mary stripped off the soiled sheets and pillowcases and remade the bed with fresh linens. The pillows, she hauled off to the dryer and tossed them with fragrant fabric sheets. Order was necessary.

By noon, David was awake and Mary was ready to go down to Dover's—wherever that was. Since she couldn't phone Drew, she called Cory Lindsey. Alexi answered his cell phone.

"Hi, it's Mary. Obviously, this isn't Cory."

"*My* Mary? Detective Andrew Taylor's *wife*? The mysterious woman who *never* stays home?" Alexi laid it on thick.

"Yes, it's *that* Mary." Her chuckle released some tension. "I need to speak to your hubby about Drew. Is he there?"

"Out back, mowing the yard," Alexi reported. "If you're calling long distance, I can have him call you back."

"No, no, I'm actually home," Mary said.

"Great! Are both boys with you?"

"Just Little David. Lazarus has custody of Andre."

"I see . . . well, I guess Drew was excited to see you."

"Actually, he was leaving the condo as we drove in."

"My, my, you two have a strange marriage," Alexi piped. "You're like two ships passing in the night and never dock."

Mary couldn't argue with that.

"Are you home for good this time?" Alexi asked.

Mary didn't know how to answer that question, either.

"Are you going to tell me about your trip?" Alexi asked.

"Yes, I will, when the time is right." Mary hitched a breath. "Okay."

"How's your pregnancy coming along?" Mary asked.

"Much better this time round, I've barely been sick."

"You're a good mom, Alexi. Do you know the sex?"

"It's a boy, and Cory is beside himself."

"Have you heard of a place called Dover's?" Mary queried.

"No, is that where you are now?"

"Alexi, go get Cory for me."

"Okay." The cell phone clinked on the counter.

Mary waited a couple minutes.

"Mary?" Cory said. "What do you want?"

"Sorry to interrupt your yard work, Cory."

"No problem, what's this call about?"

"Do you know of a place called Dover's?"

"Yeah, it's a warehouse located out on Highway 64 East," Cory replied. "Guy died that owned it. Used to house his creative arts business—making concrete statues and yard items."

"It's a vacant building?" Mary probed.

"Not anymore. The Fernwood PD is occupying the space until a new station can be built with state or federal funds."

"I didn't realize the earthquake took down the station."

"Place was ruled unsafe for occupancy. Actually, our town got a lucky pass compared to other communities west of us." He paused then asked, "What's this sudden interest in Dover's?"

"Drew was arrested this morning and I need to speak with him," she replied. "He's in some kind of legal trouble."

"Wow!" Cory internalized the idea. "I had no idea."

"Don't you two ever talk?"

"We've both been busy," Cory replied. "You want me to meet you at Dover's? It might help if I'm there."

"No, I haven't had a chance to talk to Drew since I returned from Rome," Mary replied. "Sarah was hauling him off in a squad car last time our eyes met. We seriously need a one on one."

"I'm glad you're back, Mary. Drew is only half human without you around. If you think of any way either Alexi or I can help, please don't hesitate to call on us."

"Is Cat still away?" Caitlyn was Cory's younger sister and seriously involved with illegal underground Christian ministry.

"She phones occasionally, but I never know specifically where she is at the time. Best I don't know since Christian evangelism is against international law." He fell silent. "I miss her."

"I know you do. And Cory . . .?"

"Yes?"

"I may need help with Little David if I can't get a sitter." Mary hoped that Grace Riley would be available for full-time hire.

"Of course, we love having David visit, and Miracle plays marvelously with him," Cory added. "Anything else?"

"No. Take care, Cory."

Mary found Grace's phone number scribbled on a tablet inside the kitchen's junk drawer among other miscellaneous items. She used her prepaid phone to make the call. The line rang twice.

"Hello," a mellifluous voice came back.

"Mrs. Riley, this is Mary Taylor."

"Oh, hi."

Grace seemed less than friendly.

"Are you currently working for anyone?"

"No, I'm between jobs," Grace replied.

"Well, I could really use your help with my son today," Mary said. "I need to run an errand. He's been fed and bathed, so there nothing for you to do but watch him. I shouldn't be too long."

"How soon will you need me?"

"Now, if you're available."

"Sure, I'll be there in fifteen."

Mary prepared David's mid-afternoon snack then made a chicken-salad sandwich for Grace, just in case her trip to Dover's took longer. Sweet tea and soft drinks were in the fridge, plus the pantry was stacked with Doritos and snack crackers.

Always punctual, the nanny arrived fifteen minutes later.

"Here is my cell number if you need me." Mary laid the written number on the breakfast bar. "I'll be gone for at least two hours, maybe longer. Is that a problem for you?"

"I have no other plans today." Grace smiled.

"Good. Thank you so much. I'll let you know within an hour how soon I will be home." Mary snagged Drew's SUV keys off the gold hook and left the condo through the front door.

She was at Dover's Concrete Statues and Figurines twenty minutes later. The huge warehouse was surrounded by black-and-white squad cars. Four black SUV's were parked under shade trees.

Mary pulled into a vacant space, let the windows down a few inches, then climbed out. After locking up, she stared at the warehouse. She crossed the gravel driveway and pushed open the oversized front door. A guard was seated at a table to her right.

"Your name and reason for the visit?" the female officer inquired. Her nametag read Selena Walters.

"I'm here to see Sheriff Boswell," Mary reported.

"Sorry, but you'll have to be patted down."

Mary was searched by a young rookie named Jimmy. He seemed to enjoy every moment of his task.

"Sheriff's over there." Selena pointed across the space.

26

Wednesday afternoon in Mexico City

HEZEKIAH DIDN'T KNOW anyone in Mexico when he felt the Holy Spirit wooing him there. In viewing the world map, he had decided the city named after the country was just as good a place as any to begin his ministry. Unable to speak Spanish, he trusted God to make a way. So here he was, about to land on foreign soil.

Hezekiah was the 144,000[th] male Jew to volunteer online for the Messianic Jihad—his joke. Not about to kill himself or others on behalf of a pagan god who embraced terror, Hezekiah intended to do the exact opposite. Help people discover New Life and forgiveness in Christ Jesus. He wanted sin eradicated from souls.

After receiving Christ's seal on his forehead, an emblem of the Cross of Calvary, Hezekiah met with a counselor concerning his new ministry. He needed to put behind his old life so the new one could take hold. Willingly, Hezekiah embraced his calling.

Hezekiah had a fine past. He came from a great family and had always felt blessed. In 2020, he had graduated from Emory University in Atlanta, Georgia with a major in physics. While earning a Masters at Georgia Tech, he studied architecture on the side and discovered a knack for mechanical drawing. In 2025, he was hired on by a company that developed new flying machines.

Another joke, *ha!*

OSBURG was contracted by the U.S. government to build military aircraft. With an I.Q. pushing 180, Hezekiah soon became a superstar. But failing to share the ethics of many of his coworkers, to his chagrin, he rarely fit in social situations. Uninterested in wild parties where sex was exploited and drunkenness condoned, he had no interest in experimenting with mind-altering drugs.

No, Hezekiah dreamed of enjoying a future much like his parents had, hoping one day to marry a beautiful Jewish girl who embraced his same family values and wanted a dozen children.

Hezekiah's father, Alfred Saul Goldberg, was a devout Orthodox Jew born to French immigrants that migrated to America during the early twentieth century. Hezekiah's mother named him after the famous king in the Old Testament, the son of King Ahaz and grandson of King Uzziah. All three kings ruled over Judah during their lifetimes, a territory inherited by one of Jacob's twelve sons. If anyone possessed knowledge of Jewish history, Hezekiah-in-the-present qualified. He knew from reading the Bible that God had healed King Hezekiah of a boil certain to end his life.

When the king prayed to Jehovah God to heal him, he was granted an extra fifteen years of life. During his kingship, he restored the Temple in Jerusalem and reinstituted worship.

Soon after the Temple was completed, the Passover Feast and Feast of Unleavened Bread was celebrated by the people. King Hezekiah ordered all of the pagan shrines in the land torn down. He even destroyed Moses' bronze serpent, which had become an object of praise for the people. Only later in the king's life did he displease God. Pride eventually destroyed pure worship.

Hezekiah-in-the-present did not want to make the same mistakes as the King-of-Old. But he did identify with the king in one way. He'd come from a womb that was formerly barren.

Ingrid Goldberg never listened to the doctors who said she could not bear children, rather trusted in prayer to alter her circumstances. About the time she'd given up believing God would give her a son, she became pregnant. Joy filled the Goldberg home.

Rewarding Ingrid's faithfulness, Hezekiah-in-the-present was born after fifteen years of waiting. *Fifteen years.* Just like the king in the story. It was a story he often told when he had a listener.

Hezekiah had liked working for the aeronautic company that designed and built military planes, but was often accused of being too serious by his coworkers. To fit in, he'd told dumb jokes to make others laugh. Fitting in was worth acting stupidly.

After studying the New Testament, he'd begun to visualize how his choices in life could make a difference in helping others.

Hezekiah had no interest in amassing wealth. Fame meant nothing to him. Nor designing planes to fly faster or carry bigger bombs. When he'd searched the mysteries in the Book of Revelation and learned that 144,000 Jews would be sealed and commissioned to evangelize the world for Jesus, it struck a chord in his heart! He knew that he was called to serve a higher purpose.

When Hezekiah informed his parents of his decision to serve, they were beyond thrilled. Formerly devout Orthodox Jews, they'd converted to Christianity soon after millions of believers vanished from the earth in 2025. Faith put them on a new trajectory.

So, here Hezekiah was, stepping off a plane, his one-way ticket from Jerusalem to Mexico City paid for by a non-profit Jewish fund. Wearing special attire—not like the fancy suit he wore to corporate parties. Nor the casual slacks and short-sleeved shirt he worked in.

No, he was dressed in a white linen tunic similar to what Moses wore when he called down Holy Spirit fire at the Commissioning Service in the Valley of Jezreel. Just thinking of that, excited him.

He thought the few people he loosely called friends at work would mock him for quitting his lucrative job. They had not.

Rather, they stared tongue-tied in disbelief.

In a way, that was Hezekiah's best joke.

With his sandaled feet planted on solid Mexican soil, he felt hilariously giddy. He was finally on a mission to save souls.

"Excuse me," a teen tapped Hezekiah on the arm as he walked down Mexico City's dusty street, praying about where to go next.

"Are you one of *those* guys?" the lad asked.

"Yeah, I'm one of those regular guys." Hezekiah laughed.

It was the first time he felt *regular*, and accepted into a brotherhood. It was great. He was one of THOSE guys.

The lad no more than twelve ran alongside Hezekiah asking all kinds of questions, curious about why he was in Mexico.

Excited, Hezekiah realized that he understood every word the boy said in Spanish although he'd never formerly studied the language. He assumed the gift of interpretation was a portion of the anointing when Moses called down the power from Heaven.

"You speak good Spanish," the boy switched to English.

"Actually, I'm an American," Hezekiah admitted.

"How did you get to be one of *them*?"

He shrugged. "My mother always believed I was a gift from God, so I guess I am," he replied. "What's your name?"

"Carlos." The dark-eyed boy did a cartwheel then walked backwards while facing Hezekiah. "My mom runs a bed-and-breakfast," he said. "Do you have a place to stay?"

"You speak good English," Hezekiah complimented the lad. "And I'd love to meet your mom. If she has an extra room, I can pay her." It was great that God was sending someone to guide him in a strange city. "How far is it to your mom's house?"

The boy stopped and pointed at a sign. "At that corner, we turn right and go two blocks. Then we go left, and there it is."

"Okay, walk me there and I will become your newest renter."

Hezekiah learned that Carlos' mother was a widow who had inherited the large three-story historic home from her father.

They arrived at the destination and the door opened.

"Carlos, have you brought me another renter?"

Hezekiah understood her language perfectly, but he did not yet have the gift to speak it. In time, he would learn.

"*Sí*," he replied with the one word he knew for sure.

Carlos' kind mother said to Hezekiah in Spanish, "Welcome to my bed-and-breakfast, my name is Maria Rios."

"Mrs. Rios, I am Hezekiah." He shook her hand.

She smiled as Carlos interpreted Hezekiah's introduction.

"Mama says she saw you on television," Carlos reported. "She says you are one of them." He smiled widely.

"I heard." The evangelist smiled at Maria. "Tell your mother I am one of them but to call me Hezekiah." He laughed.

"*Si*, Hezekiah." Maria caught on. "I have a beautiful suite where you can stay for as long as you need to. And I don't want you to pay rent. It's our pleasure to serve you."

"But if I stay too long, I will pay, yes?"

Maria laughed as Carlos relayed the message.

"Ask your mother if she's a Christian, Carlos."

At hearing the interpretation of the question, Maria's enormous brown eyes bloomed with light.

"*Si*," she said, "I am born again."

"If I'm not allowed to pay rent, ask your mother what I can do in exchange for her kindness?" Hezekiah addressed Carlos.

Carlos relayed the message.

Maria's petite frame of five-feet-two trembled as she wrung her small hands. "I have another son who is five," she said. "He was born deaf and dumb. Will you pray for him to be healed?"

"I will certainly consult Jesus, and we'll see."

"He says he will, Mama," Carlos relayed the response.

Grabbing Hezekiah's hand, Maria exclaimed in Spanish, "Oh thank you! Prophet of God, we are so glad you have come!"

This was a new title Hezekiah greatly appreciated. Prophet of God had a certain ring about it. Maria instructed Carlos to carry Hezekiah's suitcase up the stairs to the third-floor suite.

"If you are ready to go up, follow my son."

"*Gracias, Senorita.*" Hezekiah bowed slightly, catching on to the language faster than he'd anticipated. *God is so, so good.*

"Carlos will help you with whatever you need, so you will be comfortable," Maria said. "Please, allow us to serve you."

Carlos led the way to the third-floor suite. It was a large room with an heirloom bed pushed against the back wall. Hezekiah glanced around at the furniture. The dresser was ample-sized as was the matching antique armoire. Plus, there was a sitting nook with a big window that overlooked the street. He was pleased that the hall bath had piped in running water, both hot and cold.

A very livable space, he thanked God.

"This is a great, Carlos. Did your mother design the suite?" Hezekiah's sandals sank into the thick multicolored woven carpet.

"No, my auntie did. She's an interior decorator."

"Well, be sure and thank Auntie for making my stay with you so comfortable. What time shall I come down for supper?"

"You should rest first. A siesta is customary in the middle of the afternoon," Carlos informed Hezekiah. "Mama will prepare a snack and bring it up to you soon." The lad beamed with joy. "Help yourself to the clean towels in the bathroom cabinet."

"Thank you, Carlos, I will be fine."

* * *

Downstairs in the large kitchen, Maria rejoiced at the coming of the Messianic evangelist. She'd seen the Commissioning Service on the large screen TV in the Commons, a formal living room that once had been a smoking parlor where her father had entertained his wealthy male guests, many of them vested in agricultural products. Wine and marijuana were popular export items in Mexico.

The products brought enormous prices, particularly in Europe and America. But, with smoking forbidden in Maria's house, the Commons was a place where guests could relax, visit and socialize, read a book from the library shelf, play a game, or enjoy a video.

The kitchen conveniently adjoined the Commons and had French doors that opened into a lush courtyard at the side of the house. Maria's sister had dressed out the brick patio with trellises of climbing green ivy thick enough to keep out strong sunlight.

Over the years, Maria used a portion of the monthly rent to purchase half-a-dozen wrought-iron, glass-topped tables. Scattered across the garden floor fashioned from red bricks, Maria had covered the tables with linen cloths set with an old-world, floral-pattern china. Maria joyfully treated her guests like royalty.

Partly because her ancestors had been ultra-wealthy.

Not so fortunate, after Maria's husband passed, she'd lived with her father in this house that had once belonged to her great-grandfather. The house had passed down through the generations and undergone many changes. After finally owning the property, Maria decided to establish a Bed & Breakfast business.

Presently, soft music infiltrated the patio. Siphoned through hidden speakers, the whimsical melodies gave the outdoor garden space an ambiance that guests enjoyed during family-like meals.

Here was where Maria read her Bible and prayed every morning. Today God had sent her a special gift. He'd heard Maria's cries during the night. God had sent His ambassador to her house.

Hezekiah would pray for Padre's healing.

27

Dover's

SARAH LED MARY ACROSS the warehouse and they entered a cranky elevator lift installed decades before. It clinked and jerked all the way up to the second level where Sarah claimed an office.

"It's not much, but it's out of harm's way." Sarah gestured for Mary to sit down. "How much do you know?"

"Drew said he'd messed up," Mary recalled their last phone conversation before she left Rome. "Is he in legal trouble?"

"Are you aware he's been seeing a professional counselor?"

"We talked about it." Mary had a catch in her throat.

Where is the Sheriff going with this?

"Dr. Susan Parrot is a licensed psychiatrist hired by the state to counsel troubled law-enforcement personnel." Sarah's lips twisted to one side as her brooding eyes drooped with dread.

"Okay, I didn't know that," Mary admitted.

"Well, it seems they've been dilly-dallying a bit." Sarah avoided the word affair for Mary's sake. It didn't work.

"My husband is involved with his counselor?" The idea stunned Mary. "There must be more to it, Sheriff Boswell."

Sarah adjusted the AC to cooler. "Gets too hot up here in the middle of the day." She returned to her chair behind the desk.

"Tell me, I can handle the truth," Mary said.

"Dr. Parrot has filed a formal complaint against Drew," Sarah said. "She claims he raped her during a counseling session."

Mary actually laughed. "That's ridiculous! Drew doesn't have to commit rape to get sex! Have you seen the way women look him? There's something missing in that woman's brain."

Sarah smiled. "I agree. And I'm glad you feel that way. Drew has another side to tell. I suppose you want to see him."

"Yes." Mary stood up. "Is he downstairs?"

"Actually, he's on a bus on his way to Nashville to be booked," Sarah reported. "Is that a problem?"

Mary sighed. "Yes. No, I'll need to make arrangements for Little David before I drive over. Where was he taken?"

"He'll be booked later today at the Nashville City Jail."

"Okay, thanks. I'll find my way there."

"Better if you put off your trip until tomorrow. "

"Why is that?" Mary asked.

"The legal process will probably take the rest of the day. Dozens of the accused felons for various crimes feed into the Nashville facility every day," Sarah reported. "They're bused in from West Tennessee PDs due to damaged jail facilities."

"The quake. . ." Mary nodded.

"You won't get inside to see Drew today," Sarah added.

"Thank you for seeing me." Mary abandoned her chair and walked over to the lift, turning around to ask another question.

"Has the news media got wind of Drew's arrest?"

"I haven't said anything, but people talk."

Mary nodded, offering no further comment.

"I'll go down with you and see you out," Sarah said.

After leaving Dover's, Mary stopped for a cup of coffee before going home. Grace was there watching David.

"Grace, can you stay all day with David tomorrow?"

"Thursday?" She checked her phone calendar.

"If you can't, I'll make other arrangements."

"No, I'm free," Grace said.

"Do you still have a key to the condo?"

"Officer Taylor never asked for it back."

"Keep it." Mary debated over whether to tell the nanny about Drew's legal problem. "Grace, you may hear rumors about my husband, please ignore them." She dreaded what lay ahead.

Grace's lips pushed out. "It was already on TV."

Mary groaned in her spirit. "Was it awful?"

"Are you askin' whose side I'm on?"

"Just so you know, Grace," Mary said, "Drew is not guilty of those bogus charges. And somehow we're going to prove it."

Grace nodded. "Do you need me to stay longer today?"

"No, but be back in the morning by eight o'clock."

"Sure, and I'm truly sorry trouble has knocked."

Spontaneously responding to the nanny's kindness, Mary hugged her. "Thank you, Grace, your support means a lot."

"Just so you know, I don't think he's guilty either."

After Grace went home, Mary played with David for an hour, hoping Drew would use his one call to talk to her.

His call came in at 5:10 p.m. "Mary?"

"Yes, Drew?"

"I'm so sorry."

"I know, we'll work through it," she said with a hitch in her voice. "Now tell me exactly what happened with your counselor."

With only a few minutes to use the jail's landline, Drew explained how Susan took advantage of him when he was at his lowest. He believed their marriage was over and was drinking again.

"Susan flirted at every opportunity and I took the bait."

Mary fought back tears. "I should have been here for you."

"It's not your fault, honey. When I kissed Susan at her office, I didn't expect her to strip off her clothes and jump me."

His words sparked anger in Mary for the first time. "But you did submit to an adulterous act. You are not entirely innocent."

"Yeah, you're right. I messed up."

"Have you hired a lawyer?" she asked.

"Will you talk to Greg Diamond and get a reference?"

"Sure." Mary glanced at the wall clock. "He's probably left the courthouse by now. I'll catch him at home."

"Okay, gotta go now. When can I see you?"

"Tomorrow, I'm driving up. Grace Riley will stay with David." She handed her son a toy to play with on the floor.

"Okay, I guess that's it for now."

"Drew, there's one more act of faith you need to do."

"Yeah . . .?"

"When this is over, remove your banking chip and come with me to Jerusalem to do God's work." It was the right thing to do.

Drew was surprised by Mary's request.

"You have to know God is using this hardship to get your attention, Drew. We're meant to be together, in ministry."

"Mary, I don't know what to say." While running from God's perfect will, he'd raced straight into the arms of temptation. Satan cleverly lures Christians into pathways of sin.

Mary heard the stress in Drew's voice. "Have faith that truth will prevail, Drew. And know that I love you. Meanwhile, we'll work through the logistics of the legal system together."

He sniffled then said goodbye.

Needing moral support, Mary bundled Little David in her arms. "Okay, buddy, let's go visit Uncle Cory and Aunt Alexi. Mommy needs some TLC from her best friends."

They always offered an encouraging word.

* * *

Cory made a pot of spaghetti and invited Mary and David to join them. "Did you talk to Drew?" he inquired as they sat at the dining room table with two highchairs sandwiched between them.

Miracle was joyfully squeezing a handful of noodles and stuffing them into her mouth as quickly as she could.

"Slow down, Pun'kin, or you'll get choked." Mama Alexi admonished her toddler. "Quit racing David to finish first."

Mary chuckled. "If I could get away with it, I'd be shoveling your spaghetti down my throat, too. The food's so good."

"When did you last eat?" Alexi asked Mary.

"I think yesterday. It's been weird since I got home."

"I can only imagine." Alexi's cameral eyes flashed in the chandelier lighting. "What was it—fourteen hours on two planes? Then you see Drew getting arrested. I wouldn't last two minutes."

Mary reached over and clasped Alexi's hand. "You are a dear friend, girl. I thought I rescued you that day on Virginia Beach. But ever since then, you have been rescuing me . . ." tears filled Mary's eyes. "If I had a daughter, I'd want her to be exactly like you."

Cory cleared his throat. "What about me? Don't I count?"

Both ladies laughed.

"Honey, not counting Jesus, you are my strength and shield." Alexi clasped Cory's hand. "I love that you love me so much."

David started banging his spoon on the table, prompting everyone to laugh. "You think he's still hungry?" Cory asked.

"Na, he's just bored with our mushy reminiscing," Mary teased. "Time to clean you up, little buddy, and get going."

"Leaving so soon?" Cory began clearing the table while Alexi cleaned up Miracle and removed her from the highchair.

"I'm going over to Greg Diamond's house to talk to him about Drew's problem," Mary said. "My husband needs a good lawyer."

"The D.A. knows a lot of competent people," Cory offered. "While you defend Drew, leave David with us for the night."

Mary's eyes alighted. "Are you sure it isn't an imposition?"

"Not in the least, we still have two baby beds set up in the nursery. Besides, Miracle loves David's company."

Mary made eye contact with Alexi. "Soon, Miracle will have a little brother of her own. You are lucky parents, blessed."

"Yes, we are." Cory lovingly looked at Alexi.

"Go on now," Alexi said to Mary. "Talk to Greg about Drew's situation. Cory and I will bathe the toddlers and put them to bed."

"I'll let Grace know you're bring David home in the morning."

"Around mid-morning is good for me," Cory said.

Grateful for their support, Mary used the restroom then took off to Greg Diamond's. She had not phoned ahead.

28

Thursday, July 22

MARY WOKE UP THURSDAY at 7:45 a.m. to the tune of Grace Riley's melodic voice. "Anyone up yet? I brought breakfast!"

Kicking off the bedcovers, Mary threw on a housecoat and called back, "Coming, Grace, be there in just a minute!"

After visiting the potty and splashing cold water on her face, Mary ventured into the kitchen. "You brought breakfast?" The odors of crisp fried bacon and sweet bread teased her nostrils.

"Yes, where is Little David?" Grace inquired as she laid out the food on the breakfast bar. "Will you make coffee?"

"Sure." Mary set the coffeemaker in process.

"How are you this morning?" Grace asked.

"A little rattled," Mary admitted.

"That's to be expected."

"Grace, I should have phoned you last night and told you to come around nine. Little David spent the night with the Lindsey's."

"Do you still need me to sit today?"

"Yes, Cory's bringing him home mid-morning," Mary replied.

"I see." Grace sat down at the bar, lacing her fingers together.

"I'm so sorry I didn't call you, Grace, but my mind is elsewhere. After speaking with the D.A. last night about Drew's situation, I came straight home and fell on my knees to pray."

The elderly nanny shrugged. "It's been hard, I know. And you don't need to worry about hurting my feelings, I'm pleased to help."

"Good, I'll probably be all day in Nashville." Mary heard the coffeemaker guzzle out its dark liquid. "One good thing came out of my visit with the D.A. last night," she told the nanny. "I have the name of a reputable Nashville attorney to represent Drew."

"Someone I may have heard of?" Grace queried.

"I doubt it. John Appleton is a friend of Greg Diamond's."

"The D.A. Well, you have a busy day ahead of you, girl." Grace fixed herself a cup of coffee. "While we have breakfast, you can talk to me. I'm an excellent listener if you need to vent."

Mary poured out her heart to Grace, how she'd come to know the Lord, even died and was resurrected after three days.

"My goodness, I had no idea."

"I fell in love with Drew but resisted marrying him for a long time because of my commitment to Christian evangelism," Mary explained. "After he was wounded by a serial killer, we decided to take the plunge. By that time, I was caring for two infants."

Grace opened her mouth then shut it.

"I know it's a lot to swallow. But it's all true," Mary said.

* * *

On the way to Nashville, Mary listened to a gospel tape she received as a gift during her missionary tour in America. Faithful Christians helped her along the way, or she would have starved.

Not having talked to Daniel Tempest in months, Mary decided to call him at his Texas ranch. The cyber connection rang several times but no message center clicked on. "That's odd."

After ending that call, she phoned Rabbi Michael Thoene in Jerusalem. Gratefully, he answered. "Michael, it's Mary"

"I assume you made it home safely."

"I should've called you sooner but it's been crazy around here," Mary hurriedly uttered. "Little David and I are doing well, but my Andrew is in serious legal trouble." She jerked a haggard breath.

"What happened?" the rabbi asked.

Michael's voice was threaded with concern. Gulping back bitter tears, she answered, "Drew cheated on me with his counselor!" she exploded. "Worse, she's accused him of rape."

"What?" Michael couldn't believe his ears.

"Oh, I know Drew didn't rape that awful woman," Mary spewed. "He's a handsome man and would never have to seduce anyone for sex." She laid out her feelings pure and simple.

Michael chuckled. "Should you be telling me this?"

"Who else can I talk to that I trust?"

"Okay, settle down, and let's think this through together," he said. "I know you love Andrew. Are you sure of his devotion?"

"Yes, he was upset because I've been away from home too often since we married," Mary said. "I'm partly the blame."

"But you didn't choose to commit adultery."

"No, I didn't." Mary fought hysteria. "At a weak moment, Drew was seduced by his female counselor. But he didn't have to take the bait. I'm so angry with him I could—"

"Strangle the woman," Michael interrupted. "Look, Mary. Perhaps something good will result from Drew's crisis." He offered a positive spin on the dire situation. "You've told me before that he has resisted removing his Mark. Maybe this is a wakeup call."

Unable to help it, Mary began uncontrollably weeping.

"Now, dear, I didn't mean to upset you more."

"Oh, Michael," Mary sputtered between words, "I do wish I were as strong as you are, but I'm crushed over his behavior."

"You need to think rationally, Mary. Hang in with Drew. Wait and see how God works in the awful situation. Have faith."

"I believed so much in us, but evidently he didn't."

"I'm so sorry."

"You said, 'Let's think through this together'," Mary recalled. "What did you mean?" She was desperate for a resolution.

"How much has Andrew told you?" Michael inquired.

"Most of what I know is second hand. Drew called me from the Nashville City Jail last night and we spoke briefly," she said.

"Communicating is good," he said.

"I'm actually on my way to visit him today."

"Good. When my wife and I disagreed on a subject, I soon learned talk relieved some pressure. God rest her soul."

"It isn't fair to burden you with my problem, Michael," Mary said. "But I know you are wise in the Lord, a prayer warrior."

She fell silent. "I want to do the right thing for my boys."

"A word of warning . . ." Michael cautioned.

"What?" Mary waited anxiously.

"Don't let your children give you an excuse to end the relationship. If you decide to leave Andrew, do it for yourself."

Mary didn't know how to respond to his suggestion.

"The children will be fine either way," he added.

"I hope so." She passed the Nashville city limit's sign.

"Do me a favor, call after you've talked to Andrew."

"Okay, I'll know by then more about what we're up against in this frivolous lawsuit," Mary concurred. "Thank you for listening."

"Always, I'm here for you, anytime."

Mary ended the call and followed the GPS directions to the jail.

After parking the SUV in the guest lot, she proceeded into the five-story brick building. As expected, she was cavity-searched, her phone and vehicle keys taken and stowed to be picked up later.

Drew was in a visitation booth waiting for her.

"Hi." She blew a kiss through the glass. "How are you?"

"How do I look?" Drew had a two-day shade of facial hair and his orange suit was rumpled like he'd slept in it.

"I guess the real perps don't like cops."

"You got that right!" He actually winked a grin. "I'm actually isolated in a cell, away from the others. How is Little David?"

She could almost feel Drew as he pressed his hand against the glass divider. "David is fine." She paused then said, "I want you to start from the beginning, Drew—when you first met Susan."

He nodded, tears threatening to flow.

"Don't leave anything out," Mary clarified. "I need to know it *all* if I'm to help you." He nodded and began his story.

Drew was referred to Dr. Susan Parrot for counseling by the State Police Department. Too traumatized to concentrate on work after being shot twice by Caroline Sullivan last November, and left with a lame leg from a stroke, he'd realized he needed help to emotionally cope with his disability and failing marriage.

"Susan is the state-approved counselor," Mary stated.

"Yes, so I met with her, in her office, twice in early March," Drew revealed. "She was empathetic, helpful, but after I went back to work, I didn't think I needed to continue counseling with her."

"But you decided to see her again?"

"Yeah, when you were away so much, I was stressed out."

"When you first met Susan, did you have any reservations about her sincerity to help you?" Mary inquired.

"No, she was professional and I liked her—easy on the eyes, too." He actually blushed. "Sorry, I misspoke."

"You were attracted to her from the beginning?"

"No, not really—let's just say I appreciate a pretty woman."

"Okay, I can live with that."

"When our family was together, I was content. I had my job back and thought life was going pretty well. I was wrong."

"You still had underlying issues. With us, I mean."

"Yes." Drew intensely gazed at Mary. "We hadn't been home two days from Switzerland when you suddenly took off to California. You didn't even say goodbye. I was furious."

"I'm sorry, Drew. I needed to track down the Two Witnesses and find out what was going on with the sinkholes and quakes."

"You could've told me, Mary."

"I know," she said, "but when the Spirit directs, I can only focus on my mission. I thought you understood that about me."

"Is this your way of reminding me of our marriage vows?"

"No, you took my comment the wrong way."

"Okay, let's start over." He took in a huge breath. "That first night home after Switzerland—we were so close. Surely, you remember how it was? How wonderful we felt?"

Mary's eyes glazed over. They had shared intimate moments.

"Look, baby . . . we could go on all day talking and confessing our shortcomings, but I need you to do something on my behalf."

Mary looked deeply into Drew's droopy brown eyes.

"There's this guy in Seattle, Washington." He told her about Benjamin Sawyer, relaying Susan's slant on their brief romance.

"How did you find out about Jonathan Belk?"

"His mother and mine were best friends for years. After Mom died, Cynthia Belk continued to send me Christmas cards every year. She wrote that her son Jon worked as a cop for the Seattle Police Department. I got his number from her and called him."

"You asked Jon to find Ben for you."

"Yes, Mary. He's my only lead," Drew said. "Susan claims she broke up with Ben and ran away because he was stalking her."

What a mess! Mary wanted to understand the ensuing tangled triangle between lovers. "Did she seduce him, too?"

"That's what I need to find out."

"If Susan seduced you, how did it happen?" Mary asked.

"She showed up at my condo one night after work and asked for my help. We talked about her legal situation with her former boyfriend, had a glass of wine, and ate Take-Out Chinese."

"You were concerned about her safety." Mary nodded.

"She thought someone was watching her apartment," Drew explained. "She was scared so I offered to follow her home in my truck and make sure she got into her apartment safely."

"That's because you are a good guy and she took advantage of that," Mary concluded. "You were set up, Drew."

"Yeah, unfortunately." He shrugged. "Nothing happened between us that night. It was just a friend doing a friend a favor."

"But afterwards, something changed."

"Yes, Susan began asking more intimate questions about my relationship with you." He gazed at his wife. "Sex, in particular."

Mary chuckled. "What did you tell the counselor?"

"That we never had a problem with that."

Mary's lips trembled. "We are good together."

"Later, after we had sex in her office, she invited me to her apartment for supper. She told me why she broke up with Ben."

"I bet that was enlightening."

"Susan said Ben insisted on a sexual relationship and she refused because she was a Christian. I believed her."

Humph. "But not a very loyal one," Mary concluded.

"Susan's vulnerability was appealing," he admitted.

"I can only imagine," Mary muttered.

"After we talked on the phone—that Thursday you told me you weren't coming home following the commissioning service for the 144,000 evangelists, I was ready to annul our marriage."

"I meant to come home," Mary said.

"But you didn't," Drew pointed out. "You said you had to fly to Rome first to see about Andre. I was devastated."

"I knew you were upset, but I never expected—"

"That I would be unfaithful to you," he finished her statement.

Mary glared at Drew; no words to express her disappointment.

"You always put me second, Mary. I was so depressed I got drunk. Depression set in like the plague and wouldn't let go."

"Alcohol never solves any problem," she said.

"I'm not like you." Drew rolled his tight shoulders. "The next day, on Friday, I went to see Susan for counseling. I thought our marriage was over. I needed a human touch. And she gave it."

"And apparently Susan was more than willing."

"I kissed her first then we had sex in her office."

"Do you care about her?" Mary asked.

"No, it was just . . . no, I don't love her."

"Okay, I get the picture." Mary frowned. "Your sexual acts were mutually satisfying and there was no forced anything."

Drew nodded his head. "But it's my word against hers."

"So now, you want me to locate this Benjamin Sawyer and find out what happened between him and Susan," Mary concluded.

He nodded again, the lines in his face more pronounced.

"Okay, I need to talk to Jon Belk in Seattle and see if he knows how to contact Ben," Mary concluded. "Is that all?"

Drew smiled. "It's a lot and I'm grateful you still care."

Mary's blue eyes flashed. "Of course, I care, Andrew! You are my husband. Forgiveness is part of our marital vows, or did you forget?" She stood to leave. "How can I contact you?"

"What about my defense lawyer?"

"Oh, I forgot to tell you Greg Diamond has recommended Attorney John Appleton. He works here in Nashville."

"Will you hire him to defend me?" Drew queried.

"How will I pay him?"

"Tell Abigail at the bank you need to transfer payment to Attorney Appleton if he agrees to represent me," Drew said.

Mary nodded, taking some notes.

"Ask Appleton to come over to the jail tomorrow morning and talk to me about my defense during my arraignment."

"What do you mean?" Mary made eye contact.

"I need to know if he thinks the evidence against me will warrant a court trial," he explained. "I have Susan's comments recorded, but what was said might not be enough."

"Okay, what else?"

"After my arraignment, if I don't make bail, I'll be transferred to the county jail until I'm tried before a jury of my peers."

"What if Appleton isn't available tomorrow?"

"He's my best chance," Drew uttered, "so you'd better hustle over to his office now and talk to him about representing me."

"Okay, I can do that." Mary placed her notes in her purse.

Their eyes locked for a moment.

"I should go now," she said.

His sad gaze said how sorry he was.

29

Nashville, Tennessee

ATTORNEY JOHN APPLETON was in his late fifties. A squatty man, he was bald as an eagle. But the black flint in his American Indian eyes indicated he was a fierce defender of his tribe.

"Thanks for seeing me on such short notice," Mary said as she took a seat on the sofa facing Appleton's wide Western Cedar desk.

"No problem, Mrs. Taylor. When Greg phoned and asked for a favor, how could I refuse?" His crooked smile was a charmer.

"You've known each other for a long time." Mary nodded.

"We met at the University of Tennessee in Knoxville." He smiled at the memory. "Ol' Greg used to knock a mean golf ball."

"You were on a team together?" The idea surprised Mary. Appleton seemed more the academic type.

"Oh, no, he was on the team and I carried his clubs."

Mary chuckled. "But the bond happened anyway."

"The bond stuck like glue. What can I do for you, Mrs. Taylor?" It was attorney time to get down to business.

"First of all, call me Mary," she said, then, "How much did Greg tell you about Drew's sticky situation?"

"Only that he needed a smart defense attorney," Appleton replied. "He said you'd fill me in on the good stuff."

Appleton had a sense of humor that prompted Mary to relax a bit. "Okay, I'll tell you what I know." She began her spiel.

Humph. John listened attentively then pushed away from his desk. "I need caffeine. Can I get you a cup of Joe, or tea?"

"Decaf tea," she replied. "Cold, please, with sugar."

Appleton's frumpy secretary Alicia brought in the beverages and handed them out. Dropping two message slips on her boss's desk she scooted out of the office and closed the door.

"Here's what I think," Appleton began to outline his defense.

Mary eagerly listened and thought the plan sounded good.

"Just so I have it straight," Mary said, "you are going to personally phone Jonathan Belk and see if he knows Benjamin Sawyer's whereabouts," she clarified his role in the investigation.

"Yes, but I think we should do it right now, in my office. I want to tape Jon's response—with his permission, of course."

Mary retrieved the slip of paper with Jon's cell number and handed it over to the attorney. "What if he hasn't found Ben?"

"We'll cross that street when the light's not red."

Mary smiled as Appleton dialed the number and received Jon's message center. He held up a hand for her to be quiet.

"Jonathan, this is Attorney John Appleton in Nashville, Tennessee. I need to speak with you as soon as possible."

Appleton left his office number and stared at Mary.

"What are we going to do now?" she queried. "Should I wait here until he calls back?" This was all so new for her.

"Not necessary," he said. "If you have somewhere else you need to be, go on." Appleton's plump lips twisted. "But, do me a favor and don't leave town yet. I might need you to come back."

"I really need to go home," she said. "My toddler is with a sitter for the day and I'm not sure she can stay overnight."

"If you can work it out," he said, "I want you at the Nashville courthouse tomorrow when Andrew is arraigned. Do you have a friend in the city willing to put you up for the night?"

"Yes." She thought of Tom Rave.

"Okay, I have your cell number." The attorney stood to see Mary out. "As soon as I know something, I'll phone you."

"How much do we owe you?" Mary inquired.

"You're not on the clock yet." He smiled.

"Just so you know, Mr. Appleton, we can pay you."

"It's on my nickel today." He teased. "We'll discuss my fee later after I assess my involvement with Andrew's case."

"Thank you." Mary left the office complex.

She popped the doors to Drew's vehicle and slid into the driver's seat. After turning down the AC, she focused on her recent conversation with Appleton. He was really nice, just like Greg had indicated. He would be very helpful to Drew.

Dialing Tom Rave's number, she prayed he was home.

"Tom, this is Mary Taylor," she hurriedly said.

"Hi, Mary," he returned. "How are you today?"

"I'm not exactly fine, and I'm in Nashville."

"Okay . . ." his voice lingered for more.

"Can I come over so we can talk?"

"Sure, what's this about?" he asked.

"Drew is in trouble." Mary started the engine. "I'll tell you more when I get there." She ended the call and drove out of the lot. Twenty-five minutes later, she pulled into Tom's driveway.

Déjà vu set in as she recalled her early morning visit with Tom while escaping the devastating earthquake about to take down buildings in Fernwood. Cory and Alexi, Miracle and Little David, were with her when Tom came running out of the house to greet them. She had no idea where Drew was at the time.

Later, she'd learned her husband was in Canada chasing down a lead on Priscilla Dunn, his prime suspect for stealing Sarah's murder book on Caroline Sullivan and removing two evidence boxes from the storage room in the basement of the station.

Killing the engine, Mary stepped out of the vehicle and locked the doors. Seconds later, she stood on the porch landing.

The door came open and Tom was there.

Releasing a flood of tears, Mary fell into his arms. "Oh, Tom, I don't know what we're going to do. Drew could go to prison."

"Honey," he looked both ways down the street, "things are never as bad as they seem. You and I know that God is always on our side. Whatever is going on, you will find a way to cope."

Mary looked up into Tom's strong face, his misty blue eyes as they swallowed her like hungry prey. For the first time in a very long time, she felt vulnerable to giving in to sexual comfort.

Hadn't Drew taken his fill while she was doing God's work?

She gently pulled herself off Tom. "I'm sorry."

"It's okay, I understand. You're upset."

Mary nodded and dried her eyes on her shirttail.

"Come inside. Are you hungry? I just made tuna fish salad and sweet tea." He led Mary by the hand deeper into his house. "You're shivering and it must be ninety-five outdoors."

Mary collapsed in a chair and buried her face in her hands.

"Tell me what's happened."

Mary glanced up. "Drew cheated on me, Tom."

"I know, he confessed to me right afterwards."

Mary sobered. "He did? Really? What did he tell you?"

"That's he'd messed up big time. That he's sorry and still loves you. That he tried to break up with Susan, but she resisted."

"Drew said she threatened to ruin his law-enforcement career if he ended their affair," Mary revealed. "He feels trapped."

"Hold that thought and let's eat a bite of lunch."

They went into the kitchen. Mary sat down at the small square table and Tom served her a tuna sandwich with salty chips. After placing two tumblers of iced tea on the table, he joined her.

"Let's pray," Tom said.

Mary was comforted by his words.

"Enjoy," Tom said as he looked up.

Mary didn't realize how famished she was until she took her first bite of real food. Like a dog after a juicy steak bone, she devoured the sandwich and drank half the glass of sweet tea.

"Delicious. Thank you," she said. "I feel some better."

"You're too thin, are you skipping meals?"

"Not intentionally." Overseas if was hard to find time to eat with all that went on. "I had an early breakfast." She dabbed her moist lips with a napkin. "Little David is home with Grace Riley."

"The nanny Drew hired." Tom nodded. "You were in California chasing down the Two Witnesses," he recalled.

"Elijah sent an angel and found me," Mary said. "Yeah, he warned an impending disaster was about to occur in West Tennessee. I came home to tell Drew, but he wasn't there."

"He was chasing a bad guy in Canada," Tom said.

Mary frowned. "Like Alexi says, Drew and I are like passing ships that never dock in the same place."

"Miscommunication is common in marriages," Tom said.

"I can always count on you for clarity."

Tom laughed hard. "Girl, you didn't think so when we first met in New Mexico." He shook his head. "I really miss Ghost."

"The four of you were a scary bunch," Mary recalled. "Cat, Alexi, and I must have been crazy to chase after you guys."

"So much has happened since . . ." Tom mused. "How is Baby Miracle these days? Growing like a weed, I presume."

"Miracle is a healthy, beautiful toddler."

"That's good." They took time to finish their meal.

Tom ripped open a package of oatmeal cookies.

"Care for some dessert?"

Mary snagged a cookie and broke it in half.

"Cory and Alexi seem like a happy couple," Tom noted.

"Did you know Alexi's pregnant again?" Mary licked cookie icing off her fingers. "Cory is beside himself with joy."

"Life goes on until it stops, doesn't it?"

"Never a truer word, my friend." Mary pushed away from the table. "People live like the world as we know it will last forever— that time will never run out. We are all such dumb bunnies."

"Talking about time running out, have you seen what's happening in the world with the 144,000 Messianic Jews?"

"Actually, I haven't viewed the tube in a couple of days."

"Thousands of non-believing Jews and old-school Muslims are converting to Christianity!" Tom exclaimed. "It's a very exciting time in history!" He shook his head. "But there's a flipside, too."

"What do you mean?" Mary's forehead furrowed.

"Rumors are going around that the radical Muslims are planning an attack against Jerusalem," Tom said. "From reading Revelations, we know a battle is coming around mid-Trib."

"Ezekiel 39 talks about that," Mary added. "Gog, or Russia, will support Iran and other radicals in the attack."

"Yeah, but when God rains down hailstones on the jihadists army, they will think twice about assaulting the holy city."

Mary's gaze darkened. "So much is wrong in the world."

"I'm sorry, Mary. You came to talk about Andrew."

"I just can't think about all that horror and death today." She grimaced. "I need a day-at-a-time to emotionally survive."

"We all do." He reached across the table and grasped Mary's hand. "Be patient and don't lose heart, this too shall pass."

Mary stood up and said, "I need to use your restroom."

Tom pointed. "Through that door and down the hall on the right. . ." he began clearing the dishes off the table.

After freshening up, Mary found Tom in his office on a laptop computer. "I'm printing out the latest reports on the jihadists' movement, plus the Messianic Jerusalem Report Card."

Tom always put a twist on words.

"Thank you, I'll take the report with me and read it later."

He said, "Tell me more about your trip to Israel."

Mary questioned if she should share her concern about Andre's psychic behavior. Then decided the time was not right.

30

MARY HEARD FROM ATTORNEY John Appleton at 2:56 p.m. He was at the courthouse with Drew, waiting for the bailiff to call their case number. "How soon can you get here?" he queried.

"I'm twenty minutes away," Mary replied. "Drew was scheduled to appear before the judge tomorrow, what changed?"

"I pushed for an earlier time and got it," Appleton said.

"I'll need the address." Mary opened her phone.

"No, it's easy. Exit I-40 on Broadway and turn toward town. When you see the courthouse looming on a hill, park and enter through the main entrance. Take the escalator to the second level."

"Okay." Mary made mental notes.

"When you get to the second level, you will see a bank of elevators in front of you. Andrew and I are in City Courtroom # 5 on the fourth floor. Hurry, okay?" He abruptly ended the call.

"Was that Drew's attorney?" Tom asked.

"Yes." Mary thanked him for lunch and told him she probably wasn't staying overnight in Nashville.

"Please let me know how the proceedings go."

A few minutes later, they stood on the porch landing.

"Thanks for being such a good friend, Tom."

"Always my pleasure." He waved as she drove away.

* * *

The historic Metro Courthouse of Davidson County housed the city government, the mayor's office, and the Metro Council's chambers, including city and county courts. In essence, the facility was the "nerve center" of the justice system in Nashville.

Mary parked in the underground garage complex directly underneath the Public Square Plaza that featured a green lawn with park benches, flowing fountains, and lush flower beds. Following Attorney Appleton's directions, she went inside and boarded the escalator up to the second level. From there an elevator carried her up to the fourth floor where she located the designated courtroom.

Offering a quick prayer, she went inside and glanced around.

The bailiff stood by the lectern speaking to a frowning judge, apparently distraught over some legal matter. A glance around the courtroom told Mary many concerned relatives were anxiously waiting and watching the proceedings. It was a zoo unfolding.

John Appleton waved to Mary, motioning for her to come over. He stood on the opposite side of the courtroom with Drew.

Pushing through the crowded aisles toward Appleton, Mary's gaze was drawn to her wayward husband. He looked torn, like he'd lost something of great value. Freedom, for sure.

No, something more. She waved at them.

Maybe we both lost love and it took this to realize it.

"Thanks for coming." Drew gave Mary a loose hug.

"Where else would I be?" She peered around Drew to speak to Attorney Appleton. "Did you talk to Jon Belk?"

He shook his head. "Never called back."

"What'll happen to Drew without Jon's supporting testimony regarding Susan's sexual exploits of her male patients?" It was difficult to talk over the courtroom's noisy din of crying babies, ensuing quarrels, and general clutter and scraping of moving chairs.

"We don't know for sure if his testimony will help," Appleton said. "Meanwhile, I'll petition for a reduced bail, but since Andrew has a Fernwood city address, it won't fly. He'll likely go to County."

"Jail, you mean?" Mary trembled.

"Yes," Appleton replied. "I'll make sure he's safe."

"Can you really do that?" Mary glanced around the large courtroom. "Is *she* here with her attorney?"

John nodded toward the front of the room.

Mary turned around. There stood a beautiful young woman with long blond hair wearing a tailored suit and high heels. Susan Parrot was calmly talking to her attorney, her smile engaging.

"I know . . ." Drew uttered as if apologizing. "She's gorgeous." His eyes drooped. "Maybe she'll drop the charges."

Mary frowned. "Not likely." *A woman scorned . . .*

The conversation between the huge black guy's attorney and the judge grew more intense. Neither seemed willing to compromise. "That judge is tough," Mary commented.

"And fair, so I've heard," Appleton interjected.

"Susan's smart and will work him," Drew speculated. "She utilizes her sexuality like a lethal weapon." He grounded his eyes.

"And she's probably believable," Appleton added.

Mary saw nothing good coming from the court proceedings, and no way to help Drew. From here, it could only go downhill.

"We're number nine on the docket." John glanced up front. "That's Number Seven, giving Judge Bair Keller the dickens."

"Will Drew be allowed to testify on his behalf?" Mary asked.

"Not today," Appleton replied. "The bailiff will read the charge and I'll rebuke them, then request minimum bail for Drew— which likely will be denied. The judge will then set a court date and Drew will be hauled off in cuffs to the county jail. Sorry."

"Not as sorry as I am," Drew mouthed.

"For how many weeks?" Mary asked.

"Months, you mean," Appleton clarified.

"Not if I can help it!" she barked. "Don't worry, Drew, I'll track down Benjamin Sawyer and find out what went on between him and Susan if it kills me." It was a promise she'd keep.

"Meanwhile," Appleton said, "Jon Belk has both my office and private cell number, so maybe he'll call before the day is out."

And if he doesn't? Mary's heart leaped with growing dread.

"Looks like we're moving forward," Appleton noted.

Court was called to order and the court secretary took a seat at a table beside the lectern. "Next case," the bailiff called out.

Number Eight took a plea bargain and the woman was hauled out of the courtroom in cuffs. Drew's case came next and went as Appleton predicted. Bail was denied so Drew left in handcuffs. Mary waited until he was out of sight before speaking to Appleton.

"If you don't need me, I'm going home."

31

Friday, July 23

Mexico City

HEZEKIAH WAS IN HIS bedroom early Friday at the B & B praying for the salvation of souls in Mexico City. He'd been there hours when he noticed a child standing in the doorway.

"Hi." He acknowledged the boy's presence.

The boy stared into space, like he could see through Hezekiah.

"Is there something I can do for you, son?"

The dark-haired lad stood like a statue, offering no response.

"What's your name?" Hezekiah asked the lad.

Still, the boy did not respond. Hezekiah noticed his chocolate eyes were void of recognition, like he hadn't heard a word spoken to him. Suddenly, the boy's identity dawned on Hezekiah.

"You're Padre, Maria's!" he exclaimed, motioning for the boy to come closer. But Padre made no move.

"Don't be frightened, son," Hezekiah said, more to himself.

Padre took two steps into the room and stopped. Sucking on his right thumb, he tilted his head and sighed.

"I know . . ." Hezekiah empathized with the boy. "You can't hear what I'm saying and it must be terribly frustrating not able to speak." He approached the lad and touched his shoulder.

"Don't be afraid." He knelt in front of Padre. Their faces were so close Hezekiah could feel the lad's hot breath.

Padre examined Hezekiah's beard with his hands, continuing down his thick neck and touching the flowing sleeves of his tunic.

"You like my duds?" Hezekiah removed the red sash and placed it in the boy's hand. "Hold this while I pray for you."

Hezekiah had never prayed for anyone to be healed, though he had complete faith that God could if he wanted to.

With his hands on the Padre's shoulders, Hezekiah began uttering words that didn't make sense to him, the language of the Holy Spirit, he presumed. The prayer went on for fifteen or more minutes, and Padre did not move. It was as if the lad understood what was taking place between him and his Creator. So, Hezekiah kept on praying in the strange tongue that only God understood.

Suddenly, the boy let out a blood-curdling scream.

Hezekiah popped Juan's ears with his hands. "In the name of Jesus, hear!" Then he touched his lips. "In the name of Jesus, speak with understanding. Blessed be the name of the Lord!"

Hezekiah didn't have an opportunity to question Padre about what he was experiencing since he took off running. His footfalls struck the stairs in a maddening pace as he raced down three flights of stairs. By the time Hezekiah reached the bottom of the staircase, Maria Rios was standing there, her charcoal eyes wide with mystery.

"Padre called me Mama for the first time," she told Hezekiah.

He nodded, feeling warmth saturating his body.

"Other than that, he's speaking a language I've never heard before," Maria said. "Do you know what's happening to him?"

While Hezekiah held Maria's hands tightly, Padre's big brother came into the foyer. "What's happened?" Carlos asked.

"Good things," Hezekiah replied. "Come closer, Carlos, and interpret all that I am about to tell your mother."

"Maria, Padre is speaking the language of the Holy Spirit," Hezekiah reported. She heard the interpretation and smiled.

"Do not be afraid or interrupt Padre while God is whispering in his ear. In time, as he hears you talk, he will speak Spanish."

Carlos told his mother what Hezekiah had said. In response, she fell to her knees and kissed Hezekiah's sandaled feet.

He pulled Maria to her feet. "Carlos, tell your mother not to perform an act of worship on me. Ask her to give all of her praise to the One True God who heals her son! Blessed is Jesus!"

After hearing the interpretation, Maria hugged Hezekiah around his torso. A foot taller than her, it was as far up as she could reach. The gesture pleased Hezekiah and reminded him that he had a wonderful family and how much he missed his own mother. Later today, he would call home and report the good news and thank them for all their prayers flowing across the miles over his ministry.

"Oh, thank you, Great Prophet of God!" Maria exclaimed in a rapid Spanish tongue. "Whatever you need from us, *Rigalo de Dios*, whatever you want, all that we have is yours, only ask."

Rigalo de Dios meant "gift from God." Hezekiah was honored.

"Do you attend a church?" he asked Maria.

Carolos quickly relayed the question in Spanish.

"I'm Catholic," she replied.

"I heard," Hezekiah said. "Maria, take Padre to church with you on Sunday and tell your friends about his healing. If he can speak by then, let him thank God by giving his testimony."

Maria listened to Carlos and nodded.

"I will do that." She grinned.

"My ministry has just begun in this city. People will hear of Padre's healing and seek me. Many sick will receive God's healing," he told Maria. "But those who oppose the Gospel of Jesus Christ, those who reject salvation, great affliction will fall upon them."

"What do you mean, Hezekiah?" Carlos asked.

"I will demonstrate God's powers, just like Moses did when he instructed the Egyptian Pharaoh to release God's people from their bondage of slavery. I can command clouds to withhold rain, or call forth storms with great hailstones to fall upon the city. I can pronounce skin boils to form on sinners so that they suffer greatly. If I summon locusts, they will fly in swarms from afar and invade every pantry in the city. I can—" As Hezekiah spoke, Carlos translated the message to his mother until she could take no more.

"Stop, please!!" Maria held up a hand. "I don't want to hear about more destruction! Haven't the earthquakes and floods been enough? What about the hundreds of thousands who have died when sinkholes opened up beneath their feet? Isn't God good?"

Hezekiah smiled at Maria's passion. "God is great! God is good!" He whispered in her ear, "That's why He's doing it."

"Mama, Mama," Juan uttered, clinging to her.

"Now, dear, tend to your sheep while I attend to God's," Hezekiah said as he walked out the front door into the light.

* * *

Fernwood

Little David was up early Friday and crying out for Mary from his baby bed. "What is it, little guy?" She gathered him in her arms.

He tugged at one ear and whimpered.

"You have a bad ol' earache?" She cuddled him to her breast and headed off to the hall bath. "Let's get a few drops of liquid Tylenol down your tummy so you'll feel better."

Forty-five minutes later, when David was still bawling, Mary gave up and called his pediatrician to set an appointment.

David barely ate his cereal and his forehead felt hot. "I'm afraid you've developed a nasty infection," she told him.

He only made a sad face and whimpered.

"Hang in there, buddy, you'll be better after you see Dr. Majors this afternoon." She handed him a Sippy cup of apple juice.

The toddler drank like he was thirsty.

Fifteen minutes later, he calmed a bit. The Tylenol was doing its job so Mary set him in his playpen and dug out Jonathan Belk's phone number, praying he would answer his phone this time.

But again, his voice mail clicked on.

"It's Mary Taylor again!" she exclaimed. "I've been trying to reach you for the past two days. Don't you check your messages?"

She heard a distinct click then a grumpy male voice cut into the message and piped, "I'm answering now, whaddaya want?"

Some respect, she thought. "Is this Jonathan Belk?"

"Speaking," he uttered.

"You don't know me, Jonathan, but it's urgent that I locate Officer Benjamin Sawyer," she hurriedly spit out her cry for help.

Mary heard the cop yawn. Considering his foul mood, she didn't have long to get her point across. "Look, Jon, I apologize for waking you, but I must speak with Officer Benjamin Sawyer. My husband Drew talked to you a few days go. Remember?"

She prayed Jon wouldn't hang up on her.

"Who did you say you were?" Jon yawned again.

"Mary Taylor. I really need your help, Jon."

"Well," he yawned again, "Actually, I did ask around and learned that Sawyer lost his job and moved out of state."

"Okay . . ." Mary needed more information.

"Chicago, Illinois, I was told by a friend of a friend."

"Do you know if he's working for a police department?"

"Oh, no, it's rumored he went to court over some abuse charge and served six months in county," Jon reported.

"Really?" Mary's interest piqued.

"That's all I know, lady."

Mary thanked Jonathan for his efforts then ended the call. The next person she phoned was Drew's defense attorney.

"Mr. Appleton, thank you for taking my call." Mary hurriedly relayed the message she'd been given by Jonathan Belk.

"So, all we know is the plaintiff's former boyfriend lost his job with the Seattle Police Department for an abuse charge and served jail time." John made some notations in Andrew's folder.

"Also, a friend of a friend said Ben moved to Chicago, Illinois," Mary repeated Jonathan's information. "Does this help Drew?"

"Maybe, I can work with that info."

"How?" Mary wanted specifics.

"I'll call to the Office of the Washington State Prison System and petition information regarding the charges filed against Police Officer Benjamin Sawyer," Appleton replied.

"Will they give that to you?"

"Maybe we'll get lucky with that and obtain a current address."

"Without Benjamin's testimony to illustrate Susan's past history of patient abuse, Drew won't have a leg to stand on," Mary fussed. "It's his word against a licensed psychiatrist."

"Okay, let me work on it," Appleton said.

"I'll have my cell phone on all day, so call me if you learn anything more," Mary said. "How much do we owe you so far?"

"Nothing yet, I'll let you know," he said.

Mary ended the call and checked on Little David. He was fast asleep. After fixing herself a cup of strong coffee, she sat down to rest, contemplating the reason why Appleton ignored her billing. She suspected Greg Diamond had called in a favor and Drew's case was *pro bono*. Like Greg said, John Appleton's a good guy.

Mary spent the remainder of the morning writing a Bible Study to post on her internet blog. The subject was *Persecution*.

And she had plenty to say on the topic before it was time for David's appointment with the pediatrician later today.

32

Sunday, July 25

The Vatican

NEWS TRAVELS FAST WHEN it involves miraculous events. The healing of a Catholic priest during the Conclave spread like wildfire throughout the world. Since Andre was scheduled to speak from the Sistine Chapel's balcony at ten a.m., a number of indigent folks—some crippled or with advanced illnesses—waited patiently in St. Peter's Square to hear from Pope Benedict XXI.

What did they hope for? Lazarus pondered. That a two-year-old boy would raise his hands and pronounce a blanket healing upon them? He had used his gift more often to destroy rather than heal. He'd once stopped an elderly pope's heart at his brother's request.

Andre was even more gifted, a scary scenario.

But Lazarus was encouraged by acts of kindness Andre displayed on occasions. It was an indication that he was paying attention to his biological daddy more than his *other* one.

Not that the trances had ceased. In fact, Andre experienced them practically every night. Sometimes, Lazarus found him sleep walking and put him back to bed. The next morning, he had no recognition of what had happened. Mary Worry-Wart believed Satan was influencing Andre's thought patterns. If that were so, they would all be in danger. What if murder came to Andre's mind?

Lazarus didn't want to think of such. Though not a believer in Jesus or His kingship, he trusted a Higher Up watched over little children—sort of like the Tooth Fairy. He grinned at his silliness.

If God had an adversary, it was none of Lazarus' business. However, it was obvious that bad people committed evil deeds on a daily basis. So, if Andre chose to use his psychic gifts to harm people rather than help them, society would turn against him.

"Why do you think that, Daddy?"

Lazarus came out of his reverie and spied Andre standing in the doorway of the library. "Do you think I'm bad, Daddy?"

"No." Lazarus knelt so he'd be eye level with his son. "Did you finish your homework like I asked?"

"Boring . . ." the boy frowned.

"Education is important, Andre."

Inquisitive olive eyes stared up at Lazarus. "I speak three languages, isn't that enough? All I need to know is Latin."

"Why do you think that, son?"

"Two reasons," Andre said. "I am the Pope."

"And the other reason?" Lazarus played along.

"That's all my other daddy ever speaks."

Lazarus bit his lip. "Son, there is no *other* daddy. You need to quit talking about him. It's all in your imagination."

Andre shook his head. "He said the same thing."

Lazarus gathered his son in his arms. "What same thing?"

"That I should not talk about him, because people wouldn't believe me when I said he was real," Andre explained.

Lazarus blinked. "Okay, whatever, have you looked out the window this morning?" he asked. "People want to see you."

"I know . . ." Andre rolled his eyes.

"Don't you want to pray for those sick people?"

"Not really, it would be better if they died."

Lazarus mussed Andre's dark locks of hair. "You don't mean that, son, you love people. That's a pope's job."

"My other daddy says those people aren't worth saving."

"Stop . . . talking . . . about your OTHER daddy?" Lazarus lost his temper and blew out the bulb in the glass lamp.

"Anger is good!" Andre clapped. "It brings great power."

Lazarus took in a huge breath and held it.

"You're mad at me." Andre pouted.

"I love you, Andre, but sometimes you tax my patience. Don't I give you anything you want? You should be grateful."

"You don't think I'm qualified to be the pope anymore," Andre read his daddy's mind. "You think I'm a bad boy."

"No, I don't." Lazarus placed Andre on the floor. "But it's your job to go out on the balcony and pray for those people."

"Do I have to?"

"Yes, so mind me or no dessert after lunch."

"Okay!" Andre stamped his foot. "I will!"

"Don't be disrespectful, son."

"Sometimes it's good to vent your emotions."

"Is that something your mother told you?"

"Nope." Andre's lips twisted into a stubborn knot.

Lazarus was not about to ask how a nearly three-year-old came up with that conclusion. Certainly, he would not like the answer.

"Let's go and please my audience," Andre said, grabbing his little white toga and holding it up to his small frame. "Soon, it will be too small for me and I'll need a bigger and better one."

"That's my boy!" Lazarus laughed. "Be nice to the people."

"Of course, it's what they expect."

* * *

Twenty minutes later, shortly before 10 a.m., Andre stood on a stool overlooking Saint Peter's Square. In addition to the indigents hoping to receive a healing, a number of faithful Catholics—many from foreign countries—had joined the throng in anticipation of the Pope's comments during mass.

Andre read from a Latin script then quoted a prayer from a book. Then mass was over. The little boy raised his hands.

Lazarus watched his son with amazement. The people loved Andre. No, they adored him. In a mood to socialize, Andre went out into the courtyard and mingled among the people. Many of them remarked how adorable he looked. He gave them hope.

After the crowd had dismantled and they were in the papal apartment again, Lazarus ordered lunch sent up for them.

"You did good, son. The Catholics adored you."

"I know." He confidently shrugged.

"I'm curious. Why didn't you heal someone?"

"Are we having pizza for lunch?"

"Yes, but answer my question first."

"I just didn't feel like healing anyone."

A knock was at the door. Pizza delivery.

"Okay, let's eat." Lazarus doled out the cheesy food on paper plates. Andre snagged a slice and put half of it in his mouth.

"Mind your manners, son. Slow down or you'll get choked."

Andre only ate faster and guzzled more cola in defiance of Lazarus' request. "Isn't ignoring people's pain inconsiderate?" he asked Andre, but was interrupted by his dinging phone.

"It's Mama, isn't it?"

Lazarus glanced at the I.D. caller. "How did you know?"

"I know lots of things, Daddy."

"I'm sure you do. Now go and play on your computer while I speak to your mother." He cradled the phone to his chest.

Andre toddled off and slammed the office door.

"Hi," Lazarus said to Mary.

"Am I calling at a bad time?"

"No, Sunday mass was over an hour ago."

"How is Andre?" she asked.

"At mass, he did beautifully."

"That's not what I meant, has our son experienced any more trance episodes?" The idea of his spirit wandering around the globe spooked her. That was the Holy Spirit's job.

"He never says, but I'm watching for signs." Lazarus hoped to reassure Mary that he was a good father. "I don't think you called at this hour to ask how we're doing, so what's going on with you?"

"I'm in a difficult situation and need to vent."

Lazarus laughed. "It must be bad for you to call me."

Mary said nothing.

"Talk to *me* about what? That's not like your normal self."

She half laughed. "Normal is not a perk I often experience." Her negativity was showing. "Andrew has been arrested."

"For what—he's a cop!" Lazarus reacted.

"Cops make mistakes, too," Mary said. "Drew's female counselor has filed a complaint against him."

"What did he do? Not listen to her?" Lazarus chuckled.

"She says Drew raped her."

"Did he do it?"

"He says he didn't, that the sex was mutual."

"Well, I'm glad we got that out of the way."

"It's not funny, Lazarus. Drew could spend time in prison."

"Sorry. How is Drew's defense counsel?"

"An attorney from Nashville is working on his case," she replied. "Appleton keeps putting off telling us what we owe him for his services. I'm worried about how we'll pay him."

"What kind of name is Appleton?" Lazarus asked.

"He's American Indian." Mary yawned from fatigue.

"Do you need money from me, is that what this call's about?"

"No, that isn't even close." She'd walked into that one.

"Okay, you need to talk, I'm listening."

"The manager at Drew's bank tells me that if he's convicted of a crime and goes to prison, his Mark account will be closed and his banking chip physically removed," she reported.

"Isn't that what you've always wanted—for Drew to remove the Mark of Satan or else bust Hell wide open?"

Mary needed a wakeup call. *Hello!*

"Of course, I do. But Drew needs to do it voluntarily."

"What can I say? You find fault in everything."

"I just don't know how God will view Drew's commitment to obedience if the state requires the removal of his chip."

"Well, most people need money to operate, Mary. Some people have to pay their bills—like for rent and food."

"Why are you being like this?" Mary asked.

"I'm not up to pity parties, and I'm not in the best of moods, either. Sorry," Lazarus apologized. "I know you're upset."

"I just thought you should know what was happening on my turf," she explained. "My future is unclear. If Drew serves prison time, I'll be forced to move out. The bank will foreclose on his condo, so David and I will be forced to leave Fernwood."

"You and David," he clarified. "Are you coming here?"

"No, Jerusalem, probably."

"That's a terrible idea, Mary."

"I have a good friend there," Mary said. "In a few years, Jesus Christ will step down on the Mount of Olives and transform how society operates. I want to be there when that happens."

"Different strokes for different folks." If anyone came down, it would likely be the aliens that astronomers reported seeing circling the planet. The Jews should worry more about that.

"How soon will you move?" he asked.

"Attorney Appleton said it might be months before Drew is tried. Until then, I'm staying put." She was troubled over her uncertain future. "I'll come for a visit before long."

"When?" Lazarus feared Mary's response to Andre's increased stubbornness and allegiance to his *other* daddy.

"Did you keep the high-rise apartment?"

"Yeah, I go there a few days a week to check on things," he said. "It gives me a chance to get away from all of this."

"All the Catholic fanfare, you mean."

"Yeah," he muttered, "that, too."

"I wish I could visit my son now, but I'm tracking down someone who may be helpful to Drew's case," Mary said. "This so-called counselor is a piece of work. She seduced Drew."

"I suppose that's his side of the story."

"It's mine, too. I believe my husband."

"Do you want to talk to Andre?"

"Yes, please." She waited a couple of minutes.

"Hi, Mama," Andre timidly said.

"I miss you so much, sweetheart."

"You must address me as Pope Benedict the Twenty-first," the toddler replied. "Show some respect, Mother."

"Okay, Mr. Pope, I hope you are enjoying your time with daddy at the Vatican." Andre sounded so grown-up.

"I've been learning languages, Mama."

"You have? Which ones?"

"Spanish and French," he replied, "but I prefer Latin."

"But that's a dead language," Mary offered.

"It's all my other daddy speaks," Andre said. "All the spirits talk in Latin, so it's hardly a dead language."

"Son, you must know that's a fantasy."

"No, Mama, it's really, really, true."

"Andre, put your daddy back on the phone."

"Here, Daddy, Mama wants to talk to you."

Mary heard the footfalls as Andre ran away.

"He likes to play computer games in my office," Lazarus told Mary. "Did you need to add to our conversation?"

"What's all this talk about Latin and the *other* daddy?"

"It's just a passing phase, don't worry about it."

"Maybe you should take Andre to see a child psychiatrist."

"Goodness no, he's the Pope for Christ's sake!"

Lazarus used the name of Christ in a dishonorable way, but he was correct. The Pope's sanity must never come into question.

"Okay, I should go. David has been sick and I need to give him his meds. Please take care of Andre, he's dear to me."

As soon as Mary ended the call with Lazarus, she rang Michael Thoene's cell number and received a voicemail to leave a message at the beep. "Where are you, my friend?" A darkness closed in around her. Never had she felt so alone. She suddenly wept.

33

Monday, July 26

Nashville, Tennessee

MARY WAS AT THE county jail shortly before 2 p.m. on Monday. After being searched for contraband, her phone with her purse was stowed in a cubbyhole behind the desk. She was shown to a waiting room where others had gathered to visit their friends or loved ones.

It wasn't long before the throng was led down a long hallway and into a spacious room resembling a senior citizen's center.

Mary smiled. At any moment, it felt like someone might break out the Bingo number boards with individual playing cards.

She located a vacant table near the back and sat down. It was 2:11 p.m. by the wall clock. Time felt like it wasn't moving.

Yes, momentarily, a group of inmates—both male and female—were guided by guards into the visitation room. They quickly dispersed and joined their visitors at the tables.

With watchful eyes, prison personnel mingled about the room to ensure no rules were broken. Physical contact with prisoners was forbidden, whether to show affection, give or receive items, or act in disruptive ways. Breaking a rule insured consequences.

Mary only brought hope, but was that enough?

David was with Grace Riley for the day, still running a low-grade fever. Dr. Majors had recommended a series of allergy shots but Mary believed he was too young. But, if he continued to get sinus infections, she would need to rethink her decision.

The inmates were still filing into the room. After visitation was over, Mary had an appointment with Attorney Appleton. He'd phoned while she was parking the SUV, said he had news, but did not indicate if it were good or bad. "Just tell me," she'd said.

Appleton declined, claiming it was a face-to-face discussion.

Perturbed, Mary ended the call. If the attorney had good news, wouldn't he have said so? Mary kept sharp eyes on the door as inmates continued to file into the room. *Where is my husband?*

How would Drew react when he learned she'd failed to contact Benjamin Sawyer, Susan's former boyfriend? The one person who could shed new light on her naughty character. Without Ben's testimony, Drew would likely serve time in prison and his law-enforcement career would be over. There was no good solution.

Drew was the last person to slouch through the door. He looked haggard, like he hadn't slept well, and he'd lost a good bit of weight. How could she not worry about him? If other inmates learned he was a former detective they might assault him.

What if he dies in prison? Mary repressed tears as Drew dropped into a metal chair across the table from her.

"I wondered if you'd come," he sourly said.

"That's a terrible thing to say to me!" She badly wanted to reach across the table and grasp his hand, acutely aware a guard stood nearby watching them closely. "I love you, Drew."

Do you? The question was written in his expression.

"Have they been treating you well?"

He shrugged. "I'm still in isolation, which is good."

"Don't you go out in the courtyard to get exercise?"

"I work out with a physical therapist twice a week for my lame leg." He half smiled. "In something like a kiddy pool."

"That's good." Mary nodded.

"Food's okay, not the best, but digestible."

"Then why have you lost so much weight?"

He leaned forearms on the table. "Who can eat or sleep when I'm looking at serious time behind bars for rape?"

Changing the subject, Mary said, "I talked to Mr. Clooney at the bank about your account. It will continue functioning until your court trial," Mary revealed. "But, if you are convicted of the crime, the account will be closed and your Mark removed."

He nodded. "I expected as much."

"Why do you say that?"

"The other prisoners have scars on their left wrist."

The subject of money was closed.

"Did you talk to Jonathan Belk?" he asked.

"He finally answered his blame cell." Mary came close to cursing. "His information about Ben Sawyer was nebulous."

He nodded, "Guess Jon doesn't want to be involved."

"I don't think that," Mary countered. "What Jon knows about Ben is second-hand. He was convicted and served six months in jail, rumored to have moved to Chicago. That's all Jon knew."

"Dead end, I suppose."

"Maybe not, Attorney Appleton is going to contact the Washington State Prison and ask for Ben's forwarding address."

Drew blinked, said nothing.

"Ben's really your best chance to refute Susan's charge."

"My word against hers since my tape of our conversation the night I went over to see her didn't yield results." He frowned.

The dark circles rimming Drew's red-streaked eyes were worrisome. "Don't assume the worst, okay?" Mary remained hopeful. "All we can do now is act prudently and tell the truth."

"And pray—did you forget about prayer?" he asked.

"No, of course I pray every day."

His words stung like bees. It was not God's responsibility to bail a person out of trouble every time they messed up. There were no permanent rose gardens in the world. Thorns messed that up.

"All I'm asking God for is mercy," Mary told Drew.

He nodded. "Sorry, that comment was out of line."

They stared at one another for a long moment.

"Does Lazarus know I'm in prison?" he asked.

"We talked recently about Andre. And, yes, he knows."

"Did he jump for joy?"

"That was unkind, Andrew."

Drew let out a long breath. "So how is your son?"

"He's still has trances and talks about his other daddy."

"Who the hell is this *other* daddy?"

"Drew, that was uncalled for." Mary detested cursing.

"Sorry, I'm on edge these days."

"Do you have a Bible to read?" she asked.

"Forbidden," he said, "like other holy texts."

She nodded. Big Brother had tried to eliminate religious zeal from the lives of world citizens. Blending was the key to peace.

"How about Little David?" Drew inquired.

"He's been sick with an ear infection," Mary replied. "Dr. Majors wants to start allergy shots but I think he's too young."

A bell sounded and people began to abandon tables and move around the room. "It's time for you to go," Mary said.

Drew nodded. "Thanks for coming, it means a lot."

"You know I love you very much." Tears threatened to gush from her eyes. "I'm doing everything I can to help you."

"I just hope it's enough."

Drew stood to leave. A guard nudged his arm to get in line. When he looked back, Mary spied the hopelessness in his gaze.

"Will you still be here next Thursday?" Mary called out to him.

"As far as I know," he mouthed and waved her off.

She watched the inmates line up like third-grade students and march out of the visitation room. It was heartbreaking.

* * *

Mexico City

Monday afternoon, Hezekiah was at one of the public parks operated by the Mexico City Parks Commission. A number of curious walkers, some riding bikes, had stopped to stare at him in his odd dress and to inquire why he was there. Hezekiah explained to the gathering group that God's Son, Jesus Christ, had sent him to warn the people that judgment was coming upon the world.

One guy wearing an expensive Armani suit and a pair of Italian loafers, scoffed at Hezekiah's message of doom.

"Don't believe that homeless guy, he's full of baloney!"

"Excuse me, sir," Hezekiah said, "Come a little closer."

"Why? Are you going to strike me dead?" The arrogant businessman was close enough to rub noses with Hezekiah.

"No, sir, not at this moment," Hezekiah teased.

The people watching laughed and pointed at them.

"My job, Mr. Businessman, is to let you in on a secret."

"My, my, and what secret is that?"

"Now, I know you don't like to suffer. You probably have a family and some good friends you don't want to see hurt."

"And I suppose you are an authority on how not to suffer."

"As a matter of fact, I am," Hezekiah said. "If you want to live forever in a safe place, you must denounce your bent for sinning and accept that Jesus Christ is Lord of your life."

The middle-aged Mexican businessman threw his head back and laughed hard. "I'm not a candidate for change. I love my life. I'm successful, so go practice your witchcraft somewhere else!"

"Excuse me, Julio Alvarez?" Hezekiah called out to the man as he started walking away. "That is your given name, correct?"

The guy angrily spun around. "How did you know that?"

"An inside tip," Hezekiah teased. "The Holy Spirit told me."

The smugness tucked in Julio's furrowed expression was replaced by a flickering spark of fear. "Have you been stalking me?"

"No, but God has." Hezekiah chuckled.

"Who told you my birth name?"

"I serve a God who knows everything."

Julio frowned. "Whatever your game is I'm not playing."

"Your choice, but I know your last name was changed when your mother remarried Dr. Gonzales," Hezekiah reported. "I also know that you are not a happy man and your wife's leaving you."

"Who are you?" Julio asked, staring hard into Hezekiah's bronze-colored eyes, deep as an ocean yet bright as a star.

By this time a large crowd has gathered to observe the odd Spanish conversation taking place in the public park.

"I'm someone who cares deeply about the condition of your soul," Hezekiah explained. "God sent me to warn the Mexican people to repent of sin and accept the true Savior of the world."

Julio stared down at his pristine loafers.

"Jesus, right?"

"You're getting the picture, Julio."

The man looked up. "It's too late for me, Mr. Chosen. I am a man of great greed and deception. I hide my sins well."

"Let's make this really simple, Julio." Hezekiah smiled. "God loves you very much, and he's already made a way for sin to have no impact on you. His Son Jesus Christ died on a Roman cross for people just like you. Accept God's grace now, or not."

"Just like that?" Julio snapped his fingers.

"Just like that—salvation is a free gift."

"I wish I could, but I can't."

The businessman turned and walked away.

"I accept Jesus!" a woman wearing a red scarf fell at Hezekiah's feet. "I accept, too," another woman hollered.

At least two dozen onlookers asked Hezekiah to pray with them for God to forgive their sins and save their souls. Seeing a bubbling fountain, he baptized them by immersion.

The park attendant wasn't happy. But it was a very good day in Mexico City. And a wonderful day for Hezekiah.

Three Months Later

34

Monday, October 25

Fernwood

MARY COULDN'T BELIEVE MONTHS had passed since Drew's arrest. In weekly contact with Attorney John Appleton, she'd learned that Dr. Susan Parrot's former lover, Benjamin Sawyer, had failed to report to his parole officer after being released from a Washington State prison. It was reported he had fled America and now resided somewhere in northern Canada. Without Ben's testimony to support Appleton's allegation that Susan preyed upon her male patients, it was likely Drew would serve time for rape.

The court trial was set for 2 p.m. Monday, October 25th.

Mary was preparing to drive to Nashville as soon as David's sitter arrived. Outdoors, the weather had significantly cooled with the onset of autumn's first welcome frost in West Tennessee.

On almost every front porch of neighborhoods sat carved pumpkins on haystacks beside a standing scarecrow. Halloween was on the mind of ordinary folks everywhere in America. Teens were excited and planning hayride parties. The weatherman predicted a full golden harvest moon would rise on October 31st.

Downtown Fernwood was not to be outdone. Retail stores had staged their windows with manikins dressed in gloomy attire to depict witches and warlocks. Celebrating *All Hallows Eve* was a welcome diversion from the scary persecutions people faced daily.

"Thank you again for coming over to stay with Little David," Mary told Grace Riley when she entered the condo. "You've been such a great blessing to me during these past several months."

"I enjoy helping people." Grace picked up Little David and hugged him like she owned him. "I love this little guy."

"I know you do." Mary snagged her lined blue-jean jacket from the hall closet. "That's a great comfort to me."

"I see you're preparing to move, if it comes to that." Grace noted the packed boxes in the den. "I'd miss both of you so much."

"Life goes on, Grace. Right now, I have to concentrate all my efforts on Drew and what's about to take place in Nashville."

"Go on, we'll be fine, so don't be mommy-concerned in the least." They locked eyes. "I'll pray that Drew somehow gets off."

Under the circumstances, Mary didn't see that happening, although Sheriff Sarah Boswell and Detective Georgie Adams were set to testify in court regarding Drew's impeccable character.

"Where will you move after the trial?" Grace asked as Mary checked inside her large vinyl purse for her phone and makeup essentials, just in case she decided to stay overnight in Nashville.

Tom Rave had been very supportive in the past months when Mary visited Drew in prison. She could not have a better friend.

Somewhat physically attracted to Tom, Mary was grateful God was leading her to Jerusalem. She felt safer around Rabbi Michael Thoene, the father-image she never had. The last thing she needed was a romantic entanglement with yet another good man.

"Okay, I guess I'm ready to go." Mary hugged David and patted Grace on the back. "My plans haven't changed, Grace. I'm moving to Jerusalem if Drew is convicted and serves time."

Grace nodded with bleary eyes. "I'll miss both of you, but Little David the most. I've become very attached to him."

"No grandmother could treat him better," Mary offered. "I can tell by the way he fingers your face he adores you."

"As I him. Be careful on the road, the quake that shook West Tennessee put cracks in some of the state highways."

"I will," Mary said. "I'll Google the Highway Department and make sure my route is open. Meanwhile, keep David safe."

"I usually go outdoors in case my house falls in."

"Not if a sinkhole opens up beneath your feet," Mary warned. "I have a safety leaflet in the kitchen drawer you should read."

Grace inhaled deeply. "I hate waiting for something bad to happen. I wish we were at the end of the seven years and Jesus was already here. I'm traumatized by all this talk of disaster."

"That's how it's supposed to affect people," Mary pointed out, tugging on her jacket. "Persecution drives people to think about death and the afterlife. God's grace is sufficient."

"I wish I had your confidence," Grace said. "I believe in Jesus, but death scares me." She placed David in his playpen.

"It shouldn't," Mary refuted. "All you do is stop breathing. It's the easiest thing you'll do in this life. And then you are there."

"In Heaven, you mean," Grace said.

"Or the alternative," Mary remarked.

* * *

On her way to Nashville, Mary phoned Attorney John Appleton. "Is the trial coming off as scheduled?"

"No indication it has changed. Judge Lamar Stanton is the presiding judge. In the past, he's been very fair in dispensing justice." John fell silent. "Are you on your way here?"

"Yes," she replied. "Have you heard from Sheriff Boswell or Detective Adams this morning?"

"They're already here, seated in the anteroom with my secretary. I served them ham croissants and coffee."

"Good, that crew is always hungry."

"Where exactly are you, Mary?"

"About to exit I-40, approximately ten minutes from your office," she answered. "Can I pick up anything for you?"

"No, just get here as quickly as possible, I want to go over the proceedings with the three of you. To make sure there are no glitches in giving a positive testimony on behalf of Andrew."

"Thank you, John. I'll see you soon."

Mary ended the call and dialed Tom Rave's number.

"It's Mary," she said when he answered.

"How are you holding up?" he asked.

"Better than I ever thought I would."

"Good for you!" Tom said.

"No, God is good. I've been fasting for two days and praying that Susan will decide to drop her complaint and end this silly game of wills. The counselor is a damaged woman, out to prove her authority over the male population." Mary declared.

"Well, you have a nose for those kinds of things," Tom said.

"Drew's attorney did some digging into Susan's background and discovered she was abandoned by her father at age eight."

"What about her mom?" Tom asked.

"She was a workaholic and a closet drunk."

"Bitterness has its consequences," Tom concluded.

"Susan was a brilliant student," Mary recalled John's report. "She left home at sixteen and entered a work program for runaway teens in Michigan. After graduating high school, she applied for scholarships to colleges and continued her education."

"How did Drew's attorney find out all this?"

"FACEBOOK is a marvelous tool of information."

"That's why I stay off of it." Tom huffed.

"Later, Susan was accepted by the University of Florida into their graduate program to earn her masters in psychology. She graduated with honors and worked as a teen counselor."

"I thought she was a psychiatrist," John recalled.

"Yes, she went back to school and earned her doctorate two years ago," Mary explained, becoming an expert on Dr. Parrot.

"The only thing Dr. Susan Parrot failed to learn was how to control her passion to punish the men in her life," Tom reasoned.

"It cannot be refuted that Susan is one determined female bent on punishing the men who reject her," Mary said.

"I hope the judge sees it that way."

Both took a moment to reflect on the upcoming trial.

"Will Attorney Appleton have the opportunity to present Susan's background?" Tom suddenly inquired.

"If her attorney opens the discussion of Drew's character flaws, then yes," Mary replied. "But it's still her word against his."

"So, you expect the rape charge to stick."

"I hope it won't." Mary cringed. "My prayer is that the judge will be fair in his sentencing. Drew could get up to five years."

"Okay, I'll see you at the courthouse."

"I'll look for you," she said.

"Be vigilant and trust in the Lord."

"As always, I am his servant."

Mary ended the call as she pulled into the parking lot of John Appleton's building. Locking up Drew's SUV, she entered the foyer and took the elevator up to his office. It looked like the three of them had a party going, but Mary knew it was only comfort food.

35

The Metro Court House

THE GROUNDS OF THE Metro Courthouse looked exactly as Mary remembered when she'd been there three months before. What had changed was the weather, now much cooler. The foliage on plants and trees had been transformed from shades of green to golden browns, raging reds and oranges, and purple hues. It was a rare day Mary would rather spend outdoors with Drew and the boys. A family picnic, a walk in the park, or just hanging out together.

Susan Parrot had stolen that time from them.

Mary stared at the courthouse and took in a huge breath.

The four of them exited John Appleton's car and passed a group of college students holding signs stating STOP ABUSE OF WOMEN. The publicized rape case attracted the local media outlets and various organizations for women's rights. John had forewarned Mary that hecklers might be present. And they were.

They went up the escalator and boarded the elevator up to the fourth floor. They entered the courtroom and walked down the center aisle. John took a center seat at the defense table while Mary, Sarah, and Georgie found seats behind him on the second row.

The noise level was excruciating. But it wasn't long before the accused was ushered into the courtroom by an officer.

Drew wore a brown suit with a striped tie and loafers. His hair had been recently cut and he'd shaved. He was more handsome than Mary remembered. Her heart lurched with love for him. After his handcuffs were removed, he sat down at the table next to John.

Mary strained to hear their whisperings, but the spectators were far too noisy to interpret their conversation.

"What are they saying?" Mary nearly shouted to Sarah.

"Can't hear my own thoughts for the noise."

"I think Drew looks pretty good, considering . . ." Georgie meant considering he'd survived in a county jail for three months.

Dressed up for the slaughter about to take place, Mary thought.

The court stenographer took her place at the table on the left side of the lectern. The bailiff stood nearby, glancing often at his wristwatch. It was 2:03 p.m. and Judge Stanton was running late.

The door behind the lectern suddenly opened and a tall, thin man wearing a silky black robe swept into the courtroom with fanfare. His skin was as black as ink against his flame-blue eyes.

Mary was shocked. John Appleton had not mentioned their judge was a black man. But he'd said Stanton was fair-minded.

"All rise," the bailiff shouted. "Be seated" immediately came from the judge as he rapped the lectern with his wooden gavel.

"Is the defendant present in the courtroom?" Stanton peered at the defense attorney over his silver-rimmed spectacles.

Appleton nudged Drew and he stood up. "I am."

"Please read the charges against Andrew Carson Taylor," Judge Stanton instructed the bailiff as quiet settled over the courtroom.

"How do you plead, Mr. Taylor?"

It was no longer *Officer* or *Detective* Taylor, since Drew's credentials had been stripped away. "Not guilty," he said.

"Is the prosecution ready to present their case?" Stanton asked Attorney Adam Quincy, his gaze shifting upon the lovely Dr. Susan Parrot. Their eyes met momentarily then fell apart.

"We are," Quincy replied with utmost confidence.

"Bailiff, bring in the jurors and instruct them to be seated."

While the twelve jurors filed into the courtroom the judge waited until they were seated then advised them that both the prosecutor and defense attorneys would present a summary of their cases before any evidence or testimony would be heard.

Mary watched the proceedings with apprehension. Susan's lawyer went first and summarized her complaint against Drew. He presented a compelling case of physical abuse by a trained law-enforcement officer who was much larger than his female victim.

It was inconceivable that the counselor appeared so calm and collected while Mary was imploding with terror. Trying to appear confident, Mary was aware staff reporters were ogling her.

Defense Attorney John Appleton's turn came next. He summarized Drew's testimony, pointing out there was no physical evidence to convict Detective Taylor. Dr. Susan Parrot had not reported the rape nor gone to a hospital to be tested. Although in possession of an illegally taped conversation between his client and Dr. Parrot, John could not to use it. However, he moved for a dismissal of the case. "Denied." The judge rapped his gavel.

"Present your first witness for the plaintiff," Stanton said.

Attorney Quincy put Susan on the stand.

The lovely counselor walked over to the lectern where she was sworn in and took a seat in the witness box. Susan's back was straight, her aquamarine eyes alert, and her long blond hair tied in a profession knot at the back of her long neck. When their eyes met, Mary spied a smirk in Susan's expression. *I always win.* Mary wanted to leap across the bench like a super hero and throttle Susan.

"State your name and occupation for the jury," Quincy addressed Susan, gazing at the jury to assess their interest.

Susan repeated much of what Attorney Appleton had already told Mary regarding her professional counseling credentials.

"Will you tell the jurors in your own words how you came to know Andrew Taylor?" Quincy stepped back a pace.

"Yes." Susan calmly explained that the State Board of Health had referred her to the Fernwood Police Department when they requested a qualified counselor to meet with troubled officers.

"Objection," Appleton quipped. "Counselor had not yet met with Detective Taylor to determine if he was *troubled.*"

"Sustained," Judge Stanton announced from the bench then faced Susan's defense counsel. "Instruct your witness not to make judgmental statements regarding the defendant before they met."

"Dr. Parrot?" Quincy moved on. "When did you begin counseling sessions with Detective Taylor?"

"In early March," she replied.

"What was your relationship to Mr. Taylor at that time?"

"Very professional," Susan replied. "He didn't want to talk about his feelings at first—not uncommon for patients who resist treatment," she explained. "In time, he opened up more."

"Object," Appleton said, "judgment call again."

"Overruled," Judge Stanton said. "Dr. Parrot is qualified to make a judgment regarding her patient."

Quincy took that as a signal to resume his interrogation of Susan. "Dr. Parrot, please clarify for the jury what reason Mr. Taylor gave you for seeking psychological treatment."

"Drew was bitter about a murder case he'd been working on for over a year. The serial killer had shot him twice, once in the head that caused a stroke. Though he survived, his left leg is not fully functional," Susan reported as she glanced at the jurors.

"Isn't it true that Mr. Taylor stopped treatment after only a few counseling sessions?" Quincy said. "Why was that?"

"Yes, Andrew was worried about his mounting bills. He'd recently married and was caring for a wife with two young children. He worried how he would make his co-pay for treatment."

"Were you able to help him resolve his worry over finances?"

"Yes, I immediately petitioned the State Board of Health to waive his co-payment so he could continue counseling with me."

"Then you resumed his counseling on a weekly basis."

"Yes, we met again in mid-May," Susan reported. "Andrew was irresponsible about keeping appointments. He failed to call my office to cancel. So, I called him once to ask him why."

"Did he give you a plausible reason?" Quincy asked.

"Andrew said he was handling things better. I suggested that he finish his twelve paid counseling sessions, recognizing he still had issues regarding his ability to do his job," Susan explained.

"So, he resumed treatment," Quincy said.

"Yes, in June."

"On that Friday in July, the day you were raped, what happened?" Quincy got to the meat of the trial.

"Objection, prosecution is leading the witness!!" Drew's defense attorney barked from his perch at the table.

"Sustained," Judge Stanton said. "Rephrase your question, Attorney Quincy," he sternly directed.

"Dr. Parrot, will you tell the jury what happened on Friday, July sixteen, during your counseling session with Mr. Taylor?"

Quincy looked flatly into the faces of the twelve jurors.

Calm-and-collected Susan explained how Drew came into the office as scheduled then immediately embraced and kissed her. Resisting his caress, she had asked him to please take a seat so they could discuss his rash action and what had prompted him to kiss her. Not answering, he'd begun unbuttoning her blouse.

Drew leaned over and whispered to Appleton, "It did not happen that way, she's lying through her teeth."

The judge heard the comment and shook his head at Appleton.

"I told him to stop but he didn't," Susan continued. "Rather than fight him because he was stronger than me, I let it happen."

Susan's words were a catchy moment. A few reporters stepped out into the hall to get a jump on the unfolding events in the courtroom. Hot and sizzling tales like this drew audiences.

Quincy asked, "Afterwards, when you were alone, why didn't you go the hospital and report the rape, Dr. Parrot?"

"I was ashamed." Susan broke down in tears.

A glance at the jury box told Mary the liar had earned the sympathy of the seven women and two of the five male jurors.

Shuttering, Susan added, "In my last job in Seattle, I had a similar problem with a male officer," she explained. "If I reported the rape, I was afraid my license would be revoked."

"Of course, you were scared. What woman wouldn't fear recrimination? You felt helpless. That's what rape does."

"Objection!" Appleton fired as he stood up and pointed at Quincy. "Assumption of the plaintiff's feelings."

"Sustained," the judge said, nodding for Quincy to continue.

"I'm sorry you were subjected to this heinous crime, Dr. Parrot." Attorney Quincy empathized with the victim.

"Objection again!" Appleton exploded. "Assumption of guilt."

"Sustained!" Stanton rapped the lectern. "Attorney Quincy, one more remark like that and I'll hold you in contempt."

"I apologize, Judge Stanton," Quincy said.

"The jury is to disregard the opinion of the prosecutor."

"After your sexual encounter with then Detective Taylor in your office, how did that make you feel, Dr. Parrot?"

"Devastated and frightened," Susan rasped. "I'm a single woman and my livelihood is my job. It isn't right for a man to take that from me, an officer of the law hired to protect me!"

But there was much more to the testimony.

"Thank you, Dr. Parrot, you may step down."

36

ATTORNEY QUINCY PETITIONED THE jurors to diligently consider Dr. Susan Parrot's testimony. A licensed psychiatrist, paid by Tennessee's State Health Board to counsel troubled law-enforcement officers, she had no other option but to file a rape charge against then Detective Andrew Taylor after he forced her to have sex with him twice more in her apartment. "Fearing for her life and her livelihood, Dr. Susan Parrot saw no other way out."

Shocked over the statement, the courtroom spectators came alive with comments. Judge Stanton rapped on the lectern and shouted to the spectators. "Quiet! Or I *will* clear this courtroom!"

On a roll, Quincy continued, "Therefore, I ask you, the jury, to render a guilty verdict. Officer Taylor should not be allowed in the public venue to prey on women because he has a badge."

Jurors uncomfortably glanced at one another, nodding.

"Not a good sign," Mary whispered to Sheriff Boswell.

Mary might have been convinced of Drew's guilt had she not been the wiser. When it came time for Appleton to present his defense on behalf of Drew, he called Sheriff Sarah Boswell first, and then Detective Georgie Adams to the stand. They were effective witnesses. Both testified that Detective Taylor had never acted unethically toward any female while at work. He was married and loved his wife. What Dr. Parrot claimed was a fantasy.

"Andrew Taylor is a good man," Georgie vouched for him.

Next Appleton called Susan to the stand. "Dr. Parrot, isn't it a fact that the day before you claimed Detective Taylor raped you, on Thursday, July sixteen, you showed up at his private residence and complained to him that a former boyfriend was stalking you?"

Susan replied," Yes, I was afraid to go home."

"Furthermore," Appleton continued, "you accepted a glass of wine from Detective Taylor then ate take-out Chinese with him. Isn't socializing breaking some kind of patient/counselor rule?"

"I didn't see it that way." Susan explained that she was fairly new in town and did not want to involve the police. Since Andrew was a detective, she'd decided to seek his help instead.

"Who is Benjamin Sawyer?" Appleton inquired.

Susan admitted counseling Ben. They clicked and dated for a while, but when he'd become verbally and physically abusive, she ended their relationship and moved out of state to avoid conflict.

In response, Appleton hit Susan hard with the fact she had formerly filed a rape charge against Benjamin Sawyer, a man who was at the time still employed by the Seattle Police Department.

The jury reacted with surprised expressions.

"Dr. Parrot, isn't it true that you were counseling Office Sawyer when your relationship crossed the professional line?"

That one statement hit home with the jurors.

On a redirect, Prosecutor Quincy pointed out, "All of this is hearsay. Where is the witness to verify what has been said?"

"Is Mr. Sawyer present in the courtroom?" the judge asked.

"No, he could not be located," Appleton replied.

"Remember, jurors," Judge Stanton stated, "in rendering a decision as to the guilt of Detective Andrew Carson Taylor, you must be convinced beyond a shadow of a doubt that he committed the crime. Otherwise, he is innocent until proven guilty."

Mary was grateful Judge Stanton clarified that point with the jury. Emotions were running high. Female jurors tended to empathize with Susan, regarding Drew as a bullying officer.

This is probably why Appleton said Stanton was fair.

Susan stepped down from the hot seat.

"Judge Stanton," Quincy said. "May I introduce one more item that will shed light on the character of the accused?"

"Objection!" Appleton said. "I know of no other document pertinent to this case." His face turned beet red.

"Attorney Quincy, have you given the defense a copy of the statement you're holding in your hand?" Judge Stanton asked.

"No, it has just come to my attention." He walked over and handed Appleton a copy of the document.

"I request a ten-minute recess to review this doc with my client," Appleton petitioned the judge.

Stanton glanced at his watch. *4:18 p.m.* He dismissed the jury for a thirty-minute break. Court would resume at 4:48 p.m. sharp.

* * *

Only half of the spectators returned to the courtroom.

Mary, Sarah, and Georgie found their seats again. Once court was in session again, Quincy presented the letter from Alcoholic Anonymous and a drug-treatment center in Fernwood, Tennessee.

"I submit these letters to the court, verifying that the accused was previously treated for alcohol and drug addiction before he worked in law-enforcement. He called Dr. Parrot and requested counseling. He admitted to her he had difficulty performing his job due to handling his disability. And he was having marital problems."

Quincy looked directly at Drew. "Detective Andrew Taylor may have been a good man and law officer in the past, but that has changed. He was drinking, upset, and angry at the time he sought treatment from Dr. Parrot. He admitted to being depressed over his finances and failing marriage. He accepted prescribed anxiety pills from Dr. Parrot. Susan Parrot did everything a professional psychologist could do to help Andrew Taylor emotionally cope."

Quincy grew still. "And he paid her back by raping her."

As if infused with a huge wind, Attorney Quincy lashed out one final thought. "It's obvious from Mr. Taylor's history that he has numerous reasons to be angry. He is a disturbed individual."

The Q ball rolled into the slot.

"Based on Dr. Parrot's expert testimony, and the two documents presented into evidence," Quincy inhaled deeply, "is it not reasonable to believe that Detective Andrew Taylor mentally snapped and lost control when he raped Dr. Susan Parrot?"

The air in the courtroom seemed to take a slow breath.

"I ask you, the jury, to find the accused guilty of rape."

Again, Mary would have been convinced that Drew raped Susan had she not believed her husband. But, in all honesty, the testimony of the defense had not swayed the jury to their side.

The prosecution and defense summarized their cases and rested. By then, it was 4:45 p.m. The judge directed the jury to discuss the case and render a decision of guilt or innocence for the accused. After the gavel rapped the lectern, court adjourned.

The bailiff directed the spectators to stand as the judge exited the courtroom. Phones flashed as photos were taken of Drew as he left the courtroom wearing handcuffs and a scowl on his face.

Mary faced Attorney Appleton. "Why didn't you present the recording of Susan's flirtatious remarks toward my husband the night he was wired and asked her to drop the charges?"

"Drew had no warrant giving him the right to tape her."

"Is there anything else we can do to help my husband?"

"No, we wait for the jury's decision."

"Then what?" Mary asked.

"Then we decide if we contest the decision."

Sarah and Georgie went home. Tom Rave took Mary to O' Charlie's for supper and tried really hard to cheer her up.

"I know things look bad for Drew," he said, "but I hear Judge Stanton is fair on sentencing." He hoped to diffuse her depression.

"Even I was almost persuaded that Drew is guilty."

"Susan Parrot was very convincing," Tom noted.

"She's a liar and cheat, and has to be stopped!"

Tom frowned at Mary. "What are you saying?"

"If Drew's convicted, I'm not through with her," Mary said. "I'll find Benjamin Sawyer wherever he is and we'll demand a retrial. Dr. Susan Parrot will get what she deserves in the end."

"You almost sound bitter."

"I am." Mary's blue eyes glazed over. "It's not that I'm not interested in Susan's soul, but she cannot be allowed to do this to one more innocent male. I believe God understands."

Tom suppressed a chuckle. "I hope you're right."

* * *

The jury verdict came the following morning. Judge Stanton sentenced Drew to five years in the Tennessee State Prison east of Nashville. The last time their eyes locked, Mary spied Drew's misery and regret. But there was nothing more to be done but live with the consequences of his mistakes. It was a sad commentary.

Mary was home by mid-day Tuesday. Grace had put David down for his nap. After hearing the verdict and Drew's sentencing, she realized her services would no longer be needed.

"You're leaving town, when?" Grace asked.

"As soon as I can get a flight to Rome," Mary replied.

"I thought you were moving to Jerusalem."

"Eventually," Mary said. "I'm shipping a few necessities to Rabbi Michael Thoene's house in Jerusalem and donating everything else. Drew's not going to need his things anymore."

"What if he gets out of prison, where will he go?"

"He'll come to Jerusalem with me," Mary said. "Everything in Drew's life is about to change." She was operating on five cups of caffeine, her mind jetting in a hundred different directions.

"Can I do anything to help you?" Grace asked.

"No, I'll phone the Good Will people in the morning and have them pick up the furniture and Drew's clothes," Mary said.

"It sounds like you have it all together."

Mary's eyes misted. "I don't have anything together, Grace. I've lost my biological son, my home, and my husband. There's just me and David left to make do. I'm only doing what's necessary."

Grace spontaneously hugged Mary. "I'm sorry."

That was all the sympathy Mary needed to give her suppressed volatile emotions a voice. She let out a scream and began bawling. The scene woke up Little David and he cried, too.

Grace joined into the boohoo rally and all three railed raucously for the next thirty minutes until no tears were left to cry.

37

Wednesday, October 27

THE MORNING AFTER DREW went to prison arrived early for Mary. Sleepless in Fernwood, she'd been assaulted by weird dreams until she finally gave up the mental fight and climbed out of bed.

The sleepy sun had not peeked through the window blinds. However, as if sensing her unrest, Little David was wide awake. She found him cooing and playing with his toes in his baby bed.

The antibiotics Dr. Majors prescribed had kicked in during the night and he was mimicking the antics of a normal healthy toddler.

For that, Mary gave God all the glory.

After both of them had breakfast, David played with his toys in his playpen while Mary sat on the sofa emailing Rabbi Michael Thoene on her laptop. He was sorry to hear Andrew was convicted of rape and would serve prison time. With good behavior, Drew might get out in three, she'd told Michael. Then her cell phone dinged. She glanced at the I.D. caller and smiled.

"Good morning, Michael."

"I'm so sorry about Andrew."

"Life is what it is," she stoically replied.

"What are you going to do?"

"Now . . . with the rest of my life?"

"I guess I left myself open for that, didn't I?"

"Well, for certain I'm not staying here," she said. "I can't bear to live in Drew's condo with memories of what might have been. Besides, I have no money to pay the rent."

"I thought Andrew had a bank account."

"It's being shut down and his Mark removed."

Silence can also be a statement of grief.

"Hey, don't be so negative," Michael said. "You can move to Jerusalem where you have good friends. I'll see that you have a place to stay and help you find a job in Christian ministry."

"Taking care of us is not your responsibility, Michael."

"It is if I'm willing to help out a friend."

"I don't want anybody's pity," Mary said.

"I'm not suggesting a free ride," he said. "Financial gifts are still coming into the Jerusalem Fund daily. The collateral is there to support Christian ministries, and you certainly qualify."

"Thank you, I can't think of a location on the globe where I'd rather raise my adopted son," she remarked, feeling encouraged.

"When can I expect you to arrive?" he asked.

"Not immediately, I'm going to Rome first."

"To see your biological son," he gathered.

"Yes. Andre's in trouble, Michael."

"He's not safe?" The idea was troubling.

"No, he's plenty safe. Incarcerated at the Vatican, Andre's every move is monitored," Mary spewed. "It's apparent to me that Lazarus and his brother are using my son's psychic gifts for political purposes. I just don't know their end-game."

"You're referring to Dr. Luceres Ramnes," Michael clarified.

"Yes, Papa's been supportive of me in the past, but I don't trust him. He's skeptical of Christianity and socializes with a known terrorist," Mary pointed out. "I can't totally ignore him since my son's father, his twin, is tied to him like a horse to a carriage."

Michael snickered. "You forgot to mention dangerous. As the chairman of the Committee of Ten, Luceres collapsed world markets and installed the international banking Mark."

"That, too," Mary mouthed. "But I don't think Luceres views the banking system as a negative. It spreads the world's wealth among poorer nations and lifts many out of extreme poverty."

"You almost sound like a globalist."

"Trust me, I'm not," Mary said. "But only because I've read the Word, and know my future in relation to biblical prophecy."

"You're right-on, sister! Christians have an advantage over non-believers because we are privy to Christ's end-game."

It was Mary's time to chuckle. "But that still doesn't tell me what's going through the minds of the Committee members who try to control every aspect of society. My vote is for freewill."

"Perhaps the Committee's goal is simpler than you might imagine," Michael suggested. "The submission of the Catholics to the dictates of world-government rule goes a long way."

"What do you mean?" Mary puzzled.

"The Muslims want war so they can usher in a Caliphate to rule the world. Sharia Law is their only acceptable form of government. ISIS, a bunch of Islamic terrorists, revitalized the movement a decade ago. Although suppressed, it's still lurking in the shadows."

"You believe the Catholic Dioceses will support the regime?"

"Yes, I do. Cooperating Catholics, obeying the dictates of the Committee of Ten, go a long way to keep the peace. Even more important, let's keep you and David safe in this troubled world."

"I don't know what to say, Michael."

"Say thank you and move to Jerusalem."

"Thank you, Michael. You're a good friend."

"Now, regarding Andre . . ."

"Yes?"

"Didn't you tell me your son could heal people?"

"Yes, but he also has the destructive gene."

"Are you frightened of him?"

"No." The idea stunned Mary. "He would never hurt me."

"You've heard of the False Prophet in Revelation."

Mary's heart nearly stopped beating. "My son is not the False Prophet, Michael! He's a child preyed upon by his uncle!"

"You can't be sure of that, Mary," Michael countered. "Satan has been granted power on earth for a season. If he's using your son to propagate his purposes, you won't be able to save him."

"But Jesus can," she countered.

"Only if Andre is willing," Michael pointed out. "Our Heavenly Father never overrides free will."

"How can a small boy know the difference?"

"I can't answer that," he said. "How did God discern between Cain and Abel's gifts? One offered grain, the other a slain animal. We can't second guess God's motives."

"Well, I can't let that idea go uncontested," Mary said. "I'm going to Rome and see what's going on—what hasn't been told me over the phone. And Lazarus will tell me, or I'll beat it out of him."

Michael laughed. "Go, girl! Get all that frustration out before you show up at my house. I can't deal with a scorned woman."

The air went out of Mary's lungs like a deflating balloon.

"You're right, Michael. I can't force the issue."

"Then be your sweet self, Mary. Listen, see, seek, and pray, and God will surely show you if Andre is truly in danger."

Mary's tears spilled down her cheeks. "You are such an inspiration to me. Ari is sick but you keep on trucking."

"Trucking? What does that mean?" he asked.

"I'll explain when I see you. Now, I need to get moving."

David cried out from his playpen.

"Motherhood is calling," she said. "Thanks for the advice."

"Anytime, keep in touch."

Mary ended the call, feeling more relaxed, more able to cope with her uncertain future, yet still determined to help Drew prove he did not rape that awful Susan, a harlot of the worst kind.

38

Saturday, October 30

Rome, Italy

ON THURSDAY, THE BANK manager had purchased two airline tickets to Rome, Italy, for Mary and David. Mr. Clooney had reassured her that Drew's funds would be safely held by the bank until the time he was released from prison. However, in five years Jesus' millennial reign would be in progress and money worthless.

Even more important than saving the man she loved from a prison stint was serving God. Mary had been commissioned by the Holy Spirit to help people realize how much they needed God's love, forgiveness, and daily guidance. That meant putting her present persecutions behind and walking into a strange new reality. With God's help she'd forge ahead with purpose.

All of this drama was threading Mary's thoughts as the plane landed in Rome on Saturday and she deplaned with David. A good baby, he was easily managed. Having slept most of the flight, he was awake and squirming to crawl on the floor.

"Not yet, buddy. Mama's got you."

Steadily moving off the plane with the flow of traffic, Mary realized letting go of Drew and their marriage was like packing a huge bag with everything you owned then tossing it out the window while still in flight. Their history was deadweight on her future.

The last thing she needed was more baggage.

With David's diaper bag slung over one shoulder, and her huge purse weighting the other, Mary entered the busy concourse. Conversations in various languages buzzed around them as they joined the toddling crowd following the signs to BAGGAGE.

Pulling David along by one hand and her rolling bag with the other, Mary prayed her strength would be enough to get them through the concourse and outdoors where Lazarus promised he would be waiting. About to pause to rest, a young man approached and offered to wheel her bag and walk them to the exit. An answer to her prayer, she saw no reason not to accept his kind offer.

"Where are you headed?" he asked with a crooked smile.

"To visit with my son, he's with his daddy," she replied.

"Then who's this little guy?" The young stranger knelt to face Little David, who pinched his nose and giggled.

"My adopted son—it's a long, sad story," Mary explained.

He stood up. "I'm not one to pry, just a helper."

"Thank you so much, I was at my wit's end." Mary welcomed his kind assistance. "Are you from here?"

"I'm from all over. Timothy, at your service."

"Pleased to meet you. Be sure and thank your parents for raising such a thoughtful young man." Mary grinned at him.

During their long trek through the concourse, Timothy had little to say about himself, asking Mary more questions about her life than she chose to answer. She could tell he was a kind soul.

As they approached the revolving glass doors leading out of the terminal, Mary stepped through first with David then turned to thank Timothy for his help. Strangely, he wasn't there.

Humph. Mary considered if the helpful Timothy was actually one of those "angels unaware" mentioned in the Bible.

Outside, a salty Mediterranean breeze assaulted Mary's face as she glanced around for Lazarus. The late October weather was pleasantly cool. Above her, the sun glittered like a jewel in the noonday sky. God had created a perfectly beautiful world.

"There you are." Lazarus hauled Little David into his arms. "Golly, he's a bundle to carry around. Just look at you."

Mary frowned. "I know I must look a fright."

"No, in fact, you are beautiful," he said.

"Flattery will get you everywhere," she teased.

He laughed. "My driver is parked on the curb so we'd better hurry before a federal agent shoos him away."

Lazarus snagged the rolling bag, dragged it to the back of the limousine then set it inside. "I'll hold David while you get in."

Bossy, like he owned the day, Mary was pleased Lazarus was taking charge of the moment. She was weary from the trip with little ability to make a rational decision. She hopped in the backseat of the limousine and received David in her arms.

"No, I didn't bring a car seat," she answered before asked.

"You have a bad habit of losing car seats," he teased. "Not to worry, I'll purchase everything you need when you've settled in your apartment and rested." He slid in the seat across from Mary.

"I don't need much to function." She peered out the window as the limo pulled away from the curb. *Déjà vu*, just like before when she'd come to Rome. *This time I'm not going home.*

"How is Andrew handling prison?" Lazarus inquired, getting the elephant out of the way so they could address other topics.

"He's depressed, doesn't think life's treating him fairly."

"Well, he's right," Lazarus nodded, "if he's truly innocent."

Upset over the comment, Mary glared at Lazarus. "My husband is innocent, and life has not treated him fairly."

"You'll get no argument from me—shot in the head and left an invalid? I'd be depressed, too. How are you handling it?"

She ignored his question, staring out at the passing traffic.

"Okay . . . with that covered, can you at least tell me if Drew's lawyer plans to file an appeal for a new trial?"

Mary's sad blue eyes moved on Lazarus. "The rape case is complicated. If Benjamin Sawyer can't be found, it's over."

The colorful fall foliage glided past the limousine windows.

"Who's Benjamin?" Lazarus asked as they rolled over a crater in the road. "Earth tremors," he commented.

"Drew was convicted of rape," she revealed. "We believe Dr. Susan Parrot has preyed on her male clients before."

"Isn't that some kind of crime in itself?"

"Without a credible witness to prove that she's a psycho-predator, it was her word against Drew's. Susan won this time."

"This time? So, what, if you locate this Benjamin guy, you think he'll testify that his counselor lied to the court?"

"Yes, but I doubt we'll find him." She repressed tears.

"Hey. I've never known you to be so negative."

"I'm only being realistic." Mary glared at Lazarus.

They hit another huge crater on the interstate and the vehicle rolled to one side. "Goodness, Italy needs to repair its roads!"

"City crews are working around the clock," Lazarus reported. "They fix one hole then another opens up."

Mary sighed. "The world is coming apart."

"You've said that before, and I'm beginning to believe you're right." Lazarus reached over and took David from Mary.

"Thank you, I feel like my arms are dropping off."

"So, tell me, why do you think Jesus is coming back in four years?" Lazarus handed David his ring of plastic keys to jingle.

Mary hitched a breath. "You really want to know, or is this a ploy to condemn me for my Christian beliefs?"

"I really want to know," he said.

"Okay, but let's wait until we get to the apartment. I need to feed David and put him down for a nap. Then we'll talk."

39

The Vatican

AFTER LUNCH, LUCERES PACED the Pope's apartment while waiting for his brother to return. Needing to pass the time, he flew through several articles in four magazines on his Apple iPhone.

"No surprise there!" he quipped at one article. The weather was acting up like a naughty child gone berserk.

"Hardly news." Meteorologists blamed global warming on earthquakes and sinkholes. Forget about cows pooping carbon. One teen blog posted that a bunch of Jews, known as the 144,000, were Holy-Spirit sealed in the forehead with tiny glowing crosses.

"Poppycock!"

Messianic Jews, the evangelists called themselves. What a nuisance now that they had invaded the planet like scavengers.

One reporter suggested they all hang for treason.

He was on board with that.

However, they drew people like magnets. The religious acts they performed on people yielded many healings. They preached that Jesus Christ was the Savior of the world. That alone infuriated the Muslims. In a modern society relying upon medical technology, robotics, electronics, and energy sources of all kinds that enhanced their living standards, the 144,000 did not model society.

Reading the blog again gave Luceres a gnawing headache. He was in a stupor. When his phone vibrated for the fourth time, he grew even more irritated. It was Ahmed Ramallah calling.

The fanatic Muslim needed to vent. No doubt the Arab was livid at the Messianic Jews for spewing lies at his own people. Faithful followers of Muhammad had publicly denounced their belief in Allah, forsaking their trust in the Prophet in favor of salvation through Jesus Christ. Ahmed's banter was more like an old-fashioned broken record playing back the same ol' tired tune.

The last time they'd spoken, Ahmed pressed him to convince the Committee of Ten to back a war against Israel. The Muslim wanted to tear down the Jewish Temple and put up a mosque. He intended to establish a world-wide Caliphate on behalf of the Prophet Muhammad and rule as *al Mahdi*. Now the fifth ring?

Unbelievable!

As much as Luceres preferred to ignore Ahmed's calls, he could not without angering him even more. Grimacing, Luceres swiped a finger across the phone's face and placed it to one ear.

"What is it now, Ahmed?"

"I don't need you anymore," the Muslim boasted.

"Don't get cute with me."

"No, it's true. I've convinced the Russian president to join forces with my warriors and attack Jerusalem from the north."

"That's a truly stupid idea!" Luceres exclaimed.

"You promised me the temple site where our mosque formerly stood, but you haven't delivered!" Ahmad countered. "My people have just as much right to the Mount as the descendants of Isaac. Did you forget that Ishmael was Father Abraham's firstborn son?"

"All right, okay, calm down, Ahmed. It's not the right time to start a war." Luceres tried to appeal to the terrorist's rationale.

"What do you mean?"

"If you attack Jerusalem *now*, can you be certain that western nations will not join forces and fight on behalf of the Jews? Trust me, Ahmed, this evangelism stuff will eventually die down."

"Do you have proof?" Ahmed asked.

"People are innately selfish. When they've had time to think about the sacrifice they'll make as true followers of Christ, they'll turn away. Who can survive without a banking account? Think about it, Ahmed. People will be homeless and starve to death."

"I hear differently," Ahmed stated. "There's a Jerusalem Fund that has zillions of gold and silver coins stashed away. It'll be a long time before a Jew starves. Besides, I'm tired of waiting."

Luceres released a labored breath. "Okay, I understand that you are stressed out." He faked empathy. "Why don't you fly to Rome tonight and have a nice supper with me? We'll sit down and discuss a reasonable solution and come up with a solid plan."

"You'll hear me out?"

"Absolutely, I just don't want you going off all cocky and making a huge mistake. There is the right way to gain the land."

"Yeah, I've heard complaints from landowners that their private acreage has been seized by the IEPA," Ahmed said.

"That's a discussion for another day."

It was true that the International Environmental Protection Agency was procuring private land in order to set up refuges for endangered species. Jungle populations had been uprooted by the shifting land masses and sinkholes. Untold numbers of lions, tigers, and bird populations had fled their habitats foraging for food and shelter. For the first time in modern society, the animal population preyed on humans. *Guess, that's payback*, he considered.

"If I am to see you tonight, I'll need to rearrange my schedule," Ahmed said. "Can I call you back in a few minutes?"

"No problem, you have my number."

"Wait! Don't hang up!" Ahmed blurted out. "Okay, I've cancelled my afternoon appointment so I can meet you in Rome."

"Good, call me when you land and I'll tell you where we are dining." Luceres ended the call, satisfied it went well.

He heard the click of a turning knob and spun around.

"Look who's home!" Luceres spied Andre skipping through the open door of the apartment with his male nanny trailing a pace behind. The lad ran over to Luceres and held up an object.

"Look Uncle, see what I've got?"

"What is it, Andre?" Luceres leaned closed to see what was hid away in his small hands. Shocked, he spied a dead Blue Jay.

"Ain't it pretty and blue, Uncle?"

"And very dead, my young nephew." He patted Andre on his shoulder. "Be a good boy now and throw it away."

"No, Uncle! Bird's only sleeping," Andre insisted.

"Look at his eyes, Andre. They are deadpan. Birds have high energy and move fast. Your Blue Jay is dead, trust me."

"I don't think so." Andre clamped his rosebud lips.

"Okay, enough about a dead bird. Throw it away in the garbage can and wash your hands. It might have a disease."

"No!" Andre defiantly stamped his foot.

"It's rude to talk to an adult like that, Andre."

"If I say my bird is alive, he's alive!"

"Must you always be so stubborn, boy?"

"Look! I'll show you." Andre cupped the bird in his tiny hands and mumbled something weird then tossed it into the air.

As the lifeless Blue Jay began to drop like deadweight his wings expanded and it frantically flew around the room and toward the window, hitting the glass so hard it was knocked out.

"See!" Andre laughed. "Birdie's not dead."

Luceres blinked with astonishment. "How did you do that, Andre? Was it a trick? Come here, tell me."

"You only need to know one thing, Uncle."

"What is that?" Luceres played along with the fanciful boy.

"If I say a thing lives, it will." His unusual olive eyes targeted Luceres with malice. "If I say a thing dies, it does."

Caught off guard, Luceres was speechless.

"Uncle, don't ever tell me what to do again!"

Andre lingered a few seconds then raced into the office and slammed the door, the sound of it shaking the windows.

That child just threatened me!

"Sir?" The male nanny addressed Luceres. "Will you need my services any longer today?"

"No, Philip, I'll stay with Andre until his father returns."

"Thank you, Sir."

Raising the dead? Only Jesus Christ had done that.

40

MID-AFTERNOON SATURDAY AT the high-rise apartment in Rome, Mary fed David a jar of fruit and put him down for yet another nap since his schedule was messed up due to the time change difference between Tennessee and Italy. Jetting across the Atlantic Ocean so often did not give him the stability he needed. Often fretful and restless, at least he was not sick, thank God!

Can I ever provide a stable home for him in light of my work?"

Conflicted, Mary frowned at Lazarus, sipping on a glass of tea. "Really?" He locked eyes with her. "You're suffering guilt?"

She bristled. "Did you read my mind?"

He held up both hands. "No. Its written in your face."

"Please don't use that word again."

"What word?" he queried.

"Guilt. It reminds me of Drew's trial and sentencing. I can still see the despair on his face. How distraught he was feeling at the time." She was half a world away and still hurt for him.

"Is this my fault?" Lazarus complained.

"No, it's not. It's mine."

His lips wiggled. "Aren't you judging yourself a little harshly?"

"Besides abandoning Drew when he needed support most, I've been dragging David around with me back and forth across the ocean. He's never going to know where home is."

"Rome is a nice place to live."

On a jaunt to punish herself, Mary continued, "I've been so unfair to both the guys I love. David needs stability." *I need stability.*

Mary's global blue eyes filled with tears.

"You could give David up for adoption."

"That's not an option." *Is it?* She thought of Cory and Alexi Lindsey and the stable home they provided for Miracle.

"Look at it like this, Mary," Lazarus said, "home is where the heart is. I didn't have a stable home and look at me."

"Yeah, that's why I'm worried." She nervously chuckled.

"I was adopted by an American president and grew up in the White House," Lazarus bragged. "I'd say I turned out okay."

Mary laughed. "Okay, I'm going to have a hot cup of herbal tea and see if it will calm my nerves. Want a refill?"

He set his empty glass on the counter. "Coke over ice, please, and check the fridge. I sent a maid over to clean the apartment and stock the kitchen with supplies, including goodies."

"How thoughtful!" Mary opened the door and spied a large jug of fresh milk on the top shelf, two cartons of eggs, and packages of deli meats and cheeses on the lower shelves.

"You won't go hungry anytime soon," he quipped.

She glanced over at Lazarus. "Did she bring fresh bread?"

"In the pantry next to the chips," Lazarus replied. "I know how you love Doritos. And there are jars of baby food, too."

"I'm trying to wean David off baby foods and give him more table choices." Mary snagged the Healthy Nutty Bread, tore into the packaging, and made two turkey sandwiches. "Have supper with me." Mary fixed two plates with sandwiches and chips then passed one across the bar with a fizzing glass of Coke over ice.

"About Benjamin—what's his last name?"

"Blessing first," Mary uttered. "Dear God, thank you for our food. May it nourish our bodies as we faithfully serve You."

Not closing his eyes, Lazarus stared at Mary.

"What?" She bit into her sandwich.

"Tell me about this guy Ben."

"His last name is Sawyer." Mary took a sip of sweet tea. "He was formerly a Seattle cop counseled by Dr. Susan Parrot."

"I can find the guy if you'd like."

Mary dropped her sandwich, surprised at his offer.

"How will you do that, Lazarus?"

"My brother knows people all over the world," he said. "I'll get him to ask around. Benjamin can't hide from those people."

Shrugging, Lazarus took a big bite of his sandwich.

"*Those* people? That sounds pretty clan-destined." Mary bit into her turkey sandwich. "Are we talking Mafia thugs?"

"No, no, I'm just saying there are ways to find a person if you're looking in the right places," Lazarus said. "Trust me."

"Okay, but you should know it's rumored Ben is hiding out in Canada." A glimmer of hope trickled over her spirit.

"About Jesus . . .?" Reading the Catholic Bible to Andre had brought up some disturbing thoughts Lazarus wanted to clarify.

"What about the Savior?"

"I'd like to know more about how you view Him."

"Okay." Mary gave a synopsis of biblical history from Genesis to Revelation. From Lazarus' comments, it was obvious he was struggling with what was true, that he was a born sinner.

"You were trained as a Catholic priest, Lazarus. Didn't anyone explain the plan of salvation?" Mary resumed eating.

"I guess I wasn't paying much attention."

"And now you are, that's good." Mary trusted that her witness would not fall on deaf ears. Only the powerful Holy Spirit could convict Lazarus of his shortcomings. It took an act of grace to convince him he needed saving from the world's philosophies.

God is always present and active where humanity is concerned.

"You see, Lazarus, God knew from the beginning of Creation that humankind would not be able to live up to holy standards, so He prepared a sacrificial lamb before the world was formed."

"That's sort of like . . ." he grinned, "which came first, the chicken or the egg?" His mind whirred with possibilities.

"Yes, that's a good analogy," Mary replied. "You see, God stands outside of our timeline. The reason earth operates on seconds, minutes, hours, days, and years, is so God can monitor human progress. Since Jesus' died on the cross and our Heavenly Father resurrected him, we have been living in the Age of Grace."

"That's a lot to believe in."

Mary smiled. "I know, I was once where you are."

"What do you mean?"

"I didn't believe in God or the Bible," she said.

He offered no comment.

"God set His time table aside for the Jewish nation to allow an undetermined time for the Age of Grace. He wanted to give Gentiles the opportunity to be grafted into the promises of the Old Testament. A chance to accept or reject the Messiah."

"Okay . . ." Lazarus squinted his eyes. "So, God already knows what's going to happen—say in four days from now?"

"Yes, but He's operating on a different calendar than ours."

"What do you mean?" Lazarus asked.

"When Jesus removed the saved Christians from the earth on December 24th, 2025, the seven-year countdown started."

"The countdown to what?" The idea flustered him.

"To end of time as we know it," she explained.

"Judgment Day?"

"Yes."

"I still don't get the concept of free will," Lazarus said. "If God already knows what I'm going to do, and when I'm going to do it, where is my choice?" It was a reasonable question.

"You have a choice now, Lazarus," Mary said. "You can stay here with me, or go back to the Vatican apartment."

"But that's an easy choice with no eternal consequences."

"You're wrong. What if you got into a car this very minute and had an accident? But, if you left five minutes later, you might avoid injuries," Mary speculated. "Life is all about choices."

"I've already read Genesis," Lazarus said. "I know that Adam and Eve ate the forbidden fruit and sinned."

"Correct, they chose to be disobedient to God and suffered the consequences," Mary pointed out. *Like Drew*, she thought.

"God was not merciful then," Lazarus said. "God kicked them out of the Garden of Eden into a barren world."

"But God left them with instructions: till the land and bear children," Mary said. "God told them He Himself would come one day to save them and bring them back into the Garden."

"I did not know that."

"That's why humanity has been struggling with sin and failing so miserably throughout the centuries. Until the Messiah was born, there was no way for Adam and Eve and their offspring to be in the Father's good graces—so to speak." She inhaled deeply. "We are forgiven by God when we trust in His Son, Jesus Christ."

"So, if I confess my sins to Jesus, and ask God to forgive me, He will? Then I can go to Heaven when time runs out?"

"Yes, Lazarus," Mary replied. "If you truly believe in your heart that Jesus saves, and ask God to forgive you, the Holy Spirit will indwell you and help you choose what is best in this life."

"Promise?" he said.

"With all my heart," Mary replied.

Lazarus bowed his head and thought about what Mary had said. Then he looked up with tears flooding in his eyes.

"What?" Mary recognized conflict in his expression.

"I wish I could do that, Mary, but I can't. My brother would never forgive me." He put on his jacket and turned to leave.

"Wait!" Mary grabbed Lazarus in a tight hug and whispered in his ear. "Who do you want to please?"

His expression was raw. "What do you mean?"

"Why not please God Who created you?"

Saying nothing, he left the apartment.

"I tried, Jesus. But it would be wrong of me to coerce him into confessing faith in Jesus. Salvation is a choice."

41

Monday, November 1

Baghdad, Iraq

"YOU'RE TWO DAYS LATE!" Luceres fussed as his former Harvard University roommate entered the office. Last he'd heard from Ahmed Ramallah, he was on his way to Rome, Italy for supper.

Nonchalantly, Ahmed quipped, "But not a dollar short."

"How did you find me?" Luceres asked.

"Your brother." Ahmed took a seat in the glass-encased office with multiple windows overlooking Baghdad. The gleaming chrome furniture might have been confiscated from a spaceship.

"Am I interrupting something?" the Muslim queried.

"I can spare an hour." Luceres' olive eyes eclipsed as he observed the dark features of the Sunni Muslim seated on the sofa.

"What I have to say won't take that long."

Like mysterious black globes, Ahmed's eyes fell on Luceres as his muscular torso visibly tightened: the dance of a python preparing to strike. "Would you care for a cup of coffee?"

Diffuse and distract. Luceres commandeered the moment.

"No, thank you." Ahmed glanced around the modern office. "You have many more green plants than the last time I visited."

"Live plants generate oxygen," Luceres said.

Ahmed nodded, slouching comfortably into the folds of the plush leather sofa. "No doubt to counteract the carbon you extract from smoking cigars," he teased. "I'm truly disappointed in you."

The world leader smiled. "Not the first time, my friend."

"I didn't come to judge you," Ahmed said.

"Otherwise, you would not appear so casual."

"This meeting is more of a—how shall I say it? A courtesy."

Luceres laughed hard. "When have you ever done that?"

"I'm trying to be civil, Luceres."

"Forgive me if I'm wrong," Luceres said, "but from the tone of our troubling conversation on Saturday, I presume you are still contemplating war with the Jews to obtain the Temple Mount."

Ahmed shifted his gaze from Luceres to the picture window that overlooked Baghdad and the sandy hills beyond. Then his brooding eyes swept on Luceres again. "My decision is firm."

"You stood me up for supper on Saturday."

Diffuse and distract.

"I was sidetracked, but it was rude of me not to call."

Luceres sipped on his vanilla latte then placed his forearms on the gleaming surface of his desk. "It happens," he said.

"Did you know this past Saturday was Halloween?"

Odd times call for unusual conversations.

"All Hallows Eve is well celebrated by many cultures," Luceres offered. "So, my friend, how were you sidetracked?"

"I had an interesting conversation with a colleague."

"One of your many jihadists' brothers, I presume."

Ahmed's smile was like a flat white crack set into his dark Arabic face. "No, actually the man I spoke with was a brother Muslim who currently teaches at the University of Tehran."

"And what did this brother say that sidetracked you?"

"Did you know a NEO passed the earth six days ago?"

"No, I was unaware—what is a NEO?"

"A Near Earth Object," Ahmed replied.

"Where are you going with this?"

"Give me a moment and I'll explain." Ahmed parked his hands on his torso as he sank even farther into the folds of the sofa.

"I'm not interested, Ahmed." Luceres refused to waste his time on useless banter since he had been in the process of developing talking points for his committee meeting in one hour.

"What if the subject impacts the future," Ahmed said.

"You should be talking to a psychic, not me."

"Astrology is against my faith!" Ahmed exclaimed.

"It was a joke, Ahmed. Don't take it personal."

Ahmed scrutinized his Anglo friend then said, "Point taken."

"Are we done with this foolishness?" Luceres asked.

"Not quite," Ahmed continued. "The professor told me that a group of Ukrainian astronomers recently announced they had spotted a large asteroid in 2013 as it passed earth 4.2 million miles away. The 1,350-foot monster was dubbed TV135."

"Well, that's comforting to know." Luceres chuckled. "Any closer and I might have been worried."

His jest fell on deaf ears.

"Based on the asteroid's present trajectory, astronomers working for the Crimean Astrophysical Observatory in southern Ukraine predict a 1 in 63,000 chance that this same NEO will strike earth on August 26, 2032!" Ahmed reached his point.

Luceres perked up. "Go on, I'm listening."

"According to their statistics, based on former asteroid strikes, the sudden impact of TV135 would create an explosion on earth's surface the size of 2,500 megatons of TNT," Ahmed reported.

Luceres offered no comment as he imagined the damage.

"That's fifty times more powerful than the atomic bomb that America exploded over Hiroshima, Japan, to end World War II."

"Ahmed, that's all intriguing information, a bit scary I admit, but what has it to do regarding your intent to attack Jerusalem?"

"It has everything to do with the present!" Ahmed leaped to his feet. "Christians and Messianic Jews are preaching all over the world that the end of time is coming in less than four years."

"Sit down, you make me nervous."

Ahmed fell back in the sofa.

"The idea that Jesus removed His church has been rebuffed by a more believable theory. Aliens took those people. Intelligent people will not accept the idea only four years of time is left."

"You're wrong!" Ahmed jumped up and paced the office.

"Sit down, Ahmed."

The Muslim continued to stand. "Christians believe that Jesus will appear on the Mount of Olives to end time as we know it and set up a world government under his kingly leadership."

"I said sit down, Ahmed!" Luceres barked, pointing to the sofa. "Let's discuss this crazy theory like rational men."

Ahmed frowned then obeyed. "I'm listening."

"As a devout Muslim, how did you come by this troubling messianic information?" Luceres inquired.

Ahmed's stout fingers threaded his thick black mane of hair as he rolled his tight shoulders to loosen them. "I've read the Christian Bible and I've talked to people who've studied prophecy."

"I thought your kind only read the Qur'an," Luceres said.

"Know your enemy is the first commandment to defeat them," Ahmed uttered. "I am an enlightened prophet."

A smile trickled over Luceres' lips.

"Now, you are a prophet, not just a Muslim leader?"

"Think about the timing of the prophecy." Ahmed's eyes were ablaze with speculation. "It's an opportunity of a lifetime."

"To do what, Ahmed?" Luceres mentally counted off seven years beginning on Christmas Eve, 2025, and came up with 2032.

"Win the war of minds. Isn't it feasible to believe a blazing rock of that size striking earth would annihilate civilization?"

"Okay, you got me. Explain, please."

"A world-wide Caliphate must be in a position to control the masses before 2032. Otherwise, people will believe the prophecy Christians are preaching is true! Especially, the Messianic Jews."

"What about *my* position in world government?"

Ahmed's dark eyes narrowed. "I believe in Allah, the one true God. I believe in Muhammad, the true prophet of Islam," Ahmed professed. "And I believe I am to rule the religious world."

"Where does that leave me?" Luceres frowned.

"I care nothing about the logistics of controlling the masses under government guidelines," the Muslim announced. "You can handle the banking system and choose people to lead nations. But

I want Islam sanctioned by the Committee of Ten as the designated religion of the world. It's the only way to stop the bickering."

"I must admit, that's a radical idea," Luceres said.

"My friend," Ahmed pointed a finger, "I am interested only in seeing that people accept *al Mahdi* as their spiritual leader. I will require they give allegiance to the *Qur'an* and obey Sharia Law."

"And if they don't?" Luceres posed the obvious.

"Disobedience will be punishable by death."

"Is that all?" Luceres countered, actually smiling.

42

Rome, Italy

MARY WALKED TO THE nearest public park while holding Andre's small hand. Little David was riding in his baby carriage, a gift from Lazarus. Since the rent on the high-rise apartment was current and Mary's personal belongings were still there, it wasn't a leap to presume Lazarus expected that she would return to Rome.

She was alone with the boys this morning since Lazarus had a meeting at the Vatican. In fact, he appeared relieved to be free of watching over Andre for a few hours. Indeed, it was her pleasure.

It didn't take long to recognize Andre's consternation. He was almost three but acted like he was going on sixteen. He'd insisted they walk five blocks to the park rather than ride. However, his short legs required triple time in order to keep up with Mary.

Already, his role as Pope shaped his thoughts. In some ways, selfishly. Much of his parenting was beyond Mary's control.

So, she laughingly teased, "You're too big for your britches."

"My britches fit fine." Andre wore a pair of size three jean overalls with a long-sleeve flannel shirt tucked inside. The temperature outdoors was in the low sixties, still rather cool.

"I don't know why I can't dress like the Pope when I'm out in public!" Andre stared at the swing set in front of him. "Do you expect me to ride that contraption? I might fall and hurt myself."

Mary knelt, eye-level with her son. "Andre, when you are with me, you are not the Pope. You are still very young and should be having fun. You will be big before you know it."

"I can be big anytime I want!" Andre stamped his foot.

Little David sensed the tension and whimpered.

"It's okay, little one." Mary removed David from the buggy and sat him on a bench beside her. He pointed at the swing set.

"Look, your brother wants to swing, Andre."

"Let him then, I'll watch."

Andre plopped down on the grass, his lower chin quivering. His disgruntled expression reflected his displeasure.

"Better get up, son, you'll get your clothes dirty," Mary said.

"I don't care, someone will wash them."

"Okay, suit yourself. David and I are going to have some fun."

Mary placed David in a toddler swing, locked the gate so he wouldn't fall out, then began gently pushing him. One glance at Andre told Mary he was miserable. Could it be he was jealous of her relationship with David? Within seconds after that thought, David's swing began to pendulum faster, as if pushed by a ghostly hand. Mary tried to stop it but couldn't. She let go and panicked.

The swing went higher and higher with David bawling to the top of his lungs. "Andre!" she screamed. "Are you making the swing go higher?" She grabbed his arm and pulled him to his feet.

The swing slowed but David was still bawling.

"Shame on you, Andre, you scared your brother!" Mary fussed. "It's not a nice thing to do, where are your manners?"

Andre looked up at his mother. "I don't like him."

"Why not?" Mary felt a cold chill invade her body.

"He takes up too much of your time."

"Andre, you are intelligent and gifted," Mary told him. "I love you very much. But I promised David's mother I would take care of him when she died. I can't break my promise to her."

The charged angry atmosphere immediately changed, as if a raging storm had suddenly switched into a sunny day.

Andre smiled at Mary. "Okay, I want to swing now."

The extreme personality swing was disturbing. One second Andre was an obedient child; the next, a malicious and jealous spirit. Mary prayed the Holy Spirit would guide Andre in his quest to survive in life, and to prevent an evil spirit from influencing him.

* * *

Beijing, China

The Two Witnesses stood in the middle of a busy Beijing, China street. The metropolitan city was the capital of China, the heartthrob of commerce and politics for the country. Today, Moses and Elijah had a difficult assignment. "It's a shame the people are about to suffer so much!" one of them sadly quipped.

"Now, Moses, God told us our job wouldn't be easy."

"I've been here and done this before, Elijah."

"I know. When the Egyptian pharaoh refused to let the Israelites leave for the Promised Land, you did what was necessary."

"Correct, but I still find it hard to punish people I never met for their sins." Moses moaned. "Time hasn't changed that."

"Yet, you know we must convince these idol worshippers that God means business," Elijah said. "Persecution gets folk's attention. Makes them reconsider how they live their lives. What we do is necessary to provoke change. We'll point them to Jesus."

"But what if they reject, anyhow?"

"Well, at least we've done our part," Elijah said.

"I know, but rats? Can't we come up with anything better than that?" Moses shook his head. "Germ warfare, imagine!"

"Well," Elijah pointed out, "if labs hadn't sold deadly viruses to violent nations for profit, Beijing wouldn't be facing a plague."

The Witnesses were suddenly transported to a mountain peak north of the city. "You know, Elijah, the Chinese culture dates back eight centuries," Moses recalled. "This country has seven world heritage sites, including the Great China Wall. Lots of visitors over the centuries, and don't forget the famous Gobi Desert."

"Well, at least only half the population, some thirteen million residents, live inside the city and will suffer judgment," Elijah offered. "Before the Rapture, the population was twice that."

"Well, you know when we release this plague, everybody will come after us for blood," Moses noted. "I guess it's inevitable."

"The Word of God says we'll physically die here on earth for the first time," Elijah noted. "Death will come mid-point of the Tribulation Period. Then we are raised and taken into Heaven."

"Yeah, and I'm not looking forward to the experience."

"It is the time of Jacob's trouble," Elijah pointed out. "As Jesus suffered death, so will we. Time for us is running out."

"I guess we should get busy then." Moses envisioned them rejoicing from Heaven's side when they rose from the dead.

"There's much we don't understand, Moses."

"Okay, let's get this over, Elijah, and move on."

Moses lifted his staff and prayed to God in Heaven and declared: "O God of Abraham, Isaac, and Jacob, open the drains and underground streams in Beijing and release the rodents.

"Incite them to invade homes and businesses, forage for food, and attack the residents!" He raised his staff higher.

"Release a plague upon humankind and animal populations so that their stubborn wills may be broken and many souls come to the Light of Jesus." Moses stood on the wind at this point.

"So be it!" Elijah loudly exclaimed. "Amen and amen!"

The Chinese people were unaware how their lives were about to be impacted. God was about to invade their society and create chaos in order to bring religious conviction to them. Only those marked by Christ would be saved from the plague. Just as the Death Angel passed over the Israelites living in Egypt because the blood of a sacrificial lamb was on their doorposts, those cleansed by Jesus' blood—man, woman, or child—would not suffer or die.

* * *

Woo Chai, a prestigious and wealthy diplomat, dwelled in Beijing. He was a member of the Committee of Ten and a faithful Communist, always ready to serve his country and the regime.

Today, Woo was in bed with a terrible cold. The virus had relentlessly persisted for four days. Feeling too ill to leave his house, he texted Luceres yesterday and told him he was too sick to attend the scheduled meeting in Baghdad. In his place, he was sending his nephew, Chu men Ling, who had a doctorate in political science.

Woo had no wife. His young mistress visited him twice a week. He owned fifty spas throughout China, some of them involved in illegal human trafficking—but he never thought about the shame and suffering of the young women his business preyed upon.

No, Woo's mission in life was to earn more money and influence world politics. His mistress loved that about him.

While resting in bed after taking two Advil, Woo roused from his slumber at hearing scratching below him on the wood floor. Scrubbing his red matted eyes, he grabbed the bedpost with one hand then leaned over the edge of his king-size bed to see the cause.

A huge pair of scary black eyes attached to a brown hairy varmint stopped scratching and stared back at him.

"What is this!" Woo leaped from the bed and ran into the bathroom. Slamming the door and locking it, his heart thumped so loudly in his chest he thought he might pass out. *A rat . . .?*

Woo kept a second cell phone in his bathroom. In fact, he had another in the kitchen and one in the living room. Afraid someone might break into the house to do him harm, the phones were programmed with an emergency number should he need help. This time was no exception. He would not tolerate pests in his house.

Woo decided to call a friend instead, the Minister of Finance.

"Lei, this is Woo. I need your assistance."

"What kind of assistance?"

"I have a huge rodent in my bedroom!" Woo described the hairy brown varmint that was as big as a full-grown alley cat. "I'm locked in my bathroom at my house and I'm scared to go out."

"Well, join the crowd, Woo. Turn on your TV."

"I don't have a TV in my bathroom."

"Well, in addition to owning several phones, perhaps you should purchase televisions for all the rooms in your house."

"Lei, I don't need a lecture. All I want is for you to send someone over who can get rid of this menacing varmint."

"I'm afraid that's impossible, Beijing is in crisis."

"What do you mean?" The idea startled Woo. "Are we under attack by those aliens circling the stratosphere?"

"No, no, no," Lei replied. "We have an invasion of a different kind. Millions of rodents have attacked the city. They are crawling out of the rivers, streams, lily ponds, sewers, and drain pipes," he reported. "People are scared for their lives. Woo, it's a travesty."

"What am I supposed to do about my rat, Lei?"

"Protect yourself."

Lei actually hung up on Woo. He leaned against the bathroom wall, shaken over the news. Afraid to open the bathroom door, he had no idea what he'd encounter. Something crawled up his leg.

Trembling, Woo glanced down and spied a baby rat attached to the hem of his pajamas. He screamed and batted the rat away.

Then he heard terrible screeching sounds.

Woo dizzily spun around in time to spy dozens of rodents crawling out of the commode, gathering like an army on the counter sink. He screamed to the top of his lungs and fell back against the door. The rodents circled his feet like a vicious army, snarling and scratching, preparing for the attack. Speechless, he fainted.

43

Baghdad, Iraq

"I JUST TALKED TO THE Minister of Finance in Beijing, China," Hansen Solijar informed Luceres. "The city has been attacked by rodents! He thinks Woo Chia is dead."

"My uncle is deceased?" Chu men Ling exclaimed. "But he only has a cold. The Minister must be mistaken."

"Nothing has been confirmed, Chu," Luceres told Woo's nephew. "Don't assume the worst without knowing the facts."

Alarm registered on Chu's face but he nodded his consent.

"George, turn on your iPhone and Google Beijing," Luceres ordered. "Meanwhile, Chu can call his parents for an update."

George Clydesdale had once functioned as the District Attorney in the sleepy town of Fernwood, Tennessee. His political connections later allowed him to preside over the European Free Masons. He'd been invited to join the Committee of Ten in early 2011, their goal to unify nations under world-government guidelines. Their first accomplishment was the acceptance of the Peace First document that unified religious thought. Many religious sects revamped their holy books to comply with the guidelines.

Although it took some time and doing, the Committee manipulated world currencies, collapsed national banking systems, and introduced the Mark, an international banking chip.

In response, Luceres divided the world map into ten banking zones and assigned each of the Committee members a zone to manage. Today, George lived in Canada. His responsibility was to make sure the banking industries in the Alaskan and Canadian Provinces complied with the guidelines. He was a close confident of the world leader and thrived on his important role.

"It's true," George reported to Luceres. "BBC reports that millions of rodents have invaded Beijing and feeding off the flesh of its citizens. Clean water and diseases are impending problems."

George looked at Chu. "Sorry, son, but at least you're safe."

"How can this happen in our enlightened age?" Perez Mandosa, liaison for the Unified South American countries, queried in Spanish. "Rats? Whoever heard of such a thing?"

British-born Sir Lawrence Brighton, heading up the Unified territories of the United States and Mexico, interjected his thoughts, declaring, "Historically, it's happened before, Perez."

"During the 1600s," Luceres recalled, "rodents spread the Plague and killed some 200,000 London residents. The Black Death was worse. Mid-1300's, 25-30 million in Europe died."

"Is that going to happen in China?" asked Saheed Jamar, a Muslim American who now lived in Tehran, Iran. "Is it possible the Bubonic Plague, or something worse, is spreading?"

"Again, let's make no assumptions," Luceres warned. "Other diseases have been loosed on the world, like Covid-19 in 2020."

"We need to alert the World Health Council," Perez offered

"Of course," Luceres agreed. "First, I want to talk to the Director of the Center of Disease Control in the U.S. and ask him to send a team to Beijing to take blood samples of those infected."

Chu hurriedly said, "An analysis will tell us what this is?"

"Probably too late to save lives," George interjected.

"Maybe, if we hurry, we can stop a pandemic from occurring," Luceres said. "I personally know someone in the field of genetics capable of developing a vaccine to any kind of supergerm."

"Who is this person?" Chu asked, closing his phone.

"Dr. Albert Swartzenberg in Cairo, Egypt," Luceres replied. "If he'll coordinate with the CDC, we'll reward him handsomely."

"What if it's smallpox?" Saheed inquired.

"I thought that disease was eradicated decades ago!" Sergio Martourk, a Russian tsar from St. Petersburg, exclaimed.

"Don't be so naïve," Sir Lawrence Brighton cautioned. Every eye turned on the former U.S. Federal Reserve Chairman. "Scientific laboratories across the globe have stored lethal strains of all types of deadly diseases for decades. This might be terrorism."

"What if it's a mutant virus no one has seen before?" Chu chimed in. "It takes months to develop and test new vaccinations."

Olson Jobai, an Iranian Jew and watchman over the banking industry in the Israel and Palestinian territories, frowned. He was not a man of faith. He'd vehemently opposed the construction of the Jewish temple after the Islamic Mosque fell into the abyss through a sinkhole. The temple's existence on the Jerusalem Mount exacerbated the hate existing between the Abrahamic tribes.

"Olson? Do you know something that we don't?"

"Well, actually Iranian scientists have been experimenting with germ warfare for many decades," Olson offered. "I'll call a friend high up in government and ask if Iran has a beef with China."

Luceres inwardly groaned. "You do that."

"Wait!" Hansen Solijar spoke up. "Are you suggesting this outbreak may be a deliberate attack on the Chinese?"

"Let's not play dumb, gentlemen," Sir Lawrence intervened. "Muslims have been pushing for a world war in order to establish a revised world government under the leadership of a Caliphate."

George sarcastically laughed. "Conjecture. Just like all Jews are not Messianic Christians, all Muslims are not warmongers."

"I appreciate all of your ideas." Luceres raised his right hand to halt more speculation. "However, I need to know the facts, what we're actually dealing with, before the Committee takes action."

"George is right," Mahmoud Morouki said. A dark-skinned South American Muslim, he was educated in Europe and favored a world regime over a Caliphate that adhered to the *Qur'an*. "It's not right to accuse anyone specific of harming another nation."

"China should be immediately isolated from the rest of the world until we know what this outbreak is," Chu fearfully said.

"Not just China," Hansen Solijar interjected. "The border of every country should be closed to foreign trade until this matter is resolved. Or at least evaluated and solutions offered."

"Hansen in correct," Luceres agreed. "We need some talking points to prevent a panic. I'll contact BBC, FOX, CNN, and other major media organizations to arrange for a satellite linkup. People need to be warned of the danger without scaring them. From our past experience with pandemics, we are all aware that considerable economic damage occurs when international trade is halted."

"Maybe we should work in secret," George suggested.

"Is that fair to the world's population?" Gerald Bonifield asked. "As the Committee's liaison for the Provinces of Australia, I prefer to warn my people to stay home and ride out this scare."

"Sit tight, gentlemen," Luceres intervened. "Have another cup of coffee and a sandwich while I speak to Dr. Swartzenburg."

Conversations resumed among the members as their leader stepped from the boardroom down the hall to his office.

The first person Luceres called was his brother.

"It's me," Luceres said.

"Oh, hi, Bro, what's up?"

Luceres summarized the crisis and warned Lazarus to get enough groceries to last a few months. Chaos was about to break out on the streets of Rome when people learned what was taking place in Beijing. When Luceres learned that Mary Taylor was visiting in Rome, he instructed Lazarus to fetch her and the boy.

"We can ride out this storm at the Vatican," Lazarus said.

"Good idea, and don't go outside until I tell you."

"Mary won't do it."

"Be clever, Lazarus. Invite her over for supper, explain the situation, and insist that she stay with you for a few days."

44

Nashville, Tennessee

"YOU HAVE A VISITOR," the prison warden told Andrew Taylor through the bars of his cell. "Some attorney is here to discuss your case. Come on, I'll walk you down to the visitor's station"

"I didn't hire another attorney," Drew said.

"Well, maybe someone hired one for you."

"What's this about?" Drew asked.

Warden Leonard Blake opened the gate to the cell. "Don't know, # 451, why don't we go and find out?"

Drew was let out of his cell and led in handcuffs and ankle chains across the second-story corridor, down a set of metal stairs, through an electronically locked door into a long hallway, and finally into a private visiting room. A stranger faced him.

"You've got thirty minutes," the warden hawked.

The door to the room slammed and Drew heard it lock. He hobbled across the concrete floor. His visitor, a female, faced the wall monitor until it grew dark. "There, we're alone."

The brunette's hair was tied in a knot at the back of her neck. She was neither pretty nor ugly, just plain and tall.

"Attorney-client privilege has been granted," she said. "Let's take a seat and talk about your situation."

The attorney wore a navy-blue suit with gold buttons and matching pumps. The frilly fringe of her white blouse peeked out at the top of her jacket. Her shade of lipstick was a pale pink.

"Please have a seat, Mr. Taylor."

Not ready to cooperate, he asked, "Who are you?"

"Don't you recognize me?"

The slight smile did seem familiar.

"Should I?" Drew scrutinized the woman's features. "The warden said you were an attorney."

"He presumed I was an attorney," she said.

"Okay, whoever you are, let's get on with it."

Drew pulled out the molded-plastic chair with his shackled hands and sat down at the table. His leg chains rattled as he half twisted in the chair to get comfortable. The woman was smiling.

"Okay, game's over, who sent you?" he asked.

"It wasn't Attorney Appleton." The brunette laughed.

"If you know anything about me, you know you are wasting your time. Nothing's changed to warrant another trial."

"My, my, you *are* a despondent soul!"

The woman sounded almost vindictive, catching Drew off guard. Who sent this person? Someone from the drug cartel?

"With no hope, it must really be awful for you in here."

Drew gritted his teeth. This conversation was over.

"Hey, whoever you are, lady, we're through talking." Drew struggled with his leg restraints as he banged his fists on the table.

"Oh, would you look at that? Still the angry detective who resorts to force when he fails to get his way." The woman clucked her tongue. "Aren't those cuffs and chains annoying?"

If looks could kill . . . "Who sent you here to torment me?"

As if enjoying the banter, the woman tilted her head and glared at Drew. "I ask you again, don't you recognize me?"

"No, I don't. Should I?" He let out a slow breath. "Okay, let me make a stab at why you're come here," he said.

"The ball is in your court," she said, amused.

"If you're here on behalf of Priscilla Dunn to taunt me, it isn't working." He leaned in to face her. "I'm not a cop anymore."

"Priscilla, huh? Now she's a piece of work. Came to work for you then stole your murder evidence—did you ever find her?"

Drew frowned and glanced up at the monitor, dark so nobody knew what was taking place in this closed space. The woman seemed more like an enemy than a friend or a licensed attorney.

"Somehow, I believe you already know the answer to that question." He banged on the table again. "Hey, if anyone's listening out there, I'm ready to go." He was done with the woman.

"No one's coming yet."

Her face was close enough for Drew to smell her perfume.

"You want answers, okay." She removed her gray contacts and placed them in a container of surgical solution.

"What the—?"

"Now, is that better?" She craned her head.

"So what? You have dark eyes instead of gray."

"Okay, let's you and me play a game."

"I feel like we're already in progress."

"Smart detective, I like that about you."

"What do you want with me, lady?" He squirmed in his seat. "Haven't I been through enough? I've been shot—"

"Twice, once in the head with a revolver, and hospitalized in Monticello, Georgia. Suffered a stroke then lost some function in your left leg—am I getting anywhere close to your trauma?"

Drew blinked. *What is this? Did Susan send her?*

"Oh, I forgot. Your wife recently fled the country."

"You seem to know a lot about me." Drew heaved a breath and looked away. The wall clock said he'd been there ten minutes.

"That's because you're important to me."

"How so?" Drew's droopy brown eyes fell on the mystery woman. "I have no money, no family now, and no life. What's so interesting about me? You're fancy free. Probably have a decent life, so why waste your time here?" He banged the tabletop again.

"So feisty." She cocked her head to one side, grinned and ripped off the black wig and the strip on the bridge of her nose.

The woman was wearing a disguise.

"You know, Andrew, you are the fish that got away."

Drew sat up as his reflexes heightened.

"Don't pretend you don't recognize me, Detective Taylor? Let me tell you a few things that you don't know," she said.

Caroline Sullivan. Here he was, a sitting duck, locked in the room with a lunatic. "I'm listening, talk." He played along.

About Priscilla Dunn . . ." her manicured fingernails scraped the table. "It sticks in your craw you can't find her, am I right?"

"Can't argue with that," he said.

"Well, you don't have to look for her anymore."

"What do you mean?"

"Dunn is deceased."

"How do you know that?" Drew's thigh muscles tightened beneath the table. "The Fernwood PD has searched high and low for the thief!" He slammed a foot against the table legs.

"Developing a violent temper, Detective? Locked up in a cell with a smelly roommate. Your life flushed down a toilet."

Realizing he was losing the game, Drew grew silent.

"Oh, well," she shrugged, "I know about Dunn because I buried her." A glint played in her eyes. "Intrigued now?"

No longer able to contain his anger, Drew came halfway across the table, prompting his visitor to skitter backwards in her chair.

"Dunn came after me for money and I shot her."

As if the diagram of an atomic bomb suddenly became visible, Drew's mind surfed back to the time he was at the church cemetery outside of Monticello, facing off with a serial killer. He quietly rasped. "Why did you come to see me, Caroline?"

Sullivan threw her head back and cackled.

"Imagine meeting like this, Andrew."

"You are insane. You won't get away with this charade."

"Why not? Who will believe you, a liar, a rapist?"

Caroline was right. At the moment, he was defenseless.

"Finally, you get the full picture of your situation." She leaned half way across the table until they were nose to nose.

"Don't come any closer, or I'll bite off your nose."

Satisfied she'd rattled his cage, Caroline said, "I understand why you want to kill me," she uttered. "All that shackled wrath inside of you must be driving you nuts. Now you know."

"Know what?"

"How it feels to be a trapped rat."

Drew got up and headed for the door.

"And along comes the spider, Susan," Caroline said.

Drew spun around and lunged at Caroline, using his bound hands to clobber her on the head but she was too quick. She pressed a button on the wall and the door swung open.

"What's the problem?" the burley attendant asked, his gaze apprizing the situation. "Did he attack you, Miss?"

"You need to lock up this prisoner, he's dangerous."

"Get the warden now!" Drew demanded. "This woman is a serial killer!" He pointed bound hands at Sullivan.

The guard grabbed Drew by the arm and held him in a vise.

"I've spoken with his former psychologist," Caroline calmly told the guard. "Andrew has mental problems. Is he getting help?"

Drew dislodged himself from the guard's hold and threw the full weight of his body at Sullivan but was blocked by another burley attendant who put him down on the floor like a world-champion wrestler. "You wanna go to lockdown? Try that again."

Drew took in a labored breath. "Sorry," he apologized, "but I need to speak to my lawyer one more time."

Prisoner and killer locked cold eyes. Her lips wiggled.

"I'll be fine," Caroline assured the guard. "Anyhow, I need to tell my new client one more thing before I go."

"You sure?"

"Positive."

"Are we good now, Andrew?" Caroline turned to Drew, as calm as a ship in the eye of a hurricane.

The burley attendant backed out and shut the door.

"Please don't hurt anyone I care about," Drew pleaded, standing loosely by the door. "Kill me if it makes you happy."

"Oh, no, I wouldn't want you to miss the prison experience."

"How can you be so cruel?"

"Easy." She smiled. "You can't protect her anymore."

"Wait!" Drew screamed as Caroline opened the door and pranced out of the room. "Don't hurt Mary!"

About the Author

For two decades, M. Sue Alexander has lived on a farm in north Dickson County, Tennessee, spending a good part of each day writing Christian novels. She prays that the information within her dramatic storylines will spur others to research the Bible and historical events surrounding the End Times and discover more about how God operates on our planet and in the universe.

View M. Sue's Facebook page and blogs.
www.msuealexanderbooks.com